Too Different...

to be anything but enemies, Kim and Andrew have always detested each other—but now they are forced into an uneasy alliance.

Too Proud...

to confess they might have been wrong, Kim and Andrew deny the feelings growing between them as they spend long hours together, using his academic research and her Washington connections to avert a looming international scandal.

Too Human...

to let love slip away, Kim and Andrew fight for different versions of happiness, never noticing how similar they are, how alike in their hopes, their heartaches and in the strength of their newborn love.

Books by Judith Arnold

Commitments
Judith Arnold

Harlequin Books

TORONTO • NEW YORK • LONDON
AMSTERDAM • PARIS • SYDNEY • HAMBURG
STOCKHOLM • ATHENS • TOKYO • MILAN

Published July 1987

First printing May 1987

ISBN 0-373-16205-7

Foreword

Commitments are hard to keep. Sometimes they're even harder to break.

The six characters who form the nucleus of *Keeping The Faith*—Laura, Seth, Kimberly, Andrew, Julianne and Troy—all entered adulthood at the end of the 1960s, a time when people committed themselves less to their own fulfillment than to ideals, principles, the larger world. As Columbia University undergraduates during the late sixties and early seventies, they are representative of their generation in their commitment to the major issues of the time. In college they chose to illustrate their commitment to peace and justice and their respect for humanity by publishing an underground newspaper, *The Dream*.

Eventually the sixties generation grew up. Once Laura, Kimberly, Julianne, Seth, Andrew and Troy were no longer protected by the ivy-covered walls of the university, they ventured into the real world and made new commitments: to careers, to children, to lovers.

In *Promises*, the first book of the *Keeping The Faith* trilogy, Seth and Laura were able, through their love, to rediscover and satisfy the promises of their youth. *Commitments* focuses on two people who have, if anything, surpassed their early promise and who have not forgotten the priorities of their youth.

Kimberly Belmont has forged a successful career as a speech writer for a United States senator. Andrew Collins has earned a Ph.D. in political economics and joined the faculty of Amherst College. For both Kimberly and Andrew, the commitment they made to their professions has paid off. One reason they were able to make that commitment to their work is that in an equally important commitment—marriage—both of them saw their hopes and expectations shattered.

Loving another person can be difficult under the best of circumstances. For Kimberly and Andrew, it is almost impossible—not only because of their past heartbreaks, but because, when they were classmates at Columbia, they despised each other. For them to give their love the chance it deserves entails more than simply committing themselves to their relationship. They must first break the commitment they have to their memories—memories of each other and of the pain they've endured.

Breaking such commitments, they learn, can be as hard as making new ones.

Romance, no matter what one's age, no matter what generation one is a part of, involves knowing when to commit oneself, and how and to whom. It also involves promises—making them and having the courage to live up to them. Ultimately romance involves dreams: the strength and imagination to dream of peace, contentment, perfection, love...the strength and imagination to chase those dreams, even knowing that they are often unattainable.

In *Dreams*, the final book of the *Keeping The Faith* trilogy, Julianne and Troy—and all their fellow "dreamers"—will discover whether it is possible to make dreams—even those seemingly unattainable ones—come true.

Chapter One

Dating, Kimberly mused, was a lot like riding a bicycle. Once you mastered the motions they were with you for life.

The last time Kimberly had ridden a bicycle had been about three years ago, with her niece Mary Catherine. M.C. had just received a new bike for her birthday, and Kimberly had used the child's old bike, a squeaky thing with a white wicker basket hanging off the handlebars and pink paint flaking from the frame. Touring the suburban Augusta neighborhood where Kimberly's sister and brother-in-law lived, Kimberly and M.C. had coasted past the large brick houses with their expansive, well-cultivated yards, inhaling the sweet spring fragrance of the blooming magnolias, the dogwood and fresh-cut grass. Although she hadn't been on a bike in ages before that afternoon, Kimberly had had little difficulty remembering the rhythm, the flow and balance of riding.

The last time Kimberly had been on a date was over fifteen years ago. But tonight, as she left the pricey French restaurant with Whitney Brannigan for a leisurely walk back to her Georgetown apartment, she reflected on the fact that she hadn't forgotten the rhythm, flow, or balance of this particular exercise, either. She had remembered when to smile at Whitney, how to smile, when to ask him the right questions, how to react to his answers. Her date with him hadn't been nearly as much fun as pedaling around town with M.C. But as Kimberly assessed her dinner outing with Whitney, she congratulated herself on having avoided falling, wobbling, crashing.

Whitney was a suitable partner for her first date in eons. He was handsome in the right way, with the sort of crisp, clean-cut looks that had always appealed to her, even during her flirtation with hippiedom in college. Whitney was two years her senior, well educated, ruthless enough professionally to be interesting, and, as her mother would put it, "as bright as a Christmas tree light." If Kimberly ever quoted her mother's pet phrase to him, he would cringe, but she thought the comparison appropriate. He reminded her of a pointy green bulb flashing on and off, reflecting off the surrounding tinsel.

She had known Whitney for four years, ever since she had joined Senator Milford's staff as a speech writer. Within a month of her arrival on Capitol Hill, Whitney had asked her out for a date. That she was married at the time hadn't fazed him in the least. "Your old man doesn't have to know," he had coolly pointed out, as if leaving Todd in ignorance would have made Whitney's proposition morally valid.

Tonight such moral questions weren't at issue. That very morning, Kimberly had gotten to work late, having first stopped at her attorney's office on her way to the senator's suite in the Hart Building. The lawyer had handed her the folded decree and shaken her hand. "That's it, Ms. Belmont," he had announced robustly. "It's all behind you now, all history. You're free and clear."

She didn't want to be free and clear. She didn't want to be divorced. But she was now in possession of a neatly typed and signed document that declared her free and clear. Unattached. Single. Alone.

She'd never before been so completely, officially, legally alone in her life.

"Didn't Henry Kissinger use to live on this block?" Whitney inquired as they strolled along one of the brick sidewalks lined with beautifully restored town houses, many of which dated back to colonial times. The street was paved with worn cobblestones, and no longer functional trolley tracks lay imbedded in the surface. The streetlights were designed to resemble antique gas lamps. Grasping for positive aspects in her current situation, Kimberly meditated on the pleasure she took in living in Georgetown. Todd had never liked that quaint community of Washington, D.C. He needed space, he insisted, the sort of space that came with a house on the outskirts of the city.

"Goodie for Henry Kissinger," Kimberly said, her tone a touch too biting. A proper lady wasn't supposed to be sarcastic on a date. But thirty-five-year-old divorcées didn't have to be all that proper, she decided.

Besides, she knew that her escort wasn't a big Kissinger fan. A foreign policy specialist on the senator's staff, Whitney tended to view the world from a slightly left-of-center perspective, just as their boss, the senator, did. In her college days, Kimberly would have considered an old-fashioned liberal like Senator Milford faintly reactionary. But times had changed, the center had shifted, and now men and women like the senator were the standard-bearers for the New Left. "Neoliberalism," a columnist had recently coined the political shading. As a political functionary, Kimberly believed it was her duty to keep up with the terminology.

"So Todd has decided to stay on in your old house?" Whitney asked.

"I thought we weren't going to discuss my divorce," Kimberly chastised him. *My divorce.* The words tasted acidic to her, but she supposed she'd have to get used to them.

"You laid down some pretty stringent rules, Kim," Whitney teased her, combing a flopping lock of dark brown hair back from his high brow and winking roguishly. "No shop talk tonight, and no divorce talk."

"I think we did just fine, considering," she said, matching his light tone. Indeed, Whitney had chattered up a veritable storm over dinner. He had described the renovated condominium he had bought in Alexandria, and the vacation trip he'd taken in March to Club Med on Eleuthera Island, and the vicissitudes of finding time for racquetball. One of the most important dating skills Kimberly's mother had drilled into her was to get one's companion to talk about himself. "Men love to talk about themselves," Mrs. Belmont had instructed her daughter years and years ago. "Feed them the right questions, dear, and they will go on forever."

At times Whitney had definitely seemed to go on forever, but that was all right with Kimberly. She preferred listening to him talk about himself to having to talk about herself. What would she have said about her current life? *I'm free and clear. Lucky me.*

"So you're going to remain in Georgetown?" Whitney asked.

"I've been living here for a year," she pointed out. "Why should I move?"

"It's an expensive area."

"I get by," she assured him. In order to stay on in their house in Chevy Chase, Todd had had to buy out her share of the place, and she'd invested the money in a nontaxable bond fund that helped to cover her costs. She hated having to think about such things as investments and taxes; the subject of family finance had always been Todd's responsibility when they were married. Part of being free and clear, she had learned since their separation, entailed taking care of one's own money. Which was definitely *not* the sort of thing a proper lady was supposed to do. But again, "proper" didn't seem a particularly applicable adjective for Kimberly at the moment.

In truth, she had never been especially proper. Not even in her youth, when she was still in the thrall of her distant but infinitely respectable father and her imperious mother, had she managed to live within the strict limits of ladylike propriety. Proper young ladies of the South were supposed to attend schools like Sweet Briar College, not Barnard. They were supposed to major in music or early childhood education, not political science. They were supposed to wear skirts, not jeans, and drink mint juleps, not Liebfraumilch. They were supposed to join sororities, admire men wearing uniforms and keep fluffy white stuffed kitten dolls on their French provincial bureaus.

They were not supposed to live in dormitories on the edge of Harlem, read the poetry of Langston Hughes, and view Eleanor Roosevelt and Gloria Steinem as appropriate role models. They were not supposed to listen to the Rolling Stones and rile their parents by singing "Let's Spend the Night Together" and "Sympathy for the Devil" at the breakfast table.

And, no matter how intelligent they were, they were supposed to strive to be ignorant about finances. They were supposed to giggle charmingly when the bills for their extravagant indulgences arrived in the mail, and their giggling charm was supposed to guarantee that their menfolk would willingly earn the money needed to pay for those indulgences.

No, Kimberly had never been proper, not that way. If her friends at college and later at work found her to be a bit more proper than they were used to, it was undoubtedly because their basis for comparison differed from Kimberly's. To her family she was a renegade, a black sheep, quite probably touched.

"This is my place," she said, turning up the walk that led to her apartment, a ground-floor walk-through of a brownstone across the street from the playing fields of a high school. The open expanse of grass facing the building gave her basement apartment a great deal of light, and she had private access to the tiny fenced-in yard behind the town house. Once she had come to terms with the reality that she was no longer living with Todd, she had grown to adore her apartment. "Would you like to come in for some coffee?" she asked Whitney.

He smiled with delight. "I was hoping you'd ask," he eagerly accepted.

She unlocked the front door, which was located underneath the concrete stairs leading up to the main door of the town house. As she understood it, the basement flat had been built several years back as an in-law apartment, but the landlord's mother-in-law had whimsically decided, after the construction had been completed, that she didn't want to live below her daughter's family. So they rented to Kimberly, instead.

She ushered Whitney through the entry hall and into the cozy living room. "I'm sure I have something harder than coffee, if you'd prefer a nightcap," she offered graciously.

He didn't answer immediately; he was too busy surveying the living room. An overstuffed sofa and matching easy chair, upholstered in a floral print, took up much of the room. Shelves neatly decorated with an assortment of books, a television, a stereo and a few strategically placed objets d'art lined another wall. The two windows overlooking the small front yard were covered with ornate wrought-iron grills.

After satisfying his curiosity, he turned to her, loosened his tie and unbuttoned the collar of his oxford shirt. "You've never invited me into your house before."

"We've never been on a date before," she reminded him.

"That wasn't my choice," he said, crossing to the counter that separated the dining area from the kitchen.

Kimberly smiled uneasily. She wished that Whitney hadn't loosened his tie. It made him appear too much at home, and she was far from ready for him to make himself at home in her apartment. This was their first date, after all, and the only reason she had invited him in was that they were adults and associates at work, and it seemed like a polite thing to do. "Coffee?" she asked, hoping that he would choose that over liquor.

He grinned and strode around the counter to join her in the kitchen. "Let me give you a hand," he suggested.

She laughed. "You needn't act as if I'm helpless," she chided him. "I can make a fine pot of coffee all by myself."

"Skip the coffee."

She shot him a suspicious glance. "Brandy?" she asked.

"Skip that, too." He curled his long fingers around her upper arms and drew her to him.

The warmth of his palms permeated the lightweight fabric of her sleeves, but paradoxically she shivered. "Don't be silly, Whitney," she said sharply, trying to shrug out of his grip. Calling a man silly was *not* a proper thing to do—one ought never to deflate a man's ego on a date—but she'd be damned if she'd let him kiss her just because he'd paid for dinner.

"I wasn't being silly," he said, obviously not at all deflated. "I was being romantic, which, under the circumstances, seems like a good way to end the evening."

"Oh, Whitney..." She watched as his mouth descended toward her from what seemed like an inordinate height. She stood only five feet four inches tall, and even though she generally wore high-heeled shoes, she was used to looking up to men physically. Whitney's superior height didn't alarm her. She deftly turned her head, and his lips landed on the soft golden tendrils covering her ear. "I hate to disillusion you, Whitney, but I think it would be a dreadful way to end the evening."

"I'm disillusioned," he said after spitting out her hair.

"Sorry." She occupied herself preparing a pot of coffee, even though she would rather he just leave. His silence provoked her to justify herself. "We work together, Whitney. We see each other every day. It would be a bit foolhardy to risk our working relationship, don't you think?" There, she commended herself. That wasn't nearly as ego-puncturing as calling him silly.

"Are you really sorry?" He pulled the glass decanter from the coffee maker out of her hands before she could fill it with water, and set it on the counter. Then he rotated her to face him once more. "I'm all in favor of being foolhardy, Kim."

He tried to kiss her again, and she slipped out of his embrace. "Please stop this, Whitney."

"Stop what?" He seemed slightly exasperated. "You're single now, Kim. Divorced. We aren't breaking any laws."

"I know that." She backed into the corner where the counter met the wall and watched him warily. That Whitney was good-looking was irrelevant. She had viewed his cleanly chiseled face and gazed into his limpid brown eyes countless times at work, and she had never felt the slightest pinch of desire for him. Their having just shared a non-business dinner at an expensive restaurant didn't change anything. "I *am* sorry," she drawled. "But I'm asking you very nicely, friend to friend, colleague to colleague—please don't make a pass at me."

"And I'm asking you very nicely to stop being such a virginal prig," he countered as he approached her. His unwelcome nearness gave her the distinct impression that she was trapped. "It's 1987, Kim. When a woman invites a man into her home in 1987 she ought to know what to expect."

"Well, I don't," she defended herself. "I'm new at this, remember?"

"Fair enough. That's why I'm briefing you on it." He was practically upon her, and his hands alighted on her shoulders. "You're a beautiful woman. I'm a healthy man. We know each other and we like each other. So what's the hang-up?"

"The hang-up is, I asked if you wanted coffee, not if you wanted me." She didn't bother to conceal her anger. "If a woman can't invite a man into her home for a cup of coffee, period, then the world of 1987 is in pitiful shape."

"I won't argue about the shape of the world," Whitney allowed. "But it's the only world I've got, and this is how things are done in it. A man takes a woman out for dinner, and when she invites him back to her place afterward, he has every right to make assumptions."

"And she has every right to correct him if he's made the wrong ones," Kimberly asserted. She wasn't frightened by his proximity and his stubbornness. Only supremely annoyed. If he persisted in his muleheaded attempt to seduce her, she would become disgusted with him. And then, when they had to face each other the next day at work, she would be inclined to spit on him. Which would make going to work a difficult proposition. "Please, Whitney. Cool off. If you can't handle being invited into my apartment without attaching all sorts of innuendo to it, then I'll thank you to leave."

He engaged in an internal debate, apparently trying to come up with a new tactic. *Lord help us both,* Kimberly muttered under her breath, *but if he tries anything, anything at all, I'll slam the nearest skillet right into his skull.* Even proper Southern ladies—*especially* proper Southern ladies—knew how to protect themselves from wolves.

"Is it me?" Whitney asked, appearing absurdly innocent. "You don't like me?"

"I like you just fine," Kimberly retorted. "But I don't like your behavior at the moment."

He seemed totally unable to fathom the possibility that Kimberly could be rejecting him. "Your marriage fell apart a year ago. I can't believe you've been living a nun's life for a whole year. Is it someone else? You're seeing someone else, is that it?"

What she couldn't believe was how thickheaded he was behaving. She had always admired Whitney's intelligence, but right now he was acting like a genuine dolt.

Or maybe it was merely a matter of his being a man. Men were congenitally unable to accept that women could turn them down for the simple reason that they weren't interested in them sexually. They always had to grasp at farfetched explanations.

Before she could come up with a diplomatic way of telling him that although there wasn't anybody else in her life she wasn't going to go to bed with him, the telephone rang. Smiling with unbridled relief, she eased away from the counter to reach for the receiver. "Hello?"

"Kimberly?" A vaguely familiar baritone crackled through the long-distance static on the wire. "Kimberly, this is Andrew Collins."

Andrew Collins. Her acquaintance from college, her co-worker on that old, radical student newspaper *The Dream*. Until she had seen him at the reunion Julianne had arranged for the staff, Kimberly hadn't thought about Andrew Collins for fifteen years. And although they'd made amiable chitchat at the reunion, she hadn't anticipated that she would ever think about him again.

She had no idea why he, of all people, would be calling her. They hadn't been friends in college, merely fellow toilers on their newspaper. Andrew had never been particularly fond of her; he had never made any pretense of his lack of respect for her. She hadn't respected him much, either.

He had been condescending, arrogant, an egghead. He used to call her "cheerleader," pronouncing the word as if it were the highest insult. Kimberly *had* been a cheerleader in high school, and she saw nothing wrong with that. That Andrew Collins did made her distrust him during the years they had known each other.

Yet she couldn't deny a perverse joy in hearing from him now. He was a man who had never made a pass at her, who never would. He was a man whom she could invite into her house for coffee knowing that he would never misinterpret her intentions. Even if her intentions were dishonorable, he would never presume to take advantage of her.

Her large blue eyes flickered to Whitney, who was leaning against the counter and watching her with fascination. *Why not?* she contemplated mischievously. *Anything that will turn the fool off....* "Andrew!" she exclaimed into the telephone. "Andrew, darling!"

Darling?

A deep frown line dented Andrew's brow as he tried to analyze Kimberly's surprisingly affectionate greeting. By no stretch of the imagination could he and Kimberly consider their relationship one in which the word "darling" would be apt. He had phoned her because he was desperate, that was all.

It had been a long day, long and difficult. He was still reeling from it, still trying to make sense of how something that had seemed so right could have gone so terribly wrong.

Bob McIntyre had first connected him with John Wilding at the Latin American Research Council last autumn. "They're looking for an ambitious young researcher to fund," Bob had explained. "They need some data on the farm economy in El Salvador. The research that comes out of it could be infinitely helpful to you here. A few articles, maybe a book...I don't have to tell you that with your tenure decision coming up next year, another publication won't hurt you. L.A.R.C. has financial resources. They'll fund you generously. If you're interested in pursuing this, I'll put you in touch with Wilding."

Interested? Andrew had been ecstatic. Funding for extracurricular research was hard to come by in the academic world, particularly when one was a social scientist. The think tanks had their pets, and private industry supported its own economists, not assistant professors from private colleges. Andrew's specialty was the economy of Central America. Being offered nearly unlimited funding to delve into the agricultural economy of El Salvador was a gift of almost unseemly proportions.

More was at stake than simply research funding. Andrew had been teaching at Amherst College for five years, and he wanted to remain on the faculty, to get tenure, to feel secure. He wanted to know that something was his and that it wouldn't be taken away from him.

He had already published one book and numerous articles. His student evaluations were positive, and his colleagues in the department seemed to like him. With a powerful man like Bob McIntyre in his corner, tenure was almost guaranteed.

So he'd met with John Wilding. "L.A.R.C. is a private organization with some modest government backing," Wilding had explained. "Things are unstable in El Salvador, as well you know. We're trying to formulate an idea of how unstable. If you want to get some publications out of the research you do for us, I have no objections."

It had all sounded so reasonable, so pure, so believable. And Andrew was a man who needed to believe. The promise of a happily-ever-after future had already been snatched from him once. Like anyone whose faith had been severely shaken, he needed possibilities. He needed hope.

So he had accepted Wilding's offer of funding. He'd accepted L.A.R.C.'s bounty. He had traveled twice to El Salvador, driven through the rugged, revolution-torn interior to interview the sugar and coffee farmers and then conferred with agricultural experts in the government in San Salvador. He had flown to Los Angeles to meet several refugees. Then he'd compiled his data, interpolated it, put it all into a nice, neat package for the council. And patted himself on the back for a job well done.

But that morning, when he'd met with John Wilding to discuss his findings, everything had come crashing down upon him.

As soon as he had made some sense of what he was involved in, he had decided to call Kimberly. Not because he liked her, not because he admired her, but because she worked for a senator. He wasn't sure whether what Wilding was doing with L.A.R.C. was legal, whether the man had the blessings of the federal government. But if anyone was to investigate Wilding, it would have to be someone with access to government power, someone Andrew could trust. He prayed that Kimberly was that someone. She *had* to be—he had no one else to turn to.

Yet why on earth had she called him "darling"?

"Is this Kimberly Belmont?" he asked, wondering whether he had dialed the wrong number.

"Of course it is, Andrew," she replied in her unmistakable drawl. Her Southern accent wasn't overbearing, but it grated on Andrew. Southern accents made him think of such cultural icons as Scarlett O'Hara and Colonel Sanders. Southerners spoke too slowly; they made Andrew impatient.

"I got your telephone number from Julianne," he informed her, feeling that he had to justify his call. "I hope I'm not disturbing you—"

"Not at all."

"Well...there's something I want to talk to you about. Business," he felt obliged to add. "I think we ought to discuss it in person, if that's at all possible."

"Anything's possible, Andrew."

What was with her? Why did she sound so downright pleased to hear from him? "If it's all right with you," he proceeded, doing his best not to succumb to utter bewilderment, "I could fly down after my last class Friday morning. I could get to D.C. by mid-afternoon."

"That would be absolutely lovely," she purred, increasing his puzzlement. "Why don't you come straight to my office? It's in Senator Milford's suite, in the Hart Building."

"All right," he said, at a loss. "I'll met you there around three or so."

"Fine."

He hesitated. What else was he supposed to say? Should he be civil and ask how she was doing? Should he tell her he was looking forward to seeing her? That wouldn't be completely honest. The truth was, he wished he didn't have to see her. He wished he didn't have to travel to Washington and try to unravel the mess in which his career was currently tangled.

But he had to say something. "Thank you," he mumbled. "I appreciate this."

"It's my pleasure, Andrew," Kimberly responded before hanging up.

"What did she say?" Donna asked.

Andrew lowered the receiver and turned from his desk. Across the room, Donna was seated on the couch, her long, denim-clad legs crossed squaw-style beneath her, with the newspaper spread open to the crossword puzzle on her knees. She closed her pen with a quiet click and gazed inquisitively at Andrew.

For not the first time, he was struck by how much Donna resembled his wife. Marjorie, too, had been tall and slim, with short-cropped, dark hair, brown eyes that sloped down at the outer corners, a narrow, pointy nose and sharp chin. Like Marjorie, Donna gave off an aura of scholarly interest in the world. Which wasn't terribly surprising, Andrew acknowledged, since Donna was a doctoral candidate in psychology at the University of Massachusetts, just down the road from Amherst College. He often wondered whether he had taken up with her simply because she reminded him so much of Marjorie.

Becoming involved with someone because she brought to mind the woman he had loved and lost wasn't really a ghoulish thing, Andrew consoled himself. It was probably quite normal. The only problem was, he couldn't bring himself to love Donna. She *wasn't* Marjorie, and no matter how close she came, he would always be disappointed by her failure to replace his dead wife.

"I take it she's willing to see you?" Donna half asked, her curiosity brimming over.

"Yes. I'm going to Washington on Friday."

"You don't have to look so shaken about the whole thing," Donna scolded him breezily. "You said this woman is an old friend of yours. You've known her for fifteen years. You worked together on that newspaper of yours when you were undergraduates. Why shouldn't she help you out?"

"It's not seeing her that's bothering me," Andrew argued, then sighed and pulled off his eyeglasses. He rubbed the bridge of his nose with his thumb and forefinger and reflected on his edginess. The thought of seeing Kimberly did bother him, but he could think of no good reason it should.

Except that she'd called him "darling." Except that she'd claimed that it would be "lovely" to see him. Except that she'd said, "Anything's possible."

Why?

Although he had told Donna that Kimberly was an old friend of his, "friend" was hardly the word he would use to describe her. They were more like adversaries, antagonists. From the moment he'd laid eyes on her, she had rubbed him the wrong way.

Well, maybe not from that first moment. He recalled the first time he had seen her, when he and his buddy Troy Bennett had entered the classroom for the initial meeting of their advanced rhetoric class. Kimberly had been impossible to miss, with all that blond hair falling to her waist like a shimmering river of gold, and those enormous blue eyes, those delicate cheeks and perpetually pursed lips. "Who the hell is that?" Troy had whispered, nudging Andrew and pointing her out. "Somebody's date?"

It had been a joke among Columbia men at the time that there was no such thing as a pretty Barnard girl. That was an exaggeration, of course; there were as many attractive women at Barnard as at any other school. But for the most part, even those few who qualified as knockouts did their best to appear frumpy and studious. They thought they were being liberated. Evidently they wanted to attract the attentions of men with their brains, not their bodies. Barnard wasn't called "Barnyard" for nothing.

But Kimberly Belmont had done nothing to conceal her extraordinary beauty. Rather than wearing men's cut Levi's, she wore jeans that actually fit, that displayed her narrow waist and flaring hips. Occasionally she even wore eye makeup and a touch of lipstick. She smiled a lot.

How she wound up being close friends with such a bright, sensible woman as Julianne Robinson had always been a mystery to Andrew. But when, for a class project, Julianne and Kimberly, Seth Stone, Laura Brodie, Troy and Andrew decided to put together a newspaper, Andrew was forced to concede that Kimberly was truly a Barnard student—albeit an anomalous one.

She didn't seem serious enough to be a *real* student. She was always so damned chipper and ebullient. Rather than writing gritty articles for *The Dream*, she always wanted to write uplifting stories, essays not about the downtrodden residents of Morningside Heights but about the Korean immigrant who ran the produce market on Broadway. "A success story!" she would exclaim. "Let me write about someone who's made it. People want to read happy things, too, sometimes."

She reminded Andrew of those circular yellow smile faces that had been the rage at the time. Sunny, perky, superficial. She was awfully nice to look at, but you couldn't really talk to her without feeling you were stuck in the middle of a pep rally.

Now she worked as a speech writer for Howard Milford, a senator for whom Andrew harbored a modicum of respect. Not that he trusted politicians as a class, but Milford usually voted the right way on issues. If Milford trusted Kimberly enough to give her such an important position on his staff, Andrew figured she must have something going for her. Reputable senators didn't hire women as speech writers simply because they were gorgeous. Secretaries, perhaps, but not speech writers.

"Why don't we get some food?" Donna broke into his thoughts. "I'm ravenous."

He slipped his eyeglasses back up his nose and gazed at the woman across the living room. She wasn't really far away—the dimensions of his apartment, one of four in a converted old house, were tiny—but she seemed to be seated in another galaxy.

"I'm not very hungry," he said. "If you want, we can open a can of something."

Donna grinned and stretched, her oversize T-shirt draping loosely across her bony body. "Forget it, Andy. I just said I was ravenous. Take me to Friendly's for a tuna melt and an ice cream, and I might love you forever."

He forced a smile. "You're easy to please."

She stood and crossed the room. "I hate seeing you look so worried, Andy," she said, slinging her arms around his neck and planting a kiss on his forehead. "Personally, I think this whole thing is a tempest in a teapot."

"I wish you were right. But you're not," he contended. "Wilding is a dangerous man. And if I blow the whistle on him, I'm going to embarrass Bob McIntyre. And if I embarrass Bob McIntyre, I can kiss tenure goodbye. Q.E.D."

"If I were you," Donna remarked, "I'd pocket that whistle until after you've got tenure. Why make waves?"

She wasn't from a different galaxy, he realized, but rather from a different time zone. Donna was twenty-eight, and in many ways, being eight years younger than Andrew put her into an entirely different generation. She was a child of the seventies, not the sixties, a product of the "Me Generation." He had no doubt whatsoever that Donna would have done whatever it took to finish her Ph.D., land herself a dream job and keep it for as long as she wanted it. She knew how to be earnest without being committed, and that was probably a very healthy way to go about life these days.

But Andrew couldn't live like that.

He couldn't explain himself to Donna. She wouldn't understand. Andrew was a product of an older, more idealistic generation, and sometimes he acted reflexively. Sometimes, even though it risked his stable life, he felt compelled to take a stand.

"Friendly's," he said, hoisting himself to his feet. He ought to feed Donna, no matter how meager his own appetite was. He ought to feed her and bring her back to his place afterward and enjoy her company for a few hours. Whether Andrew could resolve his plight wasn't contingent on skipping meals or locking out his current girlfriend.

He pocketed his key, took her hand and accompanied her out of the apartment.

Chapter Two

Kimberly was on the telephone when Andrew reached the open door of her office. Without interrupting her phone conversation, she tossed him a quick smile and beckoned him inside with a wave. As soon as he had crossed the threshold, she held up her index finger to indicate that she would be off the phone in a minute. Then she angled her face away from Andrew and addressed her caller. "The Kiwanis may or may not be brighter than the Junior Achievers, Lee, but they *are* older. The senator is not going to give a speech written for high school students to a professional group like the Kiwanis. If you all can just cool your heels until next week, I will gladly juice up the Junior Achievers speech. But you'll simply have to give me a chance to dip into my book of anecdotes, Lee. We can't have the senator regaling a bunch of grown men with that shaggy-dog story about the time his father's car broke down on his way to the senior prom."

She listened for a moment, caught Andrew's eye and smiled helplessly. "No, he's not going to get into heavy issues," she said into the phone. "He'll be speaking after dinner. The fine gentlemen in the audience are all going to be soused. I'm sure the senator will want to avoid policy statements. That includes his views on trade tariffs."

Doing his best not to eavesdrop, Andrew tightened his grip on his battered leather briefcase and surveyed the small inner office. Kimberly's desk was impeccably tidy, her blotter clear and all loose papers stacked neatly in a wire tray occupying one corner. The perpendicular extension of the desk held a compact word processor. White file cabinets stood along a wall and an unabridged dictionary lay open on a polished oak book stand in one corner. Although the office lacked a window, it seemed uncommonly bright.

That might have been due less to the glaring overhead fixture than to Kimberly's radiant presence, he admitted. She had always had the ability to illuminate her surroundings. Andrew wasn't sure whether to attribute that ability to her lustrous blond hair, which was no less striking in its stylish chin-length shag than it had been back in college, when she'd worn it long and free-flowing, or to her beaming smile. Although her suit was a pale gray hue and her blouse a muted pink, her attire also seemed to add light to the room.

"Lee, we both know that this won't be the proper forum for enunciating policy positions. I assure you, the senator will agree with me on this. It's going to be a backslapping, I'm-one-of-the-guys speech, that's all."

Andrew shouldn't have been impressed by her end of the conversation. He should have assumed that a woman in Kimberly's position would have backbone and clout, would be able to argue decisively, would use phrases like "trade tariffs" and "enunciating policy positions." If the woman were as much of a ninny as she had so often seemed to him years ago, she wouldn't be the head speech writer for a senator.

Still, he found that listening to Kimberly haggle about an upcoming speech was something of a revelation. He had trouble reconciling his image of the delicate, nearly fragile-looking blond woman he had known in college with the high-powered, articulate professional now seated at the desk across the office from him. Seeing her in such a milieu and hearing her speak with such utter confidence was disorienting. Far from appearing delicate and fragile, she seemed dynamic to Andrew, almost nerve-wrackingly bright.

Perhaps she had more on the ball than he had ever given her credit for. He certainly hoped so. If she was going to help him, she would have to be more than a frivolous Southern belle.

"I'll have something for you next week, Lee," she said, signing off. "Stick with me on this. I know the senator will appreciate it." She hung up the phone and smiled again. "Hello, Andrew. I'm sorry I got tied up on the telephone. Please sit down."

Her greeting was only the slightest bit warmer than strictly businesslike, and Andrew was reassured by it. He hadn't yet recovered from their bizarre conversation two days ago, when she had called him "darling." But since her manner with him today was pleasantly aloof, he decided not to question her about her reasons for implying an intimacy between them the last time they had spoken.

"How was your trip down?" she asked politely.

He cautiously took a seat on the vinyl upholstered chair facing her desk and set his briefcase on the floor at his feet. Kimberly appeared so well groomed that he wished he had worn a tie. He had packed one, but he hadn't bothered to put it on when he'd stopped at the motel to check in on his way from the airport. At work he generally wore jeans or corduroys, and comfortable shirts with the collars left unbuttoned. Ties were reserved for cocktail parties and meetings with the dean of the college, not for hectic jaunts to Washington to confer with a former acquaintance.

At least his shirt was crisp, his blazer fairly new, his loafers recently polished. He was surprised to find himself so concerned about the impression he was making on Kimberly.

"The flight was okay," he answered her. "I've got to say, though, this Metro system of yours is absolutely mystifying. The train carried me from Crystal City to downtown Washington without any mishaps, but then when I got off, I couldn't get out of the station. Every time I inserted my fare card in the exit slot, the damned machine spit it back out at me. It took me a few minutes to realize that I had to pay an extra fare just to get through the gate and win my freedom."

"The Metro takes some getting used to," Kimberly agreed. "You're staying in Crystal City, then?"

"I've got a room at one of the motels there. They're cheaper than the hotels in the city."

Kimberly nodded. Andrew wondered whether she found their conversation as stilted as he did. "Would you like some coffee?" she offered.

Before he could answer, a fresh-faced young man tapped on Kimberly's open door and poked his head inside. "Ms. Belmont— Oh, excuse me," he said, belatedly noticing Andrew.

"That's all right, Barry," Kimberly assured him. "What can I do for you?"

Grinning meekly, the young man stepped inside the office. "I was just wondering if you've had a chance to look over my first draft for the 'Letter to the Constituents' flyer."

"I've gone through it," Kimberly said, lifting a stapled collection of pages from the top of her basket and extending it toward her associate. "You touch all the bases just fine, Barry, but as usual you've tended to be long-winded. Especially in the Social Security report. Cut it down and punch it up. You've got to keep it lively, or you'll bore the voters."

"Got it." Barry took the papers and headed for the door. "Thanks, Ms. Belmont. I'll get a new draft to you by Monday."

Kimberly watched his departure and turned back to Andrew. "My newest assistant," she explained. "He's very eager, but he has a lot to learn. I'm sorry for all these distractions," she apologized again.

Once more, Andrew reminded himself that he had no right to be surprised by her professional polish. If Kimberly was still a cheerleader, well, leading cheers for a United States senator was quite a different thing from leading cheers for a high school quarterback. "I'm sorry," he countered.

"What for?"

For misjudging you, he almost replied. *For thinking you were just another pretty face.* Although, damn, she was pretty. Andrew had always known that, but his awareness of her appearance seemed more acute today than it had ever been before.

"I seem to have barged in here when you're buried in work," he remembered to answer her. "If this is a bad time for you, Kimberly—"

She laughed. "There's no such thing as a good time around here," she informed him. "I'm always buried in work. Now...I was about to get you some coffee, wasn't I?"

"I'll pass, thanks," he declined with a shake of his head. He wanted to get on with it, to tell her what he had come to tell her and to see what she could do, then to leave and resume his normal life. "Let's get down to business."

She leaned back in her chair and folded her hands primly on her blotter. "I must say, Andrew, I can't wait to hear this business of yours. You surely were mysterious on the telephone the other night."

So were you, darling, Andrew responded silently. He was tempted to ask her about that "darling" comment, extremely tempted. Especially now, after he had seen her at work, asserting herself on the phone and then gently but firmly instructing an underling. Especially after admitting, for not the first time in his life, that he considered Kimberly almost irritatingly beautiful. Being called "darling" by someone like Kimberly could put any man's hormones into orbit, and even Andrew, who generally considered himself above such things, was no exception.

Business, he reproached himself. *Get on with it. Get it over with.* "I've been doing some research on the agricultural economy of El Salvador," he began.

Kimberly cut him off with a grin. "I'm afraid that's not the senator's area of expertise, Andrew. He's very involved in domestic farm policy, of course, but—"

"That's not why I'm here," Andrew said impatiently. Did she actually think he had come all the way to Washington for help on a term paper?

His sharp retort seemed to startle Kimberly. She took a moment to assess him, then composed herself and cued him with a nod to continue.

"The research was funded by an organization called the Latin American Research Council. L.A.R.C."

"I don't believe I've ever heard of it," she commented.

"It's a front for the C.I.A.," Andrew announced. At her blank stare, he added, "A phony cover."

"A proprietary," she said, using the correct term. "The C.I.A. frequently sets up proprietaries, fake outfits to disguise their work."

He gave her a hard look, trying to interpret her complacent expression. "Doesn't that bother you?"

She laughed. "Don't be so naive, Andrew," she reproached him. "The C.I.A. does a great deal of sensitive work. They have to operate sub rosa. Sometimes they're looking for particular information. They can't very well paint a billboard advertising for it."

He bristled at her patronizing tone. "Maybe you think the C.I.A. is swell, Kimberly," he muttered. "Maybe you think the secret war in Cambodia was terrific and Pinochet in Chile is one hell of a wonderful guy."

"That was a long time ago," Kimberly pointed out. "Whatever evils the C.I.A. may have perpetrated in the past, they do serve an important purpose. I suppose you think I'm a wild-eyed right-winger for saying such a thing, but—"

"No, I'll grant that the C.I.A. serves a purpose," Andrew conceded. He hadn't come to Washington to fight with Kimberly. And much as it rankled, he had to admit the nation wouldn't be able to function without the C.I.A. "The issue isn't the C.I.A. itself. It's L.A.R.C. Wednesday morning, I met with L.A.R.C.'s chief, a guy named John Wilding, and presented him with my findings. He said things that frightened me, Kimberly. He implied that he was going to do some pretty scary things with the data I gave him."

"Scary things?" Her vivid blue eyes grew wide. "What sort of things?"

"Economic sabotage. Things are unstable in El Salvador. The government is being attacked from the left and from the right. If the farm economy—shaky as it is—collapses, it would in all likelihood lead to a revolution. The only way to quash a revolution would be to install a strongman. I think that's what Wilding and his C.I.A. cronies are planning."

Kimberly tapped her fingertips together thoughtfully. Her nails were polished, Andrew noted, her hands tiny, her fingers slender and graceful. She appeared more concerned than alarmed by what he had told her. "What makes you believe this is what your Mr. Wilding is planning?" she asked.

"Things he said," Andrew replied vaguely. His answer obviously didn't satisfy Kimberly, and he mentally ran through his meeting with John Wilding again, searching for specifics. "The topics that interested him most in my report had to do with fertilizer shipments and marketing pipelines. Interfere with either of those, and you can easily destroy the farmers. Wilding wanted the names of all of my contacts down there, people who willingly spoke to me because I was an academic, but who told me in no uncertain terms that they didn't want to talk to government agents because they didn't trust them. I was sent to do research for the C.I.A. because the C.I.A. was being shut out."

"How do you know this Wilding person is really C.I.A.?"

"I don't know for sure. But he told me he was. After I handed over my report, of course."

"He *told* you?"

"He's strange, Kimberly. He seems like a man possessed." Andrew exhaled, wondering if he himself sounded like a man possessed. "I thought...since you work for a senator who happens to serve on the Intelligence Committee, maybe you could check out Wilding. And L.A.R.C. Find out what they're up to. Discreetly, if possible. Can you do that for me?"

She gazed at him for a long while, meditating. A knock on her open door jarred her, and she and Andrew turned to see a tall, dark-haired man enter. "Hi, Kim," he greeted her familiarly. "Are you busy right now?"

"You can see that I am, Whitney," she said, her tone distinctly chilly. Then she glanced at Andrew, and he detected an enigmatic glimmer in her eye. "But come right in," she welcomed the intruder, abruptly smiling, speaking in a sensuous drawl. She stood and glided around the desk to Andrew, urging him to his feet with her hand on his elbow. "I'd like for you to meet my very dear friend, Andrew Collins. I believe I've told you about him. Andrew, meet Whitney Brannigan.''

The way she said "my very dear friend" reminded Andrew of the way she had said "darling" on the telephone a couple of days ago. He recognized that she had shifted gears on him; she was suddenly exuding honey. And her hand remained on his elbow, pinching him through the tweed of his blazer just hard enough for him to know that she wanted him to follow her lead.

"How do you do?" he said courteously, offering his hand to Whitney.

Whitney shook it, then sized him up with a speculative perusal. "So you're Andrew," he said. "Yes, Kim's told me about you. You're a lucky man."

Kimberly pinched Andrew's arm again. He almost yelped in pain, and he almost burst into laughter. He had no idea what charade she was involved in, but sure, he'd go along with it for a while, just out of curiosity. "Luck ebbs and flows, Whitney," he remarked philosophically. It seemed like a safe thing to say, and given that Andrew was in the dark, he figured it best not to commit himself further.

"As a matter of fact, Whitney," Kimberly interjected, "we could use your brains right now. Andrew has just been telling me a fascinating tale about a C.I.A. proprietary he's recently had dealings with. I think some delving is in order."

She turned to Andrew and presented him with a winning smile. Her eyes bore into him, sparkling with an odd blend of humor and supplication. He gave her a nearly imperceptible nod. Typical of Kimberly to be playing some silly game with men, although Andrew thought that a married woman ought to be above such nonsense. But he wouldn't give her away. Yet.

Whitney scrutinized Andrew again. Andrew tried to guess what the sharply dressed, undeniably handsome man was thinking. "Fill me in," Whitney requested.

Without a clear idea of what was going on between Whitney and Kimberly, Andrew wasn't certain what to say. Fortunately Kimberly bailed him out. "Andrew has been working with a gentleman named John Wilding. His proprietary is called the Latin American Resource Center."

"Research Council," Andrew corrected her.

"Andrew thinks the man wants to sabotage the farm economy of El Salvador," she explained.

"Whoa!" Whitney staggered backward. "That's a pretty serious charge."

"Andrew is a brilliant man," Kimberly cooed, tightening her grip on his elbow and batting her eyes up at him coquettishly. Andrew willfully looked past her, hoping to convey that he didn't exactly approve of whatever it was she was doing. Her smile tensing slightly, she turned back to Whitney. "I'm sure he wouldn't make such a charge without having adequate justification. Could you run this John Wilding through your contacts and see what you come up with?" She spun back to Andrew again. "Whitney is one of the senator's foreign policy experts," she revealed. "He knows a lot of people who know a lot of things."

"Okay," Andrew mumbled, still at sea. He decided that, even more than her mysterious game with Whitney, he didn't like her surprisingly strong hand on him. He didn't like the faint, intoxicating scent of her perfume, the bewitching curve of her lower lip as she smiled at him. She was definitely prettier than any woman had a right to be.

"John Wilding. Latin American Research Council," Whitney recited. "It's Friday afternoon, so I don't know how far I'm going to get with this."

"Do the best you can," Kimberly requested, turning her dazzling smile to Whitney once more.

"Don't I always?" He pivoted and left the office.

As soon as he was gone, Kimberly released Andrew, and he took a safe step back from her. "What the hell was that all about?" he inquired.

She shrugged negligently. "Whitney has been courting me—in a rather obnoxious way, I'm afraid. I had to find a way to call him off, and I had to be diplomatic about it since we work together. So I told him you were my beau. I hope you don't mind."

"Don't mind?" Andrew exclaimed, astounded. "What about your husband, for crying out loud? Why don't you just tell the guy you're married?"

"I'm not," she said bluntly. She averted her eyes, but not before Andrew caught a glimpse of keen pain in them. "I've just been divorced."

"Oh." It took a minute to sink in. Kimberly, the gorgeous coed betrothed to her hometown boyfriend, wearing that ridiculous one-and-a-half carat diamond ring on her finger throughout her senior year, hurrying back to Georgia to marry her sweetheart before the ink had a chance to dry on her diploma. Divorced. "I'm sorry," he said automatically.

"Don't worry about it." She shrugged again. "It happens to the best of people."

Maybe it happened to the best of people, but why to Kimberly? What man in his right mind would let a woman as enchanting as she was get away?

Now *that* was a peculiar thought. Kimberly might be enchanting, but Andrew had always been immune to her spell in the past. Why should he question her husband's sanity in ending his marriage to her? If, in fact, her husband had ended it. For all Andrew knew, Kimberly might have been the one to do the walking. She had said she had *been* divorced, not that she *was* divorced, which implied that her husband had divorced her. But that was probably just some quaint Southern way of talking.

Yet the sadness lingered in her eyes, casting them in shadow, causing Andrew to brim with heartfelt sympathy for her. Whatever his history with her, he could understand her pain, because he had endured a similar pain himself. "I really am sorry," he said, quietly this time, fervently.

She lifted her gaze to him. Evidently she comprehended how sincere he was. "Thank you, Andrew."

He wished he could put his arm around her, hold her, comfort her. She looked so forlorn, and so far away from him. Yet he and Kimberly had never been particularly close, and there was no way he could offer her more than the most basic condolences.

So he shoved his hands into his pockets and smiled. "Can I ask you a personal question?"

She managed a smile. "Be my guest."

"The other night when you called me 'darling,' what was that all about? Did that have something to do with the guy who was just in here?"

"You are brilliant," she praised him, smiling. "Whitney was at my house at the time. It was our first—and I daresay our last—date. He was all over me. The man was like Silly Putty, Andrew, twisting and gooey and oozing every which way. And then you called, and I was able to slip out of his clutches. Saved by the bell, wasn't I?"

"Your first date and he was all over you," Andrew mused. "He did seem to have 'fast track' written across his forehead."

Kimberly chuckled. "Dating rituals have apparently changed during the years I was married. I remember a time when a decent man didn't kiss you until the third date."

"You're that old, huh?" Andrew teased her.

"I suppose I am. But you've been playing this game yourself, Andrew. Do you wait until the third date before you come on like gangbusters?"

"I—" He closed his mouth and frowned. How did Kimberly know about Marjorie? He hadn't mentioned that he was widowed to any of the women at the *Dream* reunion six weeks ago. And then he recalled that he hadn't mentioned to any of the women that he had been married, either. Kimberly probably assumed that he was still a bachelor. "I'm a decent man," he assured her with a whimsical smile. "I always wait until the third date."

"And then you come on like gangbusters?"

"I'd like to think I'm a little more subtle than that."

"You probably are," Kimberly agreed. "We've had our differences, Andrew, and I know you don't think very highly of me, but I've always considered you a decent man."

He wasn't sure whether he ought to be complimented or chagrined by her statement. At least two thirds of it was uncomfortably true. He hoped the last third was true, as well. He wanted Kimberly to consider him a decent man.

A sudden awkwardness enveloped him. Kimberly no longer looked depressed. She was gazing at him with an unnerving steadiness. In all the time they had known each other, she had never spoken so directly to him before, and he had never reacted with such overwhelming interest to how she thought of him.

He pointedly reminded himself that, for all the grit she'd displayed in her behavior with her colleagues, she had been playing a rather juvenile game with him and Whitney. She was still cutesy Kimberly, the coquettish Georgia peach.

"Let me give you my number at the motel," he suggested, digging in an inner pocket of his blazer for the card he'd picked up at the check-in desk. "You can call me when you've got the dirt on John Wilding."

She grinned. "You can wait here if you'd like."

"But you're busy."

"I worked late three nights out of the last four. I'm enti-tled to visit with an old college chum this afternoon." She gestured toward the vinyl chair, then moved around the desk to resume her seat.

Against his better judgment, Andrew sat. He didn't know what to say to Kimberly, how to make small talk with her. All he knew was that her smile was holding him in place, exerting a power over him that he was unable to combat.

"How have you been?" she asked.

"Didn't we have this conversation at Julianne's party?" he countered.

Her smile expanded. "I was busy catching up with all the others there. Now it's our turn. By the way—" her eyes be-gan to sparkle "—did you hear about Seth and Laura?"

"You mean that Stoned has gone bonkers over her?"

"They're going to get married," Kimberly told him. "Julianne called me a couple of days ago to tell me the news. Isn't it exciting?"

"Yes," Andrew said genuinely. He liked both Laura and Seth a great deal, and he was very happy for them. "I didn't know they'd taken it as far as marriage. But the last time I saw Seth, he told me Laura had turned his life around. Married, huh." He ruminated on the idea, then laughed. "Stoned is actually going to take on Laura's teenage daughter?"

"Apparently they get along well," Kimberly said. "Ac-cording to Julianne, they're all planning to live in Brook-lyn until the school term ends, and then Laura and Rita are going to move to California with Seth. I've tried to call Laura a few times, but her line is always tied up. She must be busy making plans. Lord, it's all so romantic." Kim-berly sighed.

"Do you think marriage is romantic?" Andrew ques-tioned her. "Aren't divorcées supposed to be jaded?"

Her smile waned. "I hope I never become jaded," she declared earnestly. "That's one thing that scares me. I don't want to turn bitter and nasty."

"I can't imagine you bitter and nasty," Andrew assured her. People who put one in mind of circular yellow smiling faces couldn't change their personalities overnight.

"So," Kimberly persevered, "how have you been?"

"Fine," he answered. "I've been fine. Until Wednesday, when I found out I was unwittingly working for the C.I.A."

She settled back in her swivel chair, smiling cryptically, looking oddly amused by Andrew's predicament. She lifted a fountain pen from her blotter, tapped it absently against her desk, then set it down. Her smile widened, revealing a straight row of small, pearly teeth. "How did you hook up with John Wilding, anyway?"

"It isn't funny," Andrew grumbled, irked by her good-humored attitude.

She laughed. "Oh, yes, Andrew, it is. I always think of you as so solemn, so dedicated and principled. You're nobody's fool. How in the world did you let some C.I.A. operative pull the wool over your eyes?"

"I didn't—" Andrew drew in a sharp breath and mulled over his response. The truth was, Kimberly had interpreted the situation precisely. Andrew had let someone pull the wool over his eyes. Willingly. "One of the people I work with in the economics department at Amherst made the introduction. He's a highly esteemed man, a full professor, and the fact that he recommended me to Wilding was a real vote of confidence. It implied that he was ready to champion me for tenure next year, and so...so I didn't ask the questions I should have."

"What are you going to do if all your suspicions are borne out, if you find out that John Wilding is a nut? Won't it mortify this full professor if you make an issue out of it?"

"It may well cost me tenure," Andrew admitted grimly. "And that's not a happy thought."

Whitney appeared at the doorway, empty-handed. "You know what they ought to do?" he announced grandly, marching into the office. "They ought to shut down the government at noon on Friday. You can't find out nothin', nohow, at this time of the week."

"Nothing at all?" Kimberly asked, disappointed.

"Well...all right, I found out a little. Wilding is employed by the C.I.A. His present field is Central America. He's been with the agency for twelve years. Nobody knows anything about the Latin American Research Council, but that's just safe talk."

"And? What's your educated opinion, Whitney?" Kimberly pressed him.

His gaze traveled from her to Andrew and back again. "I think we may be on to something here. It's worth digging further. If it's as juicy as your very dear friend Andrew suspects, we could get a lot of mileage out of it for the senator. So sure, I'm willing to stick with it for a while."

"How about tomorrow?" Kimberly asked. "Can you do anything with this over the weekend?"

"Better over the weekend than during the week. People talk more freely when they're at home than when they're in Langley, Virginia, being watched. I can call some people and see what we come up with. For the senator," he stressed, shooting Andrew a disgruntled look.

"Thank you," Andrew said dutifully. No matter how stupid Kimberly's act with Andrew was, he couldn't deny that he enjoyed being thought of, however mistakenly, as the "very dear friend" of a woman as enticing as she.

"This is all quite intriguing," Kimberly commented. "I can picture the senator giving a thundering oration on the subject of C.I.A. abuses—penned by me, of course."

"Of course," Whitney said dryly.

He remained hovering near the door, and Kimberly asked, "Was there something else? I forgot to ask you why you dropped in earlier."

Whitney's vision shuttled between her and Andrew again. "Just wanted to know whether you might be interested in dinner with me this evening," he said. "It's pretty clear that you aren't available."

"I'm afraid not," Kimberly said, sounding not at all regretful. "Andrew and I have already made plans."

Andrew grinned. "Yes, *darling*," he backed her up. "We've already made plans."

"Pizza?" Andrew blurted out. "I never took you for a pizza type."

Kimberly smiled. "I'm almost afraid to ask what type you took me for. Not pig's knuckles and grits, I hope."

Andrew shook his head. "More the veal cordon bleu type."

"Ah, yes, I'm so terribly refined," she said with a self-deprecating sigh. They were ambling down Pennsylvania Avenue in the shadow of the Capitol Rotunda, heading toward a restaurant. The evening was balmy; Washington's infamous mugginess rarely settled in as early as mid-April. "I'm sure you must have seen me eating pizza at some of our staff meetings when we were working on *The Dream*."

"We usually ate granola at those meetings," Andrew recalled. "Laura always came armed with a sack of it."

"That's right. Granola." Kimberly grimaced. "Hippie fuel. I used to make my folks buy granola for me to eat when I was home on vacation, just to get their goat. I loathed the stuff. It seemed more suited to rodents than humans."

"Humans have a lot in common with rats," Andrew pointed out.

"That's a fact I'd rather not be reminded of." She veered toward the front door of an elegantly decorated eatery.

"Rest assured, Andrew, the pizza here is of gourmet quality. They even serve it on dishes with pedestals."

Twenty minutes later a waiter delivered a sizzling pie on a pedestaled silver cake tray, just as Kimberly had predicted. She and Andrew had already consumed some Chianti, and she was feeling mellow.

Much to her delight, she was enjoying Andrew's company. She hadn't known what to expect from his visit, either in the business that had brought him to town or in his presence itself. But his business was indeed fascinating. Washington thrived on scandals, and given the secretive nature of the C.I.A., she believed that it deserved to be tweaked and twitted whenever possible. The senator believed that, too, and Kimberly had little doubt that when she and Whitney informed him of their investigation of L.A.R.C., their boss would make hay of it.

Andrew's presence was also fascinating. Seated across the small linen-covered table from him, she studied him intently, comparing his current appearance with the way he had groomed himself in college. Back then his face had been half-hidden by a shrubby brown beard, and when she'd seen him at the reunion in early March, she had considered his now clean-shaven jaw too jutting. But it wasn't really. It was large and square, appealingly rugged.

She also preferred his aviator-shaped eyeglasses to the wire-rimmed spectacles he had favored in college. The thin tortoiseshell frames matched his pale brown eyes. She liked the barely discernible laugh lines fanning out from their corners. And she liked the casual neatness of his dark hair, which contained a few visible strands of premature silver at his temples. All in all, he was aging quite attractively.

Back in school she had thought of Andrew as somehow gnomelike, despite his taller-than-average height and well-proportioned physique. He had always looked as if he had just climbed out from the pages of a dusty tome. Or a hundred dusty tomes. He had generally conveyed an aura of learnedness. She hadn't been exaggerating to Whitney when she'd said that Andrew was brilliant.

In the past his brilliance used to turn her off. She had nothing against intellectuals, but she had resented Andrew's habit of hiding behind his erudition. The man had a brain, but she often doubted whether he had any spirit.

She was now conscious of cracks in his intellectual armor, however, and she was thrilled by the opportunity to peek behind his scholarly veneer. She was thrilled by the fact that high-and-mighty Andrew had come to her, of all people, for assistance.

More than his professional vulnerability was seeping through the cracks. Kimberly had learned about his wife's death from Laura, who had in turn learned about it from Seth after the reunion. Andrew didn't seem to want to discuss his wife's passing with Kimberly, and she was tactful enough not to probe. But knowing that he had suffered such a tragedy altered her perception of him. The lopsided twist of his smile no longer connoted cynicism and arrogance to her. It connoted unspoken sadness.

"I've got to hand it to you," he commented after swallowing the last of his pizza slice. "This is delicious. Much better than anything in Amherst."

"What's it like up there?" Kimberly asked. She might have asked such a question of Whitney in an effort to get him to talk about himself, as one was supposed to do on a date. But this dinner with Andrew didn't really constitute a date, and she asked out of genuine interest.

"It's beautiful, in an almost unreal way," he replied. "They could have filmed the Andy Hardy movies on Amherst's campus. Rolling lawns, rolling hills, towering trees, ivy-covered buildings. Endless blue skies. It smells good there, Kimberly. The air is so clean."

"What are your students like?" she asked before biting into her pizza.

"They're sharp. A bit spoiled, though. Most of them have never had to fight for anything, so they sometimes strike me as flabby."

"Physically or mentally?" she asked, then smiled. "When I think of Amherst I think of tall young men named 'Buckey' and 'Shep,' wearing rugby shirts and Topsider shoes."

Andrew guffawed. "I hate to break the news to you, Kimberly, but Amherst has been coed for years." He mused for a moment, then laughed again. "Admittedly, I've encountered a few female students who'd fit that description, right down to the names."

"Do you have a house there?"

"No. A small apartment," he told her.

"Big homes are such a bother, don't you think?" Kimberly remarked. "They're so much effort to keep clean."

He seemed on the verge of saying something, then changed his mind. Instead he nodded and refilled their goblets with wine from the straw-wrapped bottle.

She wondered what he had been about to say. Lord, but she wished he'd open up a bit more. "There was a time in my life," she ventured, deciding to introduce a more personal note to their conversation, "when I thought all I'd ever want in life was to keep a nice house for my husband. But that palls. Running a vacuum cleaner is hardly creative."

"Is that why you went to work for Senator Milford?" Andrew asked.

"The senator wasn't elected until 1976," she told him. "I took my first job about six months after I got married. Todd wasn't too pleased about having a working wife, but we had a mighty big mortgage to pay off."

"You worked in public relations or something, didn't you?" Andrew recollected. "I think you mentioned that at the reunion."

"Yes. I got a job with one of the big P.R. firms in town. Glorified lobbying, that's what it was. Writing position papers for clients. The National Retail Merchants' Association, the National Society of Undertakers, you name it. They all had legislative axes to grind, and my job was to sharpen those axes for them."

"Did you enjoy it?"

She sipped her wine and reminisced. "I enjoyed the writing aspect of it. Ever since working on *The Dream* I've enjoyed playing with words. But I didn't always enjoy the positions I had to present. I happen to believe that undertakers ought to be held more accountable than they are." She bit her lip, suddenly anxious. Wasn't it tasteless to talk about undertakers with a man whose wife had died? If this had been a real date, she would have watched her words more carefully.

Much to her relief, Andrew didn't seem particularly troubled by her remark. "So now that you work for Milford you spend all your time trying to blunt those axes."

"I do my best." She took another sip of wine, then helped herself to a second slice of pizza from the tray. "The senator stands for some very good things. I'm proud to be on his staff. I can't say that my former job ever gave me a feeling of pride."

Andrew had lifted his goblet, but at her confession he lowered it without drinking. "You amaze me, Kimberly," he said.

She laughed. "Do I?"

"You were right. What you said back in your office about how I don't think highly of you." He gazed steadily at her, his eyes large and uncharacteristically tender behind the lenses of his eyeglasses. "I'd like to put that in the past tense, if it's all right with you."

She was inordinately flattered by his request, although it was a backhanded compliment at best. "Dare I ask what's made you change your opinion?"

"Just about everything that's happened today. Everything except that stupid game you're playing with Whitney."

So much for feeling flattered, she thought. Once again Andrew was judging her, condescending to her. "It's not a stupid game," she protested. "The man seems to be unable to take no for an answer. I tried honesty with him. I tried firmness. But Whitney's such a boob. Nothing worked. I made a mistake in accepting an invitation to dinner with him, but I'm not going to let that one mistake destroy my working relationship with him. So I'll do what I have to do." She offered Andrew a frosty smile. "I appreciate your having backed me up at the office, but if you don't want to anymore, that's quite all right with me. I'll figure out something else."

"It's no skin off my nose," Andrew hastened to placate her. "All I meant was, it's kind of stupid."

"Whitney is kind of stupid," Kimberly snapped. "Sometimes you have to stoop to your opponent's level."

He shrugged. "Fair enough, Kimberly." He hesitated, then said, "He calls you 'Kim.'"

"Not because I invited him to," she noted. She had no objection to her closest friends calling her "Kim," but Whitney had chosen to refer to her by that nickname almost from the first. It annoyed her, but she'd given up on correcting him. "I've never heard anyone call you 'Andy,'" she remarked, turning the spotlight back on Andrew.

"A few people do," he conceded. "I'm not crazy about it, though."

"It makes you think of Andy Hardy," she joked.

"Andy Hardy, Andy Devine, Raggedy Andy."

"You can call me 'Kim,'" she said impulsively. She forgave him for having criticized her ploy with Whitney. He was right—it was stupid. But, as she'd told him, she had run out of reasonable approaches to discouraging Whitney's attentions.

And even though Andrew thought it was stupid, he was going along with it, which was awfully generous of him. She wasn't used to generosity from Andrew, and she treasured his willingness to do something so utterly stupid for her.

"All right," he agreed, smiling shyly. He tried out the name, appraising the way it sounded. "Kim. Have another slice, Kim." He lifted a slice of pizza from the pan.

She waved it away from her plate. "I'm afraid I've reached my limit, Andrew. You eat it."

"It's pretty filling," he admitted, though he took the slice for himself. "So, when are you going to tell Senator Milford about L.A.R.C.?"

"If we find something really exciting we'll call him. If not, I imagine it can wait until he gets back to town."

"He's not in Washington?" Andrew looked sorely disappointed.

"No, he's home," Kimberly answered. "He comes up for reelection next year, and he's been trying to spend as much of his time as possible on the stump." She measured Andrew's crestfallen look and grinned. "You were hoping to meet him, weren't you?"

"It would have been fun," he conceded. "I happen to like the guy's politics."

"Next time you come down I'll try to set up an appointment with him for you," she said without thinking. Andrew hadn't mentioned anything about planning to come to Washington a second time. Yet she hoped he would want to. She hoped that after all this time she and Andrew could become friends.

She watched him carefully, gauging his reaction to her suggestion. He nibbled his pizza thoughtfully, then smiled. "That would be great," he said.

His words were casual, almost offhanded, but Kimberly felt a thrill of joy at their underlying meaning. There would be a next time. She would see Andrew again after this weekend. He did want to be her friend.

She felt as if she'd just received an unexpected gift—from a man who was unused to giving. Unexpected and wonderful. A warm wave of gratitude washed through her.

She raised her glass in a silent toast to their newfound friendship, then drank.

Chapter Three

"Laura!" Kimberly set down the documents she had been perusing and gave her full attention to the telephone. "Laura, I have been trying to reach you all for days, but your line is always busy. Congratulations!"

"Oh, you've heard?"

"Julianne called me a few days ago to tell me. You and Seth—it's so romantic! I can't believe it."

"I'm not sure I believe it myself," Laura agreed with a laugh. "But it's true. We're doing it up right, complete with the legal piece of paper. My mother wants to make a big thing out of it—she's only got one daughter, and how often does one's daughter get married and all that."

"Really? A full-fledged wedding?"

"Well, it's not going to be anything that traditional if I have anything to say in the matter," Laura admitted, laughing again. "We're just going to have a party at her house. Don't worry, when we get it all worked out you'll receive an invitation. Engraved, if I know my mother."

"Has she met Seth?" Kimberly asked, eager for all the details. "Does she like him?"

"She adores him. I suspect she'd adore anyone who would do right by her daughter at this late stage. Don't forget, the poor woman has been a grandmother for thirteen years, without ever getting to host a wedding first. But Seth is adorable, even if I must say so myself." Her tone became serious. "How are you, Kim? How's it going?"

"It's going," Kimberly answered vaguely. She didn't want to burden her friend with her own story about the finalization of her divorce. The fact was, she didn't feel particularly sorry for herself that morning.

Instead she felt uncommonly cheerful. The only explanation she could come up with for her elevated spirits was that she had won Andrew's friendship. She never would have expected that Andrew's opinion of her could be so important to her, but now that it had changed for the better, she was immeasurably pleased.

Their dinner together the previous evening had gone delightfully. He had let her pick up the tab, and that, too, had delighted her. She had told him that since he was a visitor to her town, the least she could do was treat him to a meal, and he had accepted her generosity without a fuss. She wanted to believe that this was one more bit of proof that he was finally ready to view her as an equal.

Outside the restaurant she'd shown him where the nearest Metro station was, and then he had waited with her until she caught a bus to Georgetown, which wasn't served by the city's underground rail system. Before she had boarded the bus, he'd opened his briefcase and handed her a folder. "You might want to read this," he'd said almost diffidently. "I'd rather you didn't show it to anyone else, though. At least not yet. I'm still hoping to get a paper or two out of it."

She had waited until she arrived home before scanning the contents of the folder. It contained the information he'd gathered for L.A.R.C., neatly organized and typed. That he would share it with her was more evidence that he trusted her.

She wanted his trust. She desired it. She longed to seep beneath his armor, once and for all, and vanquish the pain she knew was lurking there. Perhaps it was an irrational longing, but throughout a surprisingly restless night, all she could think of was that she wanted to reach him, to touch him, to heal him.

She decided not to mention to Laura that Andrew was in Washington. Clearly he didn't want it made public that he was about to have a run-in with one of his superiors at Amherst College—to say nothing of the C.I.A.

"So what does Rita think of all this?" she asked Laura brightly.

"Of all what? Seth and me getting married?" Laura snorted. "Seth practically proposed to her before he proposed to me. She's ecstatic about it. But listen, Kim..." She trailed off for a moment, then continued. "The reason I'm calling is, I have to ask a big favor of you."

"Yes. I would love to be your maid of honor," Kimberly joked.

Laura guffawed. "Kim, you know me better than that. My mother wants to make a big thing of it, but we've vetoed the processional stuff. Rita said there was no way on earth she was going to be a flower girl—only she kept calling it a 'flower child.' The way she said it, I got the distinct impression that she considers flower children one step removed from slugs."

"All right," Kimberly said. "No maid of honor. What's the big favor, then?"

"Seth wants to take Rita to Washington for a couple of days. Partly it's because once we move out to California in June she might not have another opportunity to see the capital for a while. Partly it's because I've got a ton of work to do here, packing up and closing out my case load at work, and I want them both out of my way. But mostly it's because Seth thinks Rita ought to see where he and I met."

"You met at school," Kimberly argued, bewildered.

"We met on a chartered bus heading down to Washington to march against the war, back in November of '69," Laura corrected her. "Seth thinks Rita's life won't be complete until she marches the route with him. Anyway, they're going to be arriving in D.C. next Thursday evening for a long weekend."

"Does Rita have time off from school?"

"No. I'm letting her play hooky Friday. Seth insists that visiting Washington is going to be very educational. Hah," Laura grunted. "But I'm willing to pretend I believe him for the few days of peace their absence will give me. Kim, you wouldn't believe the madhouse it's been here—Seth's junk is all over the place, my mother's arriving today to shop for a dress for me.... She keeps talking about color schemes, Kim. Color schemes! For a backyard party! I told her that given that the lawn is green we ought to go with green, but she keeps saying lilac, yellow, fuchsia, mandarin orange..."

Dusty rose, Kimberly almost blurted out. That had been the color of her wedding. Her attendants—she'd had seven of them—had worn dusty-rose gowns, and she had carried a bouquet of dark pink roses and trailing ivy, and her dress had been inlaid with pink-hued cultured pearls, and they'd drunk pink champagne.... Her mother had done most of the planning, too. A full year of planning. The catered engagement party, the catered bridal shower, the wedding, the reception—everything, from the tablecloths and napkins to the ribbons on the favors, had been dusty rose. So much pink, so much money spent, and what did Kimberly have to show for it?

No. She wasn't going to think that way. Not today, not when, for the first time since she'd moved out of the house in Chevy Chase a year ago, she was feeling happy.

"Seth and Rita in D.C.," she said, directing her thoughts back to Laura. "What do you want me to do?"

"Say hello, keep an eye on them, whatever," Laura replied. "You don't have to put them up or anything. They've got a couple of rooms reserved at—" Kimberly heard Laura fumbling with some papers on her end of the line "—L'Enfant Plaza. But I just can't shake the notion that they're going to need some looking after. The two of them, alone together—it's the halt leading the blind. Or the crazy leading the insane. Can I have them call you when they get into town?"

"Of course. Better yet, have them stop by my office Friday morning. I'll take them out to lunch."

"You're wonderful, Kim," Laura gushed.

"I won't argue that," said Kimberly. "Is Seth around now? I'd like to give him my congratulations, too."

"I'm afraid he's out," Laura told her. "He went into Manhattan to meet some independent producer for brunch. He's trying to wrangle money for his new film. It's called *Good Fences*, and it's wonderful, Kim. It's the best thing he's ever written. Unfortunately he's having quite a time convincing investors of that. But you'll see him next week. If you want, you can congratulate him then."

"Fair enough. Laura, I'm just so happy for the both of you. I mean that."

"Thank you, Kim," Laura said, sounding oddly shy. "I'm almost sorry I'm going to be moving so far away now that we've found each other again."

"We won't lose touch this time," Kimberly swore. "Take care, Laura. And stick to your guns. It's your wedding, not your mother's."

"Yeah. If only I can convince her of that," Laura grumbled before bidding Kimberly farewell.

Kimberly lowered the receiver and gazed at the papers spread across her bed. Weddings, she mused, were a much different matter than marriages. Weddings were celebrations, occasions of joy, color-coordinated. Marriages, on the other hand…well, they ought to be joyful celebrations, too, but when reality intruded, you never knew. Divorce might occur. Or death.

She banished that thought with a shake of her head. Andrew wasn't wallowing in grief, surrendering to morbid moods. In spite of his loss, he struck her as very in command of himself, very strong. He was doing just fine, teaching, writing, bucking for tenure. The papers she had read from his folder thus far indicated that he was a busy, productive man.

He wrote well. She found nothing pompous in his essays, nothing screaming of scholarship or academic credentials. But, then, he'd written well in college, too. She had always enjoyed reading his articles in *The Dream,* even though she'd never told him so. If she had, he probably would have been offended to think that some cheerleader with an inferior brain actually liked what he was writing.

She didn't have an inferior brain. And if Andrew hadn't figured that out by now, he wouldn't have entrusted her with his file—or with his professional future.

The telephone rang again. She had expected the last telephone call to be from Andrew, not Laura; perhaps this time he would be on the other end. She reflexively smoothed the satin lapels of her baby-blue bathrobe and tightened the knot of the sash, as if Andrew could see her through the telephone wire. Then she lifted the receiver. "Hello?"

"Kim? Whitney here."

She slumped against the pillow and prayed that he was calling her on business and not to find out if his presumed rival had departed, leaving Kimberly available for dinner that night. "Hello, Whitney," she said with forced politeness.

"Is Andrew there? I'd like to speak to him."

That brought her up sharply. Obviously Whitney had believed her little ruse about Andrew's being her "very dear friend." He'd believed it too well. She couldn't blame him for assuming that Andrew had spent the night at her place and not in a motel across the river. Hadn't that been exactly what she had wanted him to assume?

"He's out right now," she informed Whitney. "He—he went out for a walk." Did that sound as lame to Whitney as it did to her? Before he had a chance to question her further, she went on. "Perhaps I can help you. Have you found out anything about L.A.R.C.?"

"A few tidbits," Whitney remarked cryptically. "When is Andrew going to be back?"

"I honestly don't know," Kimberly mumbled. "Why don't you tell me all these tidbits you've found out, and I'll pass the word along."

"All I've got right now is that L.A.R.C. was set up to gather economic information on several Central American nations. It's Wilding's brain child. I'm meeting a guy for dinner who's worked with Wilding before. If I ply him with enough whiskey, I might pry some interesting stuff out of him. I'm planning to see somebody else this afternoon, and I'd like to get a little more background dope from Andrew before I go. Could you have him call me as soon as he gets back?"

"Of course," Kimberly promised. "Where can he reach you? Are you at home?"

"Yeah. You've got my number, right?"

Oh, have I ever, Kimberly muttered silently. "I'm sure it's in my book," she told him. "I'll have Andrew call you as soon as possible."

"Thanks. You know, Kim, I'm doing this for the senator," Whitney felt obliged to add. "I wouldn't kill a weekend just to satisfy your sweetheart."

"I understand that," she said, her voice cool and poised. "I'm sure my—my sweetheart understands that, too." She hoped she didn't sound as awkward as she felt using the word "sweetheart" in reference to Andrew.

"Have him get back to me," Whitney said, concluding the call.

She stared at the telephone on her night table and sighed. She truly didn't like getting herself so caught up in lies, but what alternative did she have? Whitney's closing remark was strangely reassuring to her. It implied that he was coming to terms with the fact that as far as he was concerned, she wasn't interested in pursuing a personal relationship.

Given that he was expecting Andrew to return his call, she didn't have time to waste either congratulating herself on her successful con or berating herself for her petty deception. She riffled through the folder on the bed until she found the card Andrew had given her with his hotel's number on it. She dialed and asked the desk clerk to connect her with Andrew's room.

He answered on the first ring. "Hello?"

"Andrew? It's me."

"Kim." Her nickname sounded so sweet when he uttered it. "Good morning."

"Good morning," she said, relishing the warmth of his tone. "Andrew, I just got off the phone with Whitney. He wants you to call him."

"Okay." Andrew waited, and when Kimberly remained silent, he said, "Why don't you give me his number?"

"Andrew." She drew in a deep breath, then proceeded. "He expected that you would be here at my apartment. I guess he figured that you had spent the night with me."

Andrew didn't speak immediately. "Oh?"

"I—I didn't correct him," she confessed. "I told him you were out taking a walk and that you'd call him when you got back."

Again Andrew was momentarily silent. "This is asinine," he muttered. "I can't stand this sort of game playing. It's really asinine, Kim."

At least he hadn't reverted to calling her "Kimberly." But she couldn't fail to detect his haughty attitude, his blatant disapproval of her. His attitude hurt her more than it should have, far more than it used to hurt her fifteen years ago. "Today you tell me you can't stand it. Yesterday you swore it was no skin off your nose," she asserted sharply. "I'm in a bind with Whitney. I'm sorry I thought I could count on you to help me out of it—"

"All right, all right," he cut her off with a resigned sigh. "'Oh, what tangled webs we weave—'"

"Now is not the time to discuss spiders," she interrupted him. "How soon can you get to Georgetown?"

"Why can't I call him from here?" Andrew asked. "I can tell him I'm calling from your place if he asks."

"And what if he wants to talk to me again?" she countered. "You can't very well say that I've gone out for a walk."

"Why not?" Andrew argued. "Maybe he'll think we both like to take walks by ourselves. Maybe he'll think we've got something bizarre going."

If that was what Whitney thought, he wouldn't be far from the mark, Kimberly acknowledged. "Just come here, Andrew," she commanded. "It would make life a whole lot easier."

"For you, maybe. All right, I'll come over," he acquiesced. "But I'm warning you, Kim, I've got work to do today, so you'd better let me do it while I'm there. How do I get to your place?"

She gave him the address. "The closest Metro stop is the one for George Washington University. It's rather a long walk from there, I'm afraid."

"Forget it. I'll take a cab," he said before hanging up.

A cab would take him much less time than the Metro and a major hike. If Andrew was willing to go to the extra expense of riding a cab to her home, then he was obviously willing to continue playing her game, even if he considered it asinine. No matter how condemning he had sounded on the phone, Andrew was still her friend. If he wasn't, he would have called a halt to the game right then and there.

Gratified, she sprang from the bed and hastened down the hall to the bathroom for a quick shower. Then she raced back to her room and donned a pair of snug-fitting white jeans and a pink knit jersey. She ran her brush through her hair a few times, fluffed it with her fingers and hurried to the kitchen to prepare a fresh pot of coffee. The least she could do when Andrew arrived was to offer him some refreshment.

By the time the coffee had run through the machine, he was knocking on her door. She fluffed her hair again, shaped her lips into a welcoming smile and offered a silent prayer that Andrew wouldn't use the word "asinine" in reference to her anymore that day.

She swung open the door and he stepped into the entry hall. He was dressed in brown corduroy slacks and a plaid shirt, and he carried his briefcase. His expression was inscrutable.

"Thank you for coming," she said.

"Uh-huh," he grumbled brusquely, marching past her and into the living room. "Where's the phone? Let's get this stupidity over with."

She pointed out the kitchen extension, a wall phone above the counter. Then she fetched her personal telephone book and opened it to Brannigan. She handed Andrew the receiver and began to dial for him.

"Where was I supposed to have been?" he questioned her.

"For a walk. Down Wisconsin Avenue, if he decides to ask. Tell him you went window-shopping or something."

"Window-shopping?" Andrew snorted. "The last thing I'd ever do in my life is go window-shopping."

"All right. Tell him…" She refrained from dialing the last digit as she scrambled for a better alibi. "Tell him you went out to buy some pastries."

"I don't like pastries," he objected, but she dialed the last number anyway.

"Swenson's," she whispered as he pressed the receiver to his ear. "For ice cream. Do you like ice cream?"

"At eleven o'clock in the morning?" he shot back before speaking into the phone. "Hello, Whitney, it's Andrew. Kim told me you wanted to talk to me."

His expression once again became unreadable to her. Hoping to ameliorate the situation, she filled a large porcelain mug with coffee and handed it to him. He took it with a slight nod.

"That's right," he said to Whitney. "Fertilizer shipments. They import it, mostly." Without looking at Kimberly, he lifted the mug to his mouth and sipped. "The address was Fairfax, Virginia. The few times I called him I got an answering machine. For all I know he may have been running the council out of his own home." He listened for a minute. "No, never heard of him…. No. Wilding never mentioned any other names. I assumed he was farming most of the work out to academics like me." He drank some more coffee, then tossed a skeptical smile Kimberly's way. "She's right here if you'd like to speak to her," he said. "No? Okay, then, Whitney. Keep in touch. And thanks." He handed the receiver back to Kimberly.

"I suppose you could have called from your hotel, after all," she murmured contritely as she set the receiver in its cradle.

Andrew shrugged. "He said he'd be calling back in a couple of hours. I seem to be stuck here."

She cringed at the word "stuck." She didn't like the idea that Andrew considered himself a prisoner in her home. "Well," she said crisply, refusing to let him know how much she appreciated his having come to her apartment. "You said you had some work to do. Make yourself comfortable."

He surveyed the living room, then carried his coffee to the dining table and took a seat. He pulled a sheaf of student papers and a pen from his briefcase and spread them on the table in front of himself. "What are you going to do?" he asked, less from courtesy than from curiosity.

"I've got to take some clothes to the dry cleaners," she told him. "And I'd like to finish looking through the file you gave me yesterday. I've been studying it, Andrew, and it's very interesting."

"Is it?" he asked dubiously. "Don't tell me you get off on peasant agronomy."

His withering tone caused her patience to fray. "I don't suppose you care one way or another what I get off on," she responded, keeping her voice level and detached. "I'll be back from the cleaners in a little while. Help yourself to more coffee if you want it."

With that she spun on her heel and stalked from the kitchen. Gathering up the suits she wanted cleaned and slinging the strap of her purse onto her shoulder, she left the apartment.

The late-morning air was balmy as she turned onto a side street and strode toward Wisconsin Avenue. She hoped that the mild spring weather and her brisk walk would calm her down. She didn't want to remain furious with Andrew for the rest of the day, particularly since it seemed that they were going to spend it "stuck" in each other's company, to use his unflattering term.

Yet how could she keep from being furious with him? Asinine, he had all but called her. The nerve of him!

She was going out of her way to help him, without complaint, without hesitation. Was it really demanding so very much that he pretend for a couple of days that he was her boyfriend? Was it really demanding so very much that he stop looking down his nose at her?

A couple of years ago she had read an article about an organization that was devoted to the problems of unusually good-looking people. According to the members, handsome men and pretty women had difficulty getting people to take them seriously, to associate with them as easily as they did with others. When Kimberly had read the story, she'd found the unspoken conceitedness of the club's members offensive.

She knew she was pretty, but her beauty had never worked against her. She had never had problems dealing with people because of her looks. Women like Julianne and Laura had accepted her for the human being she was. Men were frequently attracted to her, but she knew she wasn't irresistible to the opposite sex. She still remembered the adolescent heartache of having crushes on boys who wouldn't give her the time of day. She still remembered the many hours she'd spent staring at her reflection in the mirror as a teenager, comparing herself to Twiggy, feeling rejected and bemoaning her physical flaws.

But Andrew's rejection of her rankled more than anyone else's. She knew that he didn't fully accept her intelligence, and she couldn't shake the suspicion that his failure to respect her mind had something to do with her blond hair and blue eyes, her slender figure, her chipper disposition. In his snobbish view of things, a woman who had been on the cheerleading squad in high school couldn't compare to a woman who had been on the tennis team, or the yearbook staff, or the student council.

Andrew had viewed her as a lightweight even before he'd gotten to know her very well. And he still didn't know her very well. *Asinine,* she huffed.

Her visit to the dry cleaners didn't take long, and after she had dropped off her suits, she wasn't ready to return home yet. Instead she decided to take the walk Andrew was alleged to have taken.

She strolled down Wisconsin Avenue, browsing in the shop windows, contemplating which dresses she would buy if she could afford them. Getting used to living on a constrained budget had been difficult for her. Until her separation from Todd she had spent her entire life knowing that she could have anything she wanted—which was why it had been so much fun, back in her rebellious youth, to refuse the gifts her wealthy parents had wanted to lavish on her. All those lovely outfits her mother used to buy while Kimberly was away at school.... She'd come home for a vacation, find three or four new dresses spread across her canopied bed, and toss them onto the floor with vicious glee. Then she'd storm down the stairs, singing "Sympathy For The Devil" just for the thrill of watching her mother blanch.

At a *pâtisserie* she halted and studied the cakes and éclairs on display in the showcase. The hell with Andrew, she fumed. *She* liked pastries. She marched into the store, requested a box of six petits fours and refused herself the merest twinge of guilt when she handed the clerk a five-dollar bill.

Feeling rather pleased with herself, she strolled home, toting her purchase in a tissue-lined white box. If Andrew wanted to be so damned supercilious, she would take the box outside into the backyard with a glass of lemonade and a good book and eat all the petits fours herself.

When she entered her apartment, she found Andrew hunched over the table, immersed in his work. How intent he looked, peering through his eyeglasses, wielding his pen.

Like a gnome just climbed out of a tome, she reflected, then shook her head. Perhaps when he'd had his beard he had looked like a gnome, but not now, with his sharp, square jaw, with his thin lips fully visible, pressed together in a line of concentration, and his broad, strong shoulders stretching smooth the cotton of his shirt. He mumbled a greeting at her entrance, but he didn't glance up.

She set the box of petits fours on the counter and peeked at the paper he was marking with his pen. "'Bombastic, pleonastic, irrelevant bull,'" she read, struggling to decipher his nearly illegible scrawl. "Are you really going to write that on a student's paper?"

"I already did," he pointed out, permitting himself a slight grin.

"If you won't think I'm a bubble head for asking, what does 'pleonastic' mean?"

Although she had taken care to insult herself before Andrew could insult her, she knew that asking such a question put her at risk. Fortunately Andrew didn't leap at the opportunity she'd given him to belittle her. "It means redundant. The next time that assistant of yours hands you one of his wordy drafts for Senator Milford's 'Letter to the Constituents,' tell him it's pleonastic."

"I surely will," she concurred, her eyes shifting back to the paper Andrew was grading. "Bombastic and irrelevant, too? Won't your student be crushed?"

"I'm the one who ought to be crushed, having to read a paper like this. What's in the box?" he asked, his gaze drifting past her to the counter.

She chuckled. Old stick-in-the-mud egghead Andrew was conscious of the world outside his skull, after all. "Pastries," she drawled, her smile challenging him. "I'm sure you all don't want any." She opened the box with deliberate slowness, plucked one of the chocolate-covered cakes from the tissue lining and took a dainty bite.

Andrew watched her. He observed the graceful position of her hands as she held the petit four, the delicate tip of her tongue circling her lips, savoring the sweetness. Abruptly he laughed. "What is this, revenge?"

"You said you didn't like pastries," she said with feigned innocence. "I'm so sorry, Andrew. Did you want one?"

His laughter increased, and she was unable to keep herself from joining him. "It isn't as if I flee at the sight of them," he said, accepting the box from her and pulling out a petit four. "To tell you the truth, Kim, the breakfast I ate at the coffee shop in my motel was pretty awful. I'm starving."

"Would you like some lunch?" she asked.

He shook his head. "No. Just a pastry." He popped the whole petit four into his mouth.

"How about some more coffee?" she offered. Not waiting for an answer, she lifted the empty mug from the table and carried it into the kitchen to refill it.

Andrew continued to watch her, his smile relaxed and his eyes glowing with a gentle amber light. "What a well-bred lady you are," he commented. "Here I am, taking over your apartment, being rude, and you serve me coffee."

Kimberly returned his smile. "Maybe that's my revenge, Andrew," she hinted. "By being so utterly charming, I take all the wind out of your sails. You've simply got no choice but to be charming back."

"One thing I've never been is charming," Andrew declared.

Kimberly had to agree. But Andrew's shortcoming didn't bother her. Her experience with charming men had taught her that charm wasn't a particularly valuable asset in a man. Todd had been charming. He'd been ever so gracious as he told Kimberly, in no uncertain terms, that if she wanted to have children, she would have to quit her job and take full responsibility for rearing them, because he didn't have much faith in nursery schools or baby-sitters and he had no intention of being saddled with dirty diapers and formula bottles himself. He'd been ever so polite the first time he confessed that he was having an affair, ever so diplomatic as he told her, over a dignified snifter of cognac, that their marriage was obviously not working out as either of them had planned and so they might as well cut their losses.

She was glad Andrew wasn't charming that way. She appreciated his bluntness, even if he sometimes insulted her. She would rather know where she stood with a man than to have to interpret every nuance of his smile, every quirk of his eyebrow, in order to make sense of him.

"I should let you get back to work," she said, placing the steaming mug of coffee at his elbow. "If you'd like," she added, lifting the box and grinning mischievously, "I'll hide these loathsome pastries so you won't be tempted."

"Oh, you'd better," he played along. "I'm a fiend when it comes to loathsome pastries. That's why I hate them so much—I know how easily they could lead to my downfall."

Laughing, she put the box on the counter and departed for the bedroom. The papers she had been reading that morning lay scattered across the bed. She stacked them into a neat pile, kicked off her shoes and stretched out on the bed to resume reading.

An hour later the telephone rang. She had just reached the last page, and she let the phone ring twice more so she could finish the final paragraph. Then she answered.

"Kim? Whitney again. Is Andrew there? I'd like to speak to him."

She was relieved that Andrew was in fact at her apartment; it spared her the necessity of having to lie to Whitney again. But she couldn't deny being somewhat irked by Whitney's insistence on talking to Andrew rather than to her. After all, she was as much a part of the investigation as

Whitney was. Almost as much a part of it, anyway. He was doing the legwork, yes, but she had access to Andrew's papers. And to Andrew.

She didn't want to quarrel with Whitney over his attempt to shut her out of things, however. "Hang on," she said, then hollered through her open bedroom door. "Andrew? Whitney wants to talk to you."

"Okay, *darling*," Andrew shouted back before picking up the kitchen extension.

She stifled the urge to laugh. She also stifled the urge to listen in on their conversation. Resolutely she hung up the phone and waited.

Within a few minutes Andrew appeared at her bedroom door. "Well?" she asked.

He didn't speak immediately. Instead he took a moment to examine her bedroom—the heavy maple dresser with an embroidered linen runner decorating its buffed surface, the matching mirror above, the double bed with its pale blue comforter and dust ruffle, the framed Monet print of water lilies, hanging on the wall above it, and the "blue period" Picasso on the wall by the window overlooking the backyard. His gaze ultimately came to rest on Kimberly, who stared at him expectantly.

"He met with someone who worked with John Wilding several years ago at another proprietary, doing research in the Middle East," Andrew reported. "He said the man told him that Wilding had tried to take over the proprietary. He had some crackpot idea of fomenting unrest in Syria."

"What's so crackpot about that?" Kimberly asked. "I'm not crazy about Syria myself."

Andrew frowned. "For one thing, there's enough unrest in Syria without the C.I.A. adding its two cents. For another, it isn't supposed to be the C.I.A.'s job to overthrow unfriendly governments. Apparently the C.I.A. knows that, since they removed Wilding from the project and tied him to a desk for a while. L.A.R.C. is his first foray back into the real world."

"In other words, the man has a history of being naughty," Kimberly summed up.

"Something like that. Whitney told me he's going to spend the afternoon trying to track down the origins of L.A.R.C. Then he's supposed to meet someone for dinner, and if he gets home by a reasonable hour, he'll call again."

Kimberly allowed herself a minute to digest Andrew's announcement. If Whitney intended to telephone her house after dinner with an updated report, Andrew would have to remain with her through the evening.

She wondered what he thought of that. Did he feel "stuck," trapped by her "asinine" game? His eyes, partly obscured by his eyeglasses, refused to offer any answers. Neither did his mouth. He wasn't smiling, and he wasn't scowling.

"That's my folder," he said abruptly.

She was unnerved by his mildly accusatory tone of voice. "You gave it to me to read last night," she reminded him.

"Yes, but—" He smiled sheepishly. "I didn't know whether you'd bother to."

"I did bother," she informed him. "It's awfully interesting, Andrew. All these people you met and interviewed... How on earth did you find them?"

He shrugged. "It's called research, Kim. You do what you have to do to find out what you have to find out."

"I'm amazed that you got them all to open up so much to you," she remarked, then refuted herself. "No, I shouldn't be amazed. You always wrote wonderful interviews in *The Dream*, too. You obviously have a knack for this sort of thing."

"It isn't a knack," Andrew asserted modestly. "If you ask the right questions, most people are more than willing to talk about themselves."

Kimberly pondered his claim. She wanted Andrew to talk about himself. She wanted to know everything that was going on in that enormous, constantly toiling brain of his. If only she knew the right questions to ask....

"I have an idea," she said abruptly, gathering up the papers and stacking them neatly back inside the folder. "Whitney won't be calling back till this evening, you said. Let's take a drive."

Her suggestion obviously took Andrew by surprise. "A drive? Where?"

"To Fairfax." She stood and straightened her sweater. Then she crossed purposefully to her dresser to pick up her purse and keys. "Let's go look at John Wilding's house. You told Whitney he lived in Fairfax, right?"

Andrew's lips flexed as he mulled over her idea. "What's to be gained by looking at his house?"

Kimberly smiled. The most important thing to be gained, she comprehended, was that she and Andrew would be outdoors. If they spent all afternoon trapped together in the house, she would feel as much a prisoner as he would. And besides, she'd be damned if she was going to sit around doing nothing while Whitney knocked himself out learning everything there was to learn about L.A.R.C. She was tired of his refusal to include her in his investigation.

What was to be gained was that she and Andrew would be doing something together. How else would she learn the right questions to ask him?

"I'm curious," she remembered to reply. "I bet you are, too. It's a beautiful day. Let's go."

He didn't appear completely convinced, but she was already out the door of her bedroom, moving rapidly toward the front door and leaving him no choice but to follow. Reluctantly he did.

Chapter Four

"How can you afford a car like this on a civil servant's salary?" he asked.

Kimberly navigated her silver BMW through the narrow, congested Georgetown streets toward the Key Bridge. The car appeared fairly new, the plush floor mats spotless and the upholstery in showroom shape. Since Andrew hadn't gone car shopping in a decade, he didn't know much about current automobile prices. But he suspected that Kimberly's car must have cost a small fortune.

She smiled bitterly. "Todd and I bought it when we were still married," she explained, downshifting as they reached the bridge leading across the Potomac River into Virginia. "My lawyer recommended that I leave him this car and take the Mazda. He warned me that a car this expensive would foul up the accounting when we divided our assets. But we bought this car for me, and I insisted on keeping it."

"Any regrets?"

She shook her head, and her smile softened. "None at all," she swore.

The light breeze entering the car through the open sun roof ruffled her hair as she accelerated. Andrew might have expected a woman like Kimberly to own a fancy car, but he had never guessed that she would own a car with a stick shift. She had always struck him as the automatic transmission type. It seemed incongruous, a woman as delicately feminine as she was, tapping the clutch and dancing the stick through the gears with finesse. Incongruous, and oddly sexy.

He turned resolutely to the windshield, following the moderate weekend traffic with his gaze. Although he had always considered Kimberly pretty, he had never considered her sexy before.

Yes, he had. Yesterday, watching her while she fielded telephone calls and questions from underlings in her office, and later, when she skillfully ordered their pizza and then settled the check, he had found her sexy. In his mind, a woman's sex appeal related directly to her competence, her intelligence, her mastery of the world around her. By those standards, he was coming to realize, Kimberly was an undeniably sexy woman.

It was a discomfiting thought. If he had known that she would make such a disturbing impact on him, he wouldn't have come to Washington. The last thing he wanted was to find himself turned on by a pampered blond debutante, no matter how competent and intelligent she seemed.

"What's the address again?" she asked, cruising west on the highway.

Andrew shuffled through his folder until he found John Wilding's address. He read it to Kimberly. "How are we going to find his place?" he asked.

She shrugged. "When we get to Fairfax, we'll ask directions. It's a pretty small town."

"What if he's home?"

She shrugged again.

"Kim, he'll recognize me. We've met a few times. I can't very well march up to the front door and ring his bell." The more Andrew thought about it, the more he realized that this was a harebrained idea. He didn't know what had possessed him to let Kimberly talk him into driving to Wilding's house. She had seemed so excited when she'd suggested it, her face aglow, her eyes animated with sparks of light. He couldn't refuse a woman who looked as exuberant as she had.

But now, in the car, with time to reflect, he concluded that nothing productive would come out of their visit to Wilding's address. In all likelihood Wilding would be home. They would drive past his house—and if they were lucky, Wilding wouldn't happen to notice them—and then they'd drive back to Washington. Perhaps all Kimberly had wanted was an excuse to take her elegant car out for a spin on a sunny spring afternoon.

"If worse comes to worst and he is home," she opined, gunning the engine to pass a truck, "at least we'll see where he lives. We'll see if he's the sort to keep his lawn mowed. What do you think, Andrew? Is he a good-neighbor kind of man?"

"I wouldn't want him for one of my neighbors," Andrew grumbled.

Kimberly eased back into the right lane and then cast Andrew a probing glance. She remained silent for a minute, then took a deep breath and let up on the gas pedal. "What are the right questions, Andrew?"

"Hmm?" He scowled. "The right questions for what?"

"You told me before that most people like to talk about themselves if you ask the right questions. What are the right questions for you?"

He studied her face in profile. Her forehead was smooth, not a line marring the clear skin. Her tiny nose had a natural bob to it, and the skin beneath her chin cut a sleek line to her throat. He focused on her lips for a moment, then turned away. "I don't know, Kim," he said. "Ask and find out."

She lapsed into another brief silence, then said, "Tell me about your childhood."

That wasn't the question he expected. Actually, he hadn't known what to expect, but an inquisition on his childhood definitely wasn't it. He issued a short, surprised laugh, then said, "What about it?"

"Where are you from? Where did you grow up? I know so little about you, Andrew."

"I grew up in Canton, Ohio. My father owns an auto parts store. My mother is a housewife. I have two younger sisters."

She appeared astounded by his sudden outpouring. He wasn't sure why she should be; he hadn't told her anything notably intimate about himself. Yet he, too, was struck by the comprehension that in all the years they had known each other, Kimberly had never before asked him anything about his background.

"Was it a happy childhood?" she inquired.

"Happier than most, I imagine. We weren't rich, but we had everything we needed. My parents loved us. They raised us pretty well."

"Would you like to have children?"

Her innocent question caused a shard of pain to cut through him. Children. It had all started with Marjorie's pregnancy, their baby, the child they were never to have. Even though they had still been in graduate school, barely scraping by, Andrew and Marjorie had wanted that child more than anything. Compared to losing Marjorie, losing the baby had seemed almost tolerable. Almost. But not quite.

He turned away, wondering whether Kimberly had noticed his momentary anguish. His failure to answer prompted her to apologize. "I'm sorry, Andrew. I guess that wasn't the right question."

"It was a valid question," he assured her quietly, doing his best to recover. "Yes. I would like to have children someday."

She flashed a quick look his way, evidently trying to gauge the reason for his altered mood. Then she turned her attention back to the road. "So would I," she confessed. "I reckon I'm too old, though."

"You aren't that old."

"I'm old enough not to have known that nowadays men come on like gangbusters on the first date," she said with a wry chuckle.

"Women are having children later than they used to," he commented. "With all the tests they have, all the screening they can do, it's not such a dangerous risk."

Kimberly laughed incredulously. Andrew had only stated the truth, and he didn't understand her reaction. "I can't believe we're talking this way," she explained, swallowing a final laugh. "It's nice, Andrew. I miss having my old friends to talk to. I have friends, of course, but other than Julianne, I don't keep up with anyone who knew me back when. Remember how we all used to sit around rapping in the basement office of *The Dream*, back in school?"

Andrew smiled. "The staff meetings."

"There Julianne would be, at the head of the table, trying to maintain some sort of order," Kimberly reminisced. "She'd be discoursing on whether it was a mortal sin to accept advertisements from a conglomerate like A & P, and Troy would be spinning his lens cap on the table and muttering about how he was constitutionally unsuited to bureaucratic meetings, and Laura would be divvying up the granola...."

"Counting the raisins to make sure nobody got gypped," Andrew recalled.

"Right." Kimberly slowed down to read an exit sign, then sped up again, grinning as her memories took shape. "Then Seth would come barging in, always ten minutes late, wearing one of his weird T-shirts—"

"'Better Stoned Than Sorry,'" Andrew quoted. "That one was one of his favorites, wasn't it?"

"All his T-shirts were his favorites," Kimberly contended. "He had a slogan for every occasion. 'Better Living Through Chemistry,' 'Keep In Shape—Have Loose Joints,' 'I'd Rather Be Here Than In Vietnam.'"

"'Frankly, My Dear, I Do Give A Damn,'" Andrew recollected, relaxing, the last of his sorrow ebbing away. His gaze drifted for a minute, then sharpened on Kimberly. "You had a shirt that said, 'Smile—It Increases Your Face Power.'"

"I hardly ever wore T-shirts," Kimberly protested. "And certainly not with slogans. 'Smile—It Increases Your Face Power' was printed on a poster I brought to our office and hung on the wall."

"Wherever it was, the slogan was pretty damned corny," Andrew said.

Kimberly seemed temporarily riled by his provocative comment. Then she grinned placidly and remarked, "Maybe it was corny, but it was true. Smiling does wonderful things to the face."

Andrew wrestled with the temptation to argue, but he checked himself. He agreed with Kimberly; it was nice talking this way, nice sharing the memories with her. "What a cheerleader you are," he murmured. "That's what you and I used to talk about at those meetings, wasn't it."

Kimberly nodded. "Seth would race in and announce that he'd decided to write his next column on the moral bankruptcy of dancing to George Harrison's 'Bangladesh,' the tastelessness of dancing to a song about children starving. And I'd say, if George Harrison didn't want people dancing to it, he wouldn't have written such a catchy tune. And you'd squint through those granny glasses of yours and carp about how typical it was of a cheerleader to care more about the tune than the lyrics."

"I didn't squint," Andrew objected.

"Whenever you looked at me you did," she maintained somberly. "It was a squint of disapproval, Andrew, as if you couldn't bear to look directly at me."

"Oh, I could bear it," Andrew said good-naturedly. He stared across the seat at her. Looking directly at her was more than bearable. It was delightful. Her beauty was mesmerizing. He could stare at her for a long time and never feel the urge to squint. And he could have back in college, too. Did he really squint then? "Maybe I squinted because looking at you was like looking at the sun," he posed, conceding that her recollection was more accurate than his. "You were always so bright and glowing."

His compliment took her aback. "That bothered you, didn't it," she said, mildly accusing.

"Yes," he admitted. "Those were serious times, Kim. I couldn't understand how someone could be so cheerful when so many things were wrong with the world."

"I was no more cheerful than anyone else," Kimberly claimed.

"More optimistic, maybe?" he suggested. "More hopeful?"

"I don't know." She meditated for a moment, then sighed. "Maybe I was. It wasn't that I wasn't aware of what was going on in the world. It was just that…it was more fun to believe that everything would work out somehow, someday. It seemed healthier to believe that we'd all overcome and live happily ever after. The folly of youth," she concluded with a snort.

"That's one of the best things about youth," Andrew noted, not at all pleased by her self-derision. "You're right, it is more fun to believe everything will work out. It's unrealistic, but a lot more fun."

"Things didn't work out as well as I had thought they would," she mused wistfully.

"But you still had the courage to be hopeful back then," Andrew pointed out. "You were very brave, Kim. It was much easier to be a cynic, much safer. I think I envied your bravery."

She released the gear stick, reached for his hand and squeezed it. "I wasn't very brave," she disputed him. "I was just behaving the only way I knew how to behave. Ignorance is bliss, Andrew, and I was fairly ignorant."

"And you were blissful." He had been totally unprepared for her friendly hand clasp, but he was touched by it. He liked the feel of her hand in his, so small and dainty against his. He twined his fingers through hers to keep her from pulling away. "Life was strange then, Kim. I'm sorry I was such an ass around you."

"We were all asses back then," she remarked, veering onto a ramp. "Let's try this exit and see where it takes us."

They coasted to a quiet street. Andrew spotted a gas station up ahead, then turned to survey the street signs. "Slow down!" he shouted, reading a sign bearing the name of Wilding's street. "That's his address."

Kimberly braked and then turned right onto a residential road. "What number are we looking for?"

Andrew told her. As they glided past a block of modest but well-maintained houses, he began to grow apprehensive. Perhaps they were asses in their youth, but what he and Kimberly were doing now seemed far more foolish than anything they had done back then.

"That's his place," she announced, pulling up to the curb before a trim brick ranch house and halting. "It looks like no one's home."

"You can't tell that," Andrew muttered, slouching in his seat and peeking surreptitiously over the dashboard. "His garage is closed. His car could be in there."

Kimberly perused the house thoughtfully. "Why don't I ring the bell and find out?"

"What are you going to do if he is home?"

"I'll tell him...I'll tell him I'm from the League of Women Voters, doing a survey on who he's planning to vote for in the next presidential election."

"Kimberly, that's over a year away," Andrew reminded her. He found her stubbornness exasperating, but also rather appealing.

"I can still be doing a survey," she said resolutely, unbuckling her seat belt and swinging open her door.

He grabbed her arm to stop her. "If you're supposed to be doing a survey, you can't visit him empty-handed," he pointed out.

She hesitated, then eyed his briefcase, which stood on the floor between his legs. "Give me a piece of paper," she ordered.

He thumbed through the folder on his lap. He couldn't give her anything from that; Wilding might recognize the papers as photocopies of the documents Andrew had given him. Rummaging through his briefcase, he found a pen and a student paper and handed them to her. "Here," he grunted. "I'm sure most League of Women Voters people take surveys on the backs of essays on Soviet imperialism in the Western Hemisphere."

Smiling, Kimberly took the paper and pen and climbed out of the car.

Slouching lower, Andrew spied on Kimberly as she marched boldly up the walk to the front door. He was daunted by her fearlessness, unnerved by it. Never in his wildest dreams would he have imagined that Kimberly Belmont, the belle of Atlanta, was willing to meet a C.I.A. operative head-on.

Yet she didn't really seem aware of the danger in what she was doing. To her it was just another silly game. Andrew could imagine Kimberly the cheerleader taking a classmate up on a dare and stealing the ladies' room sign, or setting a thumbtack on a teacher's chair. Apparently she viewed this escapade as no more serious than that.

Sneaking a look out the side window, he watched her press the doorbell, wait, then press it again. Slowly he unwound from his cramped position. She smiled and waved him over.

Drawing in a deep breath, he pursed his lips and joined her on the front walk. As silly as her latest game was, he wasn't about to let her show him up at it. He could play it as well as she could.

"At least he mows his grass," she observed, sprinting across the lawn to a break in the decorative shrubs surrounding the house. "Let's look through a window."

"Kim—"

She ignored him, gripping the window frame and peering inside. "His living room," she announced. "Colonial-style furniture with plaid Herculon upholstery. Straight from Sears, if I'm not mistaken."

"And what does that tell you about him?" Andrew inquired indulgently.

"Well, if he's skimming, he isn't sinking the money into his house," she said, dusting off her hands and stalking around to the side of the house, Andrew at her heels. "Remember that other C.I.A. fellow... what's his name? The one who sold plastic explosives to Libya."

"Edwin Wilson," Andrew supplied. He had learned all he could about every other incident in recent history where C.I.A. agents had overstepped the law.

"That's the one. Didn't he own a showplace in horse country? That man made a fortune on his double-dealing."

"And now he's rotting in jail," Andrew remarked.

Kimberly tossed him a triumphant smile. "See? Things do work out sometimes. Boost me up, Andrew. This window's too high."

He glanced left and right, checking to see if anyone might be watching them. Then, drawing in another deep breath, he lifted Kimberly by her waist. She was unusually slim, and his long fingers splayed out over her sides. She was light, so slender and compact. The flesh of her belly was firm beneath his fingertips, the fabric of her sweater soft. Her cologne filled his nostrils.

He didn't want to be prowling about John Wilding's house. But for the chance to hold Kimberly, to take her in his arms and support her weight, the peril of being caught was almost worth it.

He brusquely shook his head clear of that notion. How on earth could he think that risking life and limb to find out God knows what—how could he think that was worth the opportunity to hold Kimberly? How, for that matter, could he have thought that she looked sexy driving a stick shift? What was wrong with him?

Nothing, he assured himself as Kimberly descended, her back sliding along his chest as she reached for the ground with her feet. Nothing was wrong with finding Kimberly gorgeous. Undoubtedly any normal man would enjoy holding a woman like her for a few minutes. There was nothing disreputable, nothing embarrassing about it.

"That was his bedroom," she whispered, turning to face Andrew as he loosened his hold on her. He let his hands linger on her hips, and she didn't object. Instead she leaned closer to him and giggled. "He has a water bed."

"He does?"

"A king-size one. Big enough for plenty of hanky-panky. Is he married?"

"I don't know," Andrew answered. "We never got that personal in our conversations."

"I bet he isn't," Kimberly guessed, slipping out of Andrew's arms and tiptoeing around to the backyard. "Most

married women wouldn't put up with a king-size water
bed.''

"Some might," Andrew argued. Water beds weren't
worth arguing about with Kimberly, but he felt a sudden
need to put some distance between her and himself. "The
world is filled with adventurous wives."

Kimberly shot him a disgruntled look. "Sure," she
sniffed. "And it's filled with men who come on like gangbusters. A gas grill," she noticed, pointing to the grill on the
patio. "How mundane."

"Admit it," Andrew teased her. "If you think a gas grill
is mundane, you probably find water beds infinitely exotic."

"I assure you, I don't," she said piously. "I'd think water beds would make one seasick."

He couldn't keep from goading her. "Maybe you ought
to try one out and see."

"Not in this lifetime," she declared with finality. "I may
be a divorcée, but that doesn't mean I'm into water sports."

"But you've already proved that you're adventurous. We
wouldn't be here if you weren't."

Kimberly pivoted to face him. His eyes wandered from
her tousled hair, which had a few dead leaves from one of
the shrubs tangled into it, to her graceful shoulders, her
bosom, the tiny waist he had briefly clutched, the swell of
her hips, her tapering legs. She *was* adventurous, and he
would be willing to wager big money that she'd have the
time of her life on a water bed.

He tore his eyes from her. This was not a productive line
of thought. He wished they'd never come to Fairfax, not
because of the inherent danger but because he honestly
didn't like thinking erotic thoughts about Kimberly.

"His garbage pail!" she exclaimed, bringing his attention back to their present situation. She jogged across the

patio to the aluminum trash can standing at the corner of the house. "Let's see what's inside it."

The entire masquerade had gone on long enough. Andrew was not about to paw through a week's worth of coffee grounds and banana peels just to satisfy Kimberly's whim. "Don't be absurd," he snapped.

"I wasn't being absurd," she protested, lifting the lid of the can and gazing in. "He smokes," she commented unnecessarily. The pail was brimming with dead cigarette butts.

"There you have it," Andrew muttered. "The secret to the man's behavior. He's a nicotine freak. Can we go now?"

Before Kimberly could reply, they heard the sound of an approaching car. Andrew grabbed the lid and set it noiselessly back onto the pail, then flattened himself to the brick wall and shifted his head a centimeter to gaze around the side. A black Cadillac had pulled up to the curb in front of Kimberly's BMW and sat idling. Two men were in the Cadillac's front seat, but Andrew couldn't decipher their faces.

"Is that him?" Kimberly hissed.

Andrew pressed her to the wall beside him, his arm pinning her against the bricks. The passenger door of the Cadillac opened, and although he couldn't see the man's face, he recognized Wilding's voice.

"Don't move," he whispered, nodding in answer to Kimberly's question. "Don't even breathe."

Wilding swung out of the car and shut the passenger door. He bent to address the driver through the open window. Andrew felt Kimberly's ribs moving against his arm, shifting slowly as she took a controlled breath, and he detected the faint flutter of her heart. It was all her fault that they were in such a dangerous position, but he wanted to protect her. He wanted to save her far more than he wanted to save himself.

They waited. The men talked for a few seconds longer, and then Wilding straightened. Andrew turned to Kimberly. "The hedge," he mouthed, tilting his head toward a hedge of yews separating Wilding's backyard from his next-door neighbor's.

Kimberly nodded slightly. Her lips were pressed together, clenched bloodlessly, but her eyes were twinkling.

Andrew twisted back to watch Wilding, who waved at his colleague and then rotated, starting toward the house across the front lawn. Andrew pressed his ear to the wall, listening for the vibration of the door opening. As soon as he heard it, he released Kimberly. They both dove for cover beneath the bushes, crawling through the dirt and emerging in the adjacent yard. "Run!" she panted, darting toward the street.

Andrew could have overtaken her easily, but he didn't. For some inexplicable reason he wanted to remain behind her, to be able to shove her out of harm's way if the need arose.

Gasping for breath, they glimpsed Wilding's house from behind the edge of the row of yews to ascertain that Wilding was safely inside. The black Cadillac was gone. They bolted for the BMW and collapsed inside. "Which way did he go?" Kimberly asked, fumbling with the key.

Andrew inserted it into the ignition for her, then fell back against the seat as the car peeled wildly away from the curb. "I think he turned left at the corner."

She didn't bother slowing down to take the turn, and Andrew was tossed against the door as the BMW skidded around the corner. Belatedly he groped for his seat belt. "There he is!" she shrieked energetically, spotting the black car just before it made another left turn.

"Slow down," Andrew cautioned her. "You don't want him to see us tailing him."

"All right, all right," Kimberly muttered, though she didn't ease her foot much on the accelerator pedal. She turned left, and they found the Cadillac waiting at a stop sign. "Diplomatic plate," she said. "Write it down—I'll be able to trace the number at work."

Andrew reached for his briefcase to get a pen, then froze. The student paper. Where was it? Still at Wilding's place? With Andrew's name incriminatingly typed in the upper right-hand margin? "Kim," he barked. "Where? Where's the paper?"

"What paper?" she asked innocently.

"The student paper, damn it! The essay I gave you!"

She turned to him, able to read the panic in his eyes. She let him fret for a second before presenting him with a smug grin. "Relax, Double-O Seven. It's in my back pocket."

He sank into the upholstery, then let loose with a laugh. "Good enough, Agent 99. Give me the pen."

She shifted to pull from her hip pocket the pen and the paper, which was wrinkled but intact. Andrew jotted down the Cadillac's license number, then surrendered to more laughter. "You're crazy, Kim," he declared. "Absolutely nuts."

She joined his laughter. "Not nuts enough to like water beds," she maintained.

He lifted his hand to her hair and pulled out two broken leaves. Cupping them in his palm, he displayed them for her. "I think you'll be thrown off the cheerleading squad for this."

"Their loss," she said, shrugging blithely.

Chapter Five

Pastel shades flattered her.

Andrew supposed that Kimberly would look good in anything she wore—army fatigues, a tuxedo, baggy chartreuse pajamas. But the soft hues of her clothing complemented her fair coloring in a magnificent way, highlighting her lucid blue eyes, giving her complexion a healthy glow.

At the moment she was attired in a peach-colored dress with long sleeves and a simple cut, snug at her slender waist and flaring down to the hem. The neckline wasn't daring, but it revealed her throat and her graceful collarbone. The only jewelry she wore was a pair of pearl studs in her earlobes and a narrow gold watch on her wrist. She looked exquisite.

Andrew tried to recall the last time he had been with a woman as beautiful as Kimberly, and all he could come up with was the hours he'd spent seated across the Formica-topped work table from Kimberly herself, in *The Dream*'s basement office fifteen years ago. She had often worn pastels then, too. But he couldn't remember her looking nearly as good as she looked now.

It was more than just the colors of her clothes that enhanced her appearance. It was their unobtrusive style and her meticulous grooming, her subtle use of cosmetics, her smooth hands, her understated perfume. She knew what to do with herself, how to make the most of nature's generous gifts.

Marjorie had been a slob. Andrew had loved her, so he hadn't cared much about the way the corduroy of her slacks was always eroded at the knees, the way her untucked shirt-tails always drooped below the ribbed edge of her sweaters, the way her sweaters themselves were always stretched out of shape and worn to near transparency at the elbows. Nor had he minded the fact that their compact apartment in the married students' housing at the University of Michigan was always a mess. Marjorie used to joke that she vacuumed once a year, whether or not the carpet needed it, and that allowing dust to accumulate on the tables ought to be accepted as a physics experiment, since dust was a product of meteors.

Andrew had straightened out the place as best he could, and he had always chosen to give her articles of clothing for Christmas and her birthday. Invariably, the first time she would wear some new sweater he'd given her, she would spill ketchup or grape juice on it.

They had argued about her slovenliness. But if Andrew had been able to view the future, if he had had any inkling of how little time together he and Marjorie were to be granted, he wouldn't have wasted so many precious minutes berating her for her carelessness and wishing she were neater. Bickering was a natural part of any intimate relationship, but if he had known how close he was to losing her, he never would have fought with her.

No, that wasn't true. Even after they *had* known that the end was upon them, they had fought. Living with Henry and Edith for that last year had been excruciatingly tough, and the chemotherapy had been wretched, leaving Marjorie exhausted and listless. But even as she and Andrew watched her life ebb away, they still quarreled over her habit of leaving books open on the floor, her failure to return record albums to their jackets when she was through listening to them and her refusal to hang her towel back on the rack when she was done with it. The things she had no control over—Andrew didn't mind any of that. He had lovingly changed the bed sheets daily and bathed her when she was too tired to bathe herself, clipped her toenails and held her head when nausea overcame her. He would gladly have done those things for her forever—if only he had been given the chance. He hadn't, though. Marjorie died, leaving him with little but his own insufferable tidiness.

Marjorie had been typical of the women Andrew had dated throughout his life: attractive, if not classically beautiful, and dazzlingly intelligent. He had never associated much with women like Kimberly.

He had liked the restaurant they'd gone to, an elegant establishment located inside the Georgetown Inn. He wondered if she had selected the place because it had pink napkins and pink flowers in the bud vases on the tables. Clad in her peach dress, surrounded by so much pink, she had appeared as gently tinted and delicate as the water lilies in the Monet print hanging above her bed in her apartment.

On their way back to Fairfax, she had driven Andrew to his motel so he could change his clothing. He had donned his tie, his tweed blazer and a pair of dark blue trousers. Although he'd brought the tie and the tailored slacks in the hope of wearing them when he met Senator Milford, he was just as happy to wear them for Kimberly.

"What was it like being a cheerleader?" he asked, genuinely interested. They had just left the restaurant, and he was in an expansive mood. He was trying to reconcile the image of a teenage Kimberly doing splits in the air with the reality of her dashing through the bushes at Wilding's house, scaling the walls, taking maniacal chances with her own life and Andrew's. Sometimes the two images coincided, and sometimes they seemed poles apart. An inveterate analyzer, Andrew needed to make sense of Kimberly. He needed to find a logical explanation for how the cheerleader had evolved into this astonishing woman by his side.

She peered up at him and smiled. "Do you want to know the truth?" she asked, leaning toward him conspiratorially. "I loved it."

"Did you really?"

"Oh, Andrew... I know you're going to think I'm a moron for saying so, but it was great. I loved everything about it—the short pleated skirts we wore, and the letter sweaters, and the saddle shoes, and riding in the team bus to the away games. I loved the megaphones and the pom-poms. Maybe I'm an egomaniac, but I loved the recognition, too. Being a cheerleader in my high school was a real coup. We were admired, we were envied.... We were popular."

"You probably would have been popular even if you hadn't been a cheerleader," he commented.

She shrugged, drawing to a stop at the corner as they waited for the light to change. "That's like saying I would have been popular if I'd been a poet, or a dog breeder. Maybe I would have been and maybe I wouldn't. The fact was, I *was* a cheerleader."

"In my high school," he recalled, "the cheerleaders were very aloof. And they always tended to be superstraight. There were three distinct cliques in the school: the jocks, the freaks and the hoods. Cheerleaders were female jocks."

"And you were a freak," Kimberly accurately guessed.

He chuckled and nodded. "I hung out with my classmates in the A-track, listened to The Doors, talked about drugs with aplomb. The jocks—cheerleaders included—tended to be Beach Boys fans and beer drinkers."

"Heavens!" Kimberly gasped in mock dismay. "In *my* high school, no proper young lady worth her salt would ever be caught drinking beer. We drank mint juleps and Southern Comfort. Beer was considered a man's beverage.''

"I'm sorry I ordered the wine at dinner," Andrew teased her. "I didn't realize that my masculinity hung in the balance. I should have asked for a pitcher of whatever they had on tap.''

"Frankly, I don't like beer much," Kimberly confessed. "I'm glad you ordered the wine." The light changed, and she started across the street, Andrew following. "It's such a lovely evening, I wish we could take a stroll to work down all that food. But we've got to get home. Whitney could be calling anytime now." Her gaze narrowed on Andrew and her smile faded. "Do you mind coming back to my apartment for a while? I know you think this is all silly, but I'm sure he's going to want to talk to you when he calls, and if you aren't there—"

"That's all right," he assured her. "I don't mind." He honestly didn't. His eyes glinted wickedly when he added, "Are you sure you trust me not to come on like gangbusters once I enter your apartment?''

Kimberly tossed back her head and laughed.

The night air was pleasantly cool. She slipped her hand through Andrew's elbow as they turned off Wisconsin Avenue and proceeded down a picturesque block of restored town houses. "This is such a delightful neighborhood," Andrew commented. "I almost feel as if I've stepped into another century. Look at these gas lamps." He paused beneath one of the decorative streetlights and gazed up at it.

Kimberly grinned. "The last time I walked down this block I was with Whitney," she told Andrew.

"And?" He noticed dimples forming at the corners of her mouth. "What's so funny?"

"Just how different you are from him," she explained. "You talk about the streetlights. He talked about whether Henry Kissinger had lived on this street."

Andrew mulled over what she'd said. He wondered what his having mentioned the streetlights indicated to her and why she was so amused. "So? Did Henry Kissinger live on this street?"

"I don't know," Kimberly answered as they resumed their stroll. "If he did, he never invited me to his house. I'm afraid he and I travel in different circles."

"I think you ought to get to know your neighbors better," Andrew chided her. "You ought to find out where they stand on the issues. Look at Wilding's neighborhood. Do you think his neighbors on that charming little block have any idea of what he's scheming?"

"Every neighborhood has its hidden snakes and flakes." She crossed the street with him. "Especially in the Washington area. Ignore these government types and they just might do something heinous, like creating a revolution in El Salvador."

"You never know," Andrew commented lightly.

"You still don't trust the government, Andrew, do you?" she half asked.

He weighed his answer. "I don't distrust it as much as I used to fifteen years ago," he conceded. "But I can't shake the notion that it tends to attract people who are hungry for power—exactly the sort of people I don't want representing me."

"Nonsense," she debated. "It attracts people who wish to serve their country. Most politicians take office because they think they can make the world a better place. Maybe you disagree with their positions, maybe you think they're going about it the wrong way. Maybe their definition of 'better' is different from yours. But their motives are usually pure."

"God, you're such an optimist," he observed with a smile. He found Kimberly's positive opinion of politicians sweet, even if he didn't quite agree with it. He envied her ability to approach the universe in such a positive manner. He had spent enough of his life being bitter, seeing the world as a bleak and hostile place. And it hadn't done him a lick of good. Kimberly's attitude didn't mark her as shallow, only as sensible.

They had reached her apartment. She unlocked the door and ushered Andrew inside. Once she shut and bolted the door, she preceded him into the living room and switched on a lamp.

"Do you think he's called yet?" Andrew asked.

Kimberly read her wristwatch and shrugged. "It's nine o'clock. If he missed us he'll call again." She crossed to the kitchen. "Would you like something to drink?"

Andrew removed his blazer and tugged his necktie loose. "What have you got?"

"Coffee, brandy, some orange liqueur..."

"No beer, huh," he joked.

Her eyes met his across the counter, and she smiled. "No beer. But being a Southerner, I do have bourbon."

"Wild Turkey?"

"Jack Daniel's."

"Sounds great."

He watched as she pulled a bottle of Jack Daniel's from one cabinet and two highball glasses from another. He was glad she was going to join him. "Ice?" she asked as she unscrewed the bottle top. "Or water?"

"I'll take it straight," he requested.

Her smile expanded. She poured two hefty portions of bourbon, left the bottle on the counter and carried the glasses into the living room. Andrew took his drink from her and sank onto the sofa. Kimberly stepped out of her shoes and curled up on the easy chair, tucking her stockinged feet beneath her. Then she took a sip. She held her glass like a lady, he observed, with her pinkie crooked into the air, but she drank her booze strong and neat, just like a man. He liked that.

Before tasting the bourbon, he glanced at the wall phone in the kitchen. He wanted to learn what Whitney had found out about L.A.R.C., but he almost wished they wouldn't be hearing from him for a while. Once they did, once Whitney called and made his report, Andrew would no longer have a good excuse to stay at Kimberly's apartment. And he wanted to stay. He wanted to enjoy a leisurely drink with a beautiful woman.

She must have noticed his gaze drifting to the telephone, because she asked, "Would you like to watch some television? Or I could turn on the stereo—"

"No, that's all right," he hastened to assure her. He didn't want her to feel obliged to entertain him. "Why don't we just talk?"

"Fine." She settled back in the overstuffed chair and took another bracing sip of bourbon. Her index finger traced the circular rim of her glass, but her eyes remained fixed on Andrew, their clear, shimmering blue reminding him of a still, deep pond in the Berkshires, mirroring the Massachusetts sky. She smiled tenuously. "Tell me about your wife," she said.

IT WAS A RISKY THING to ask. Kimberly recognized how risky it was when Andrew froze in his seat at the sound of the word "wife," his glass in midair, his eyes suddenly searing behind his eyeglasses, the muscles of his jaw stiffening. But she wasn't sorry she'd broached the subject. Maybe it was the wrong question, but she wouldn't take it back.

At his lengthening silence, she felt the need to justify herself. "I know she passed away, Andrew. Seth told Laura and she told me." When he still didn't speak, she added, "I was terribly sorry to hear about it."

He finally moved, lifting his glass to his lips and taking a long sip. But even the bourbon couldn't erase the aching pain in his eyes, the tension around his mouth and neck. She wished she had the nerve to march across the room to the couch and sit beside him, to wrap her arms around him in comfort. But she'd exhausted her supply of courage simply by giving voice to the question, and she remained where she was.

Not a word from him as he swallowed, lowered his glass to the coffee table in front of him and stared at her. "I tell you what," she offered, trying to placate him. She would do anything to ease his agony, anything to get him to open up to her again. Anything to see him bare the soul he had managed to hide from her for so long. "I'll fill you in on my sad marriage story first."

"Okay," he said softly.

Although she didn't particularly want to discuss her divorce, she intuited that Andrew's willingness to listen to her talk about it meant that eventually he would be willing to tell her his own sad story. "Divorce is such a common thing," she said, studying the dark amber fluid in her glass. "But you never think it's going to happen to you. I always figured that if you could survive the first couple of years of marriage, you were set for life. Or at least until the midlife crises struck. Todd and I aren't old enough to suffer midlife crises."

"So why did you split?" Andrew asked.

"Little things," she replied pensively. "Little things that added up to big things. He had affairs—"

"That's a pretty big thing, if you ask me," Andrew commented.

She lifted her gaze to him and smiled. He *was* a decent man. How many men in this day and age would consider extramarital affairs anything but trivial? "In the society I grew up in," she explained, "men always have affairs. A proper wife is supposed to look the other way. And I did—the first time.''

"Why the hell did he want anyone else when he had you?''

Andrew's compliment warmed her deeply. Her eyes met his, and she was equally warmed by their tenderness, their steadiness on her. Telling Andrew about her divorce wasn't as difficult as she had expected, not when he seemed so sympathetic and caring. "What Todd had was a wife,'' she distinguished. "As soon as it's legal, it isn't so much fun anymore. I guess.'' Her smile grew bittersweet. "I probably would have continued to look the other way if it hadn't been for all the other little things. He had so many confusions about me, about what I should be doing and feeling. He resented the fact that I had a career, but then he liked the income I was bringing in. He didn't mind when I worked for the P.R. firm, but he hated my working for the senator. He considers my boss a closet pinko.''

"Milford?'' Andrew guffawed. "A Communist?''

She shrugged. "What can I say? The senator believes that prayer is a private matter. He believes that we ought to negotiate arms treaties with the Soviet Union. Very suspect behavior in the eyes of someone like Todd.''

"Why did you marry him?'' Andrew asked, leaning forward and resting his forearms on his spread knees. "Didn't you know all this about him before you tied the knot?''

She chuckled sadly. "I've known Todd ever since we were children. His parents and mine were good friends. But knowing someone a long time doesn't mean you know him well. We got along fine, we were attracted to each other, we came from similar backgrounds. Even though we dated other people before we got married, it was always a given that we'd get married eventually.'' She laughed again. "If he was scandalized that I went to Barnard College up north in Sin City, he was even more scandalized that I didn't go through all the premarriage rituals with him. I was never lavaliered—"

"What?"

"Lavaliered. That's when a fellow gives you a pendant with his fraternity letters on it, and he and his fraternity brothers stand under your window and serenade you. After that you get pinned. Then you get engaged. I can just imagine Todd and his brothers driving up to Harlem to serenade me!" She chuckled at the absurdity of the idea. "I think he believed that my time at Barnard was my last fling, that I was going to 'get it out of my system' before we got married. I'm not sure what 'it' was, but it was supposed to be behind me by the time I got married."

"Kim." Andrew shook his head incredulously. "It was 1972. I can't believe people were doing that sort of thing in 1972."

"They probably weren't in Canton, Ohio," she conceded. "And they certainly weren't doing it at Columbia. But life was different where I came from. This was how things were done."

"Especially if you were a cheerleader," he ribbed her.

She looked sharply at him, anxious to ascertain that he wasn't denigrating her again. When she had confessed, during their walk home from the restaurant, that she loved being a cheerleader, Andrew had appeared fascinated. She didn't want to think he had relapsed into his original view of her as an empty-headed goose.

But his smile was gentle, not mocking. It was an utterly beautiful, nonjudgmental smile. She nestled into the chair's cushions and continued her tale. "We had a big, grand wedding. Half of Augusta was invited. Everyone told us we made a perfect couple."

"Why didn't you have any children?"

She had already told Andrew that she wanted children, so his question was reasonable. "I don't think Todd cared to become a father," she admitted. "At first he protested that we needed my income to pay for our house—which we did, I'm afraid. It was a huge place, much larger than any childless couple requires. The fact that he loved it so much led me to assume he would want to have children eventually. So I waited. I paid my share of the mortgage. I closed my eyes to his affairs. And I waited some more. After I turned thirty I began to get nervous about it. Finally I called him to account, and he said the only way he'd have children with me was if I did it his way—I'd have to quit my job and stay at home with them."

"Is there anything so terrible about that?" Andrew asked. "I don't mean to sound sexist, Kim, but lots of women—even today—stay at home with their children. My mother did, and she found it very fulfilling."

"I love my work," Kimberly argued, then meditated on her insistence, in her marriage, of maintaining her career. She sighed. "Andrew, I would have quit my job to have children if I had thought for one minute that Todd was going to be a willing father. But he truly didn't want children. He only wanted to get me to quit the senator's staff. It was like a bargain he was cutting with me—he'd let me have my children if I'd stop working for a pinko." She drank her bourbon and sighed again. "That's not the right way to have children, as some sort of trade agreement, some sort of compromise. If both partners aren't ready to put their all into parenthood, it's not right."

Andrew pondered her statement and nodded.

"Why didn't you have children?" she countered, deciding that she'd talked long enough about her divorce. The subject no longer depressed her, but she found it tiresome. Now it was his turn to talk.

He lowered his gaze to his glass, examined it intently and drained it in one long gulp. "Is it all right if I help myself?" he asked, rising.

That he was trying to evade her question was obvious. She forgave him, but she wasn't about to let him off the hook. "Go right ahead," she said generously, angling her head toward the counter where the bottle stood. Then she took another sip from her own glass and handed it to him. He refilled his glass, added some bourbon to hers and delivered it to her on his way back to the couch.

He drank. She waited. He drank some more. "How strong is this?" he asked.

"The proof must be written on the bottle somewhere," she told him. "Do you want me to check?"

"No." He inspected his glass, took a parting sip and set it on the coffee table. "I just wish I was feeling it a little more, that's all." He settled back on the cushions and smiled sheepishly. "We've never gotten drunk together, Kim."

"Stoned, either."

His eyebrows arched in surprise. "Do you smoke grass?"

"No." She returned his smile. "I'm ashamed to admit I've never touched the stuff. But it would have been fun getting stoned with you."

"Do you think so?" He ruminated, then snorted. "I didn't smoke much in college. Every time I did I got gloomy and introspective."

Kimberly didn't bother to point out that even when he wasn't stoned, he'd had a tendency to be gloomy and introspective. Well, maybe not gloomy. But dreadfully solemn and somber, as if all those heavy thoughts of his allowed no room for laughter. What had he said earlier? Something about how those had been serious times. He hadn't needed marijuana; he'd been introspective enough without it.

He eyed his glass, then bravely refused to hide behind it any longer. He seemed able to sense that Kimberly was growing impatient, that he couldn't keep stalling. "We tried to have children," he said slowly, quietly, his gaze fastened to the wall behind Kimberly. "After a long time she conceived, but then she had a miscarriage. That's when they discovered she had some abnormal cells." He grimaced at the memory. "That's how they break the news to you: 'Abnormal cells.'"

"She had cancer?"

Andrew nodded, still unable to look directly at Kimberly. "Vaginal cancer, uterine cancer, ovarian cancer.... It had already metastasized. It's such an amazing vocabulary they have, Kim. A million words ending with the suffix *oma*. As soon as you hear something that ends in 'oma' you know you're in big trouble."

"How long had you been married?" she asked.

"When she was diagnosed? Almost four years."

"How did you meet her?"

A vague smile shaped his lips as he reminisced. "We met in graduate school. She was a grad student in the physics department. We got married about a year later."

"What was her name? What did she look like? Have you got a picture of her?" Kimberly couldn't keep the spate of questions from pouring out. As impossible as it seemed, Andrew was finally opening up to her. She felt an urgent need to learn everything at once, before he rethought things and clammed up again.

He laughed dryly. "She's dead, Kim. Why on earth would I be carrying around a picture of a dead woman?"

"I don't know," Kimberly defended herself. "I'm just trying to imagine her. I want to know about her."

He raised his glass and drank. "This *is* strong," he assessed the bourbon. "I think I'm beginning to feel it."

Kimberly smiled. In any other circumstance she would abhor the idea of having a drunk man in her home. But Andrew wasn't the sort to get obnoxious and don a lampshade. If the liquor helped him to talk, then she hoped he'd get plastered.

"What was her name?" she repeated.

"Marjorie."

"Was she pretty?"

"Sure. No." He exhaled, and his gaze alighted on Kimberly. "She wasn't pretty, not in the traditional sense. But she was beautiful."

"Of course she was beautiful. You loved her," Kimberly pointed out. One of her mother's many pet clichés was "Beauty is in the eye of the beholder." Like so many clichés, that one was absolutely true.

"I loved her," he confirmed, his tone husky with emotion.

Kimberly wondered whether he was going to cry. She almost wished that he would. If he did, she would definitely cross the room to him, definitely fold her arms around him. She would welcome his tears, welcome the intimacy they would represent.

Yet he seemed resolutely dry-eyed, and Kimberly remained in her chair. "Did she suffer long? I should think it would be terrible to see someone you love suffering," she mused.

"She died about a year and a half after she was diagnosed," he said. "It wasn't a whole year and a half of unremitting suffering, though. We had ups and downs, moments of hope, good days." He kicked off his loafers and propped his legs up on the coffee table, as if making himself more comfortable would enable the words to flow more easily. "As soon as we found out how sick she was, we left Ann Arbor and moved in with her parents in White Plains so we could be near Memorial Sloan-Kettering in Manhattan. It's one of the finest cancer treatment hospitals in the world. I wanted her to have the best care available."

"That's certainly understandable."

"Unfortunately living with Edith and Henry had its drawbacks."

"You didn't like your in-laws?"

"Oh, I loved them," he corrected her. "I still do. They're great people. But . . . you need privacy. You realize how little time you have left, and you want to run away and just be by yourselves as much as possible. We had enough coming down on us without having to prop up Edith and Henry all the time." He pulled off his eyeglasses and rubbed the pale red marks they left on the bridge of his nose. "Sometimes, when I wasn't able to fall asleep, I'd go downstairs to the kitchen for a glass of milk and find Henry there, also unable to sleep. And he'd say, 'She shouldn't have gone into physics. Maybe she was exposed to radioactivity in a lab, maybe her research was what made her sick.' And I'd think, her research was one of her great joys. How could this man say she would have been better off without it? How could he be so insensitive?"

"Insensitive?" Kimberly protested. "She was his daughter. He was grieving."

"I know that. I tried not to hold it against him. But it was hard, Kim. Very hard." He turned to the window and gazed out at the darkness. "They're good people, Edith and Henry. I keep in touch with them. I see them from time to time. In some ways they're easier to take than my own parents. After Marjorie died I spent some time back in Ohio, trying to unwind, trying to pull myself together. My parents wanted to baby me. My dad wanted to give me a job in his store so I wouldn't have to go back to Ann Arbor and relive all the memories while I finished my degree. They thought they could protect me from ever getting hurt again. They still want to protect me."

"That also seems like a natural response," Kimberly asserted. "You're their son and they love you."

"Maybe." His eyes drifted back to Kimberly. "When you're trying to come to grips with yourself, the last thing you want is to have everyone else crowding you, no matter how good their intentions are."

"Is that why you don't like to talk about it?" Kimberly asked.

"I'm talking about it now." He lifted his glass, then lowered it without drinking. "I talk about it with people I can trust not to crowd me, not to pity me, not to baby me. What happened with Marjorie is a part of my life, just like breaking my arm falling off a skateboard when I was eight was part of my life, and having the neighbors call the police one evening because I was playing 'The Soft Parade' too loud, and graduating from Columbia and from the University of Michigan. Those few people who can accept it, whom I can trust...I can talk about it to them."

She recognized that he had complimented her again, a much more significant compliment than any he had ever given her before. Yet she didn't bask in Andrew's flattery. He hadn't told her he trusted her as a means of softening her up. He had simply stated a fact.

"Do you date much now?" she asked.

"What constitutes 'much'?" he returned, smiling crookedly.

Kimberly grinned. "One of the things that frightens me about being divorced is that now I have to start all over again. Dating is fun when you're sixteen, Andrew, but not when you're thirty-five. I'm too old for it."

"You aren't so old," he said, for not the first time. "And you're gorgeous, Kim. If you wanted to go out on dates, I'm sure you could have men beating a path to your door. Look at Whitney."

"Ugh. Look at him," she grunted. Then her gaze met Andrew's, and they both laughed. "Did you find it hard, starting all over again? I reckon you didn't," she answered herself. "According to the latest statistics, the odds are slanted strongly in favor of men. Single women past thirty-five may as well forget about ever marrying again."

"You want to get married again?"

"Definitely. I want to have a child, Andrew. I already told you that. I suppose I could have one by myself if I had to—and oh, Lord, wouldn't that shock my family!" She laughed. "How about you? Will you get married again?"

"I hope so."

"Are you seeing anyone now? Anyone special?"

He accepted her question as she'd intended it—not nosy, not prying, only curious. "I've dated a few women since I moved to Amherst," he told her. "The woman I've been seeing lately is a grad student at U-Mass. She's got a job lined up for next September at Cal-State Fullerton if she wants it, and she says she does. So even if she doesn't finish her dissertation in time, she's going to be leaving for California in a couple of months." He shrugged. "Obviously this one isn't going to lead to marriage."

Kimberly tilted her glass against her lips and emptied it. "How do you meet women?" she asked. Before he could answer, she stood and walked to the counter. She hesitated, then brought her glass and the bottle to the coffee table and dropped onto the couch next to Andrew. She could no longer tolerate being seated so far away from him when she felt so close to him.

She poured some bourbon into her glass, then dribbled a bit more into his. "Are we going to get drunk together?" he asked, smiling whimsically, twisting on the cushion in order to face her.

She was pleased that he hadn't questioned her decision to change her seat. His smile and the way he'd angled his shoulders toward her, sliding one arm along the back of the sofa, indicated that he was delighted by her company. "I'm not drunk," she assured him. "Now tell me, how do you go about the dating business? Do people set you up? Or do you go to bars?" At his laugh she persisted. "I'm serious, Andrew. I'm such a novice at this. I've talked to Julianne about it—she's my closest single woman friend. But she doesn't date much at all. I don't think she really cares one way or another about getting married. Whenever I ask her for advice, she tells me to accentuate the positive and things will work out."

"Once you're ready to start dating you'll have your hands full," Andrew predicted. "When a woman is available she shows it. And when a woman as pretty as you are shows that she's available, she should have no trouble attracting men."

"You really think I'm pretty?" she asked. She wasn't fishing for more compliments from Andrew. But he had never before talked to her this way, and she couldn't help wondering whether he was only complimenting her to boost her ego.

"I think..." He brushed a stray lock of her hair from her cheek. "I think you're the prettiest woman I've ever known."

"You do?"

"Oh, come on, Kim. You don't need me to tell you what your mirror tells you. You're a beautiful woman."

"Do I look available?" she asked. The question surprised her; it struck her as incredibly forward. Yet an unfathomable compulsion to know precisely what Andrew thought of her forced the words out. "Right now? Do I look available?"

He gave her a long, thoughtful examination. She watched as his lips moved, shaping his words before he gave voice to them. He had lovely lips, she noticed. Strong and thin, expressive.

He didn't say anything for a moment. Instead he lifted his hand to her cheek again, tracing the arching bone that gave it its shape. "It was good today," he whispered.

"What?" Her voice sounded tremulous to her, curiously husky. She was conscious of the narrow distance between them. Andrew was close enough for her to smell his clean scent, his woodsy after-shave. He was close enough for her to feel the warmth of his body. "What was good?"

"Going to Wilding's house."

"Oh?"

"No," he contradicted himself. "Not going there. What was good was holding you. At his house, by the bedroom window." His hand dropped to his lap, and he abruptly glanced away, as if rattled by his confession.

Her heart seemed to stop beating for a moment. What now? What to do? His words elicited a powerful yearning inside her, yet the way he averted his eyes informed her that he didn't wish to follow through. Andrew was smart; he was wisely trying to douse whatever was heating up between them. He was backing off again, before it was too late, before Kimberly could reach his soul.

Unable to ignore her disappointment, she looked at her watch. It was nearly eleven-thirty.

Andrew wrapped his fingers around her lower arm and lifted her wrist so he could check her watch, as well. "He isn't going to call," he said. "Not this late."

He raised his eyes to her. Kimberly remembered that the only reason Andrew had come home with her was to abet her in her scheme to detour Whitney's attentions. She eased her wrist from his loose grip and said, as much to herself as to him, "You probably want to leave."

"No."

His gaze remained steadfast on her, searching. She ran her tongue over her lips, a nervous reflex. She didn't know what to say.

"I'll—I'll go if you want me to," he added.

"No." She wanted him to touch her hair again, and her face and her wrist. She wanted to feel his arms around her and his beautiful lips on her. She wanted to remain in the company of this fine, decent friend, this man who had survived a pain far worse than hers.

She didn't want him to leave.

Chapter Six

The luscious flavor of his kiss lingered on her lips as she led him down the hallway to her bedroom. She had never kissed a man wearing eyeglasses before. She had thought that Michael Caine looked cute when, as a teenager, she'd seen him in *Alfie*, but she hadn't fantasized about kissing him. And if she'd ever dated a nearsighted man, he must have been wearing contacts.

She wasn't sure what she had expected. Would the frames collide with her brow? Would she bang into them and bruise Andrew's nose? Would the lenses steam up?

None of those disasters had occurred, however. Obviously Andrew was accustomed to his eyeglasses, and he knew how to angle his face, how to tilt her chin with his thumb to avoid any interference when their mouths met. His kiss had been sublime, informing Kimberly that her decision to invite him to stay the night hadn't been a mistake.

As soon as she reached her bed, his hands fell to her shoulders and turned her to him. He bowed his head to kiss her again, and this kiss vanquished her memory of the previous one. His mouth tasted of bourbon and maleness, a heady combination, and his tongue moved sensuously against hers, alluringly. How had she ever thought that this sexy man was an egghead? How had she ever considered him an intellectual snob when he had such strong arms, such firm lips and such a lean, well-toned body?

She ran her fingers up his sides, feeling his ribs through the cotton of his shirt. The knowledge that he would shortly be removing that shirt and baring his chest to her caused a thick, warm longing to course through her. She couldn't recall ever responding so rapidly to Todd.

Kimberly had never made love with anyone but her husband. She had kept her inexperience a secret from everybody except Todd, because in the late sixties and early seventies, when she was coming of age, liberated women were supposed to be sexually adventurous, experimenting, sowing their wild oats with all the abandon of their male counterparts. Kimberly had remained a virgin by choice, but she hadn't discussed that choice with her friends in college. She had listened to their exploits and only smiled enigmatically when their attention turned to her. She hadn't wanted her classmates to think she was a prude or a weirdo.

Todd had been overjoyed by Kimberly's chastity—which, she acknowledged in retrospect, ought to have given her a fair idea of how strongly he adhered to the double standard. Even after she'd accepted his proposal, he had refused to sleep with her until they were married. "You've lasted this long, Kim, you may as well go for it," he'd explained, as time after time he warded off her sexual overtures and extricated himself from her embraces. That she was a mature twenty-one-year-old woman with healthy desires didn't matter to him. *He* wasn't a virgin, but he went on and on about what a thrill it would be for him to take a virgin to bed on his honeymoon.

Perhaps it had been a thrill for him. For Kimberly it had been agony. Nearly a full year had passed before she'd finally begun to enjoy sex. Privately she conceded that the problem was her lack of experience, but she had never dared discuss her theory with Todd. He probably would have considered her a wanton slut if she had.

Andrew's lips had moved to her temple, and all thoughts of Todd dissolved in the heat of her passion for the man with her now. His hands drifted across her back to the zipper of her dress and tugged it open. She shuddered slightly.

At her involuntary motion he pulled back. "Should we be doing this?" he asked in a low, hoarse voice.

She peered up at him. His eyes were clear and heartbreakingly gentle. "Are you having doubts, Andrew?" she returned, praying that he would answer in the negative.

"No," he murmured, answering her prayers. "All I meant was . . . you've had a lot to drink, Kim. I don't want to take advantage of you if you're—"

"Smashed?" She laughed. "Let me assure you, Andrew, mingled among all my slave-owning ancestors are a few moonshiners. I know how to hold my liquor. How about you?"

"My grandfather's brother was a bootlegger during Prohibition."

"Then you've got good genes," she concluded.

"How nice of you to notice." He slid the silk of her dress down her arms and over her hips, pulling her panty hose with it and letting the garments drop to the floor. Then he took a step back to study her in her lacy pink bra and matching panties. He took a deep breath and shook his head. "It doesn't seem possible that any woman could be as beautiful as you are," he muttered, sounding strangely disapproving.

"I'm sorry," she said reflexively.

"I'm not." He reached for his tie, but Kimberly pushed his hands away and undid the knot herself. Then she unbuttoned his shirt and shoved it off his shoulders. His torso was more muscular than she had expected. Gnomes who climbed out of tomes weren't supposed to boast such rugged physiques. But, then, her impression of Andrew as a bookworm had obviously been in error.

She combed her fingernails through the dark curls of hair adorning his chest, and he sucked in another sharp breath. Her tantalizing touch was apparently driving him to distraction, but, exercising great self-control, he withstood it without protest. When her hands dropped to his belt, however, he groaned and gathered her to himself for another devastating kiss.

Refusing to break from her, he helped her to remove the rest of his clothing. He set his eyeglasses on the night table, then lifted her onto the bed and dove on beside her. "Don't you want to take off my underthings?" she asked.

"Eventually." Lying on his side, he let his hands roam along the trim of her bra and then the lacy cups, teasing her nipples through the delicate fabric. He bent to kiss one swollen nipple, his warm breath seeping through the cloth.

Todd had never paid so much attention to her lingerie. But, then, she mused dreamily as Andrew shifted to kiss her other breast, Todd had never paid so much attention to her breasts, either. With him lovemaking had centered on one part of her anatomy to the exclusion of all else.

Andrew deliberately avoided that part of her anatomy, instead taking time to explore the arching wings of her collarbone, the smooth skin of her throat, the indentation of her navel, the sleek lines of her thighs. "You're so beautiful," he said with a sigh.

"How can you even see me with your glasses off?"

He gazed at her, and once again the steady, fire-tinged light of his eyes reached to her heart and melted it. "Kim, I could close my eyes and still see you," he swore. "If I closed my eyes right now, all I'd see would be you." He kissed her with exquisite tenderness, then wedged his hand beneath her to unfasten the clasp of her bra. As soon as it was off, he turned his attention to her panties, running his finger along the elastic that stretched taut between her hipbones, then venturing beneath it to trace the edge of her hair.

Andrew had always struck Kimberly as an impatient man, yet she was the one bristling with impatience now. Her hips moved reflexively, urgently, and he obeyed her unspoken demand by stripping the panties down her legs and tossing them away. Then he stroked back up her legs to touch her.

She was unprepared for the sudden spasm, the frantic clenching of her soul in response to his caress. She was embarrassed to be reacting so fiercely, so swiftly. Proper ladies weren't supposed to be overcome by sexual need so immediately. Truly proper ladies weren't supposed to be overcome at all, if Kimberly's mother was to be believed. Mrs. Belmont had hardly been a font of information for her inquisitive daughter, but what little she had taught Kimberly about her own body bore an unfortunate resemblance to the timeworn Victorian dictum about closing one's eyes and thinking of England.

Kimberly wasn't thinking of England at the moment, or even of the glory that was Dixie. She was thinking only of Andrew, of his hard, virile body next to hers, his uneven breath, his glittering eyes, the exotic strands of silver woven into his dark hair. She was thinking of the smooth contours of his back as she trailed her hands over its surface, and the unyielding curve of his buttocks, the flat stretch of his abdomen and the eager fullness of his erection as she daringly draped her hand around it. She was thinking of how much she wanted him, how anxious her body was for him, how miraculous it was that she could be falling in love with a man like Andrew Collins.

Her touch seemed to galvanize him. A low, broken sound emanated from deep within his chest as she tightened her grip. In a fluid motion, he rolled onto his back, drawing her over him, guiding her legs around him and arching up into her.

For a moment she was dazed, unable to move. She had never before made love in that position—Todd would never have allowed such a thing—and she wasn't sure what to do. Andrew showed her, clasping her hips with his hands and imparting his rhythm to her. As soon as she took over, his hands rose to her waist and he let her lead him.

She felt free, wildly free and powerful above him, her hair tumbling into her face and brushing lightly against his jaw, her body compelling his, inciting it. The unfamiliar freedom fed her arousal, gave her strength, drove her with undue speed to the crest of sensation. She felt the dark tremors building within her, spreading through her, conquering her as she conquered Andrew. She surrendered with a breathless gasp, then sank fully onto him in time to absorb his shattering climax.

She remained on top of him, utterly relaxed, too weary to consider moving from him. Her soft flesh molded to the hard angles of his body in a surprisingly comfortable way. She hoped he was comfortable, too, because she wanted to stay exactly where she was forever.

Andrew clearly wasn't as exhausted as Kimberly. His lips browsed along her hairline and his fingers roamed the length of her spine. He bent one of his legs between hers so he could rub her thigh with his knee.

His energy astounded her. Whenever she and Todd used to make love, he had always been completely wasted afterward, interested in nothing more than drawing up the covers and going to sleep. Yet Andrew seemed invigorated by what he and Kimberly had just shared. His leg rose higher, flexing against her, getting her excited all over again. Her helpless moan caused him to laugh.

She laughed, as well. "Could you have imagined fifteen years ago that we'd end up like this?"

"No." He lifted his head from the pillow to kiss the tip of her nose, then curled his arm around her and held her close. "We're different people now than we were then."

"No, we're not," she argued. "I haven't changed that much, and neither have you. We're both just a little more tolerant, that's all."

"Tolerant?" His laughter increased. "Is that why I'm here? Because you're tolerating me?"

You're here because I'm falling in love with you, Kimberly almost said. She gazed down at him, savoring his strong, handsome features. She could nearly detect an incipient dimple on one of his cheeks. One more reason to love him, she admitted. Smiling definitely increased his face power.

"Do you mind talking?" she asked. Todd had always become irritated when she tried to embark on a conversation with him after sex. But that was because her talking had disturbed his sleep. "Do you want me to shut up?"

"What for?" He kissed her again. "Now seems like as good a time as any to debate the function of the C.I.A. in a democratic society."

"Andrew..." He was laughing too hard to hear the warning in her voice. She didn't want him making fun of her when she was so captivated by him.

"No, come on," he insisted, belying his artificially sober expression by flexing his leg against her again. He seemed inordinately pleased by her ragged sigh, but he maintained a straight face when he said, "Take wiretapping, for instance. Illegal domestic surveillance. What's your opinion of that, Kim?"

"Stop it!" she protested, succumbing to a chuckle. She tried to punch his arm, but he held her too tightly, and she had no choice but to subside on top of him again. Her fingers drew a twisting line through the hair surrounding his flat, brown nipple, and this time the ragged sigh came from him. "I like your chest," she told him.

"I like yours, too. I bet I like yours more than you like mine."

"It's probably a toss-up," she said diplomatically. Her finger skimmed upward to his broad shoulder, and she cushioned her head against his chest, beneath his chin. "I've never done it this way before, on top," she confessed.

"Did you like it?"

"Very much," she answered truthfully. She kissed the hollow at the base of his neck. "Let's do it again."

He shifted his hips beneath her, analyzing his condition. "Give me a few more minutes," he requested good-naturedly.

Amazing. It really was amazing, talking with him this way, so easily, so naturally. Why couldn't it have ever been like this with Todd?

Because Todd wasn't Andrew, that was why. Because Andrew was unique, marvelous, an incredible human being.

She wondered whether it was right for her to be comparing Andrew to Todd, even if Andrew fared spectacularly in the comparison. She wondered whether he was comparing her to the other women he had known. "Do you think about your wife when you're making love?" she asked.

She felt his withdrawal subliminally. Yet he didn't curse, he didn't shove her away. His arms remained ringed around her. His chin remained still and rigid against her hair.

"I'm sorry," she whispered. "You don't have to answer that."

"I do sometimes," he admitted, his voice drifting down to her from above her head. "Think about her, I mean." His words came haltingly. "But not now. Not with you."

She didn't know if she was supposed to take that as a compliment, but she did. "I'm usually much more tact-

ful,'' she said contritely. ''I don't know what it is about you
that makes me speak my mind this way—''

''We've always spoken our minds with each other, Kim,''
he pointed out.

That was true enough. In the past what had been on their
minds were insults. They wouldn't feel the need to insult
each other anymore. She was certain at last that Andrew no
longer looked down on her, no longer viewed her as a dumb
blonde, a pretty, trivial airhead. If he did, he wouldn't be
lying with her now, holding her, loving her.

They had always spoken their minds and they always
would. Kimberly would always be this honest with Andrew, this open to him. ''I like you,'' she whispered. She had
meant to say that she loved him, but ''like'' slipped out, instead. Yet that, too, was the truth. She genuinely liked him.

He seemed both touched and amused by her admission.
''You have a funny way of showing it,'' he teased, before
rising to kiss her. His mouth opened against hers, and the
moment their tongues found each other his body tensed beneath her. ''I think my few minutes are up,'' he declared as
he pulled his lips from hers.

''So are you,'' she joked, rocking her hips to his.

With a deep groan he filled her again. And this time she
allowed herself no thoughts of anything but him. No com-
parisons, no memories. Only Andrew, merging with her,
fusing himself to her, accepting her body, her mind, her
heart.

AT ONE TIME OR ANOTHER every heterosexual man must
have dreamed of waking up beside a cheerleader.

A cheerleader, a prom queen, a debutante, a cool, blond
goddess. A shiksa, as David Schiffman, Andrew's best
friend in high school, used to call it. ''Literally a shiksa is a
gentile girl,'' he had defined the Yiddish term. ''But spiri-

tually she's the beautiful blond girl you can never have, the unobtainable."

Andrew wasn't Jewish, but he had understood what David had meant. The shiksa was the woman you dreamed about.

But dreams didn't come true. So when you woke up, you defended yourself against the dream. You viewed the shiksas from afar and invented justifications for your inability to capture them. You talked yourself out of wanting them. You decided that they were stupid, that they were shallow, that they weren't worth your time. You assured yourself that they were stuck-up, that they took men for granted, that the lady within your reach was actually the one worth having.

His vision took in the woman sleeping at his side. Sunlight filtered through the translucent curtains drawn shut across her window and imbued her hair with glints of gold. It fell in graceful waves against the creamy skin of her cheek. Her eyes were closed, and he saw that her eyelashes were uncommonly long. If she opened her eyes, Andrew knew that their clear irises would match the delicate blue of her bedspread.

Everything about her was too good to be true. Like a dream. Now he was awake, no longer dreaming. She *was* too good to be true, and he felt his defenses rising again.

He couldn't blame the bourbon, at least not for his own behavior last night. Maybe for hers. Maybe, despite her protestations, she'd been blitzed last night, and when she woke up she'd be full of regret, embarrassed and entertaining a whopping headache. But Andrew wasn't hung over, and if he wasn't hung over he couldn't have been drunk the night before.

Then what was he doing in Kimberly's bed? Besides, perhaps, indulging in a dream?

He was in her bed because she had been using him to detour the advances of another man. He was in her bed because she had been playing a foolish game and had gotten a little carried away with the spirit of it. He didn't feel exploited—he had enjoyed himself too greatly—but he wasn't going to be irrational about the situation now that dawn had broken and he'd returned to full consciousness.

All right. A dream. That was all it was. A delightful, breathtaking dream, evanescing in the glare of daylight. Kimberly was a fun person—by definition, all cheerleaders had to be fun—and he was fond of her, but he was too much of a realist to believe that what they had experienced last night could possibly be love. Because if it were, if he let himself love her, he would lose her. He knew it instinctively; he knew he was not designed for true love with gorgeous blond-goddess cheerleaders who represented the stuff of dreams. It simply wasn't in him, any more than it was in Kimberly to love a cynical four-eyed highbrow.

And he couldn't bear losing someone he loved, not again. The last time he'd had no control over what had happened. But this time he did have control. He could take emotional precautions.

She stirred beside him, and her eyes fluttered open. As soon as they came into focus on Andrew, she smiled. "Good morning," she murmured drowsily.

Even her voice, clogged with sleep, was too good to be true. It was as creamy as her complexion, as voluptuously feminine as her body. He steeled himself against it, then presented her with a remote smile. "Good morning, Kim."

"What time is it?"

"Time to get up," he answered, shoving back the covers and swinging his legs over the side of the bed.

She twisted to see the alarm clock on her night table. "Nine-thirty," she announced, pushing herself to sit. "Whitney might be calling soon."

Of course. Whitney. That was why Andrew was here.

He located his shorts and trousers on the floor, where they'd fallen the night before, and donned them. Then he slid his eyeglasses on and reached for his shirt. "Don't put your shirt on," Kimberly requested as he slung his arms through the sleeves. Her smile became flirtatious. "I want to be able to look at your chest."

"I'm not going topless unless you do," he challenged her. "Tit for tat—no pun intended."

"I'll bet," she snorted before conceding with a laugh. She glided across the room to her closet and pulled a baby-blue satin bathrobe from the hook on the back of the door. More blue, Andrew noted, exerting himself not to let the resonant color of her eyes disarm him. She slipped on the robe and secured it by tying the sash. But when Andrew started to close his shirt, her expression reflected such strong disappointment that he let his hands drop from the buttons. Let her feast her damned eyes on his chest if it meant so much to her, he allowed begrudgingly. Probably—if he couldn't blame it on the bourbon—the only reason she'd made love with him last night was that she admired his build.

He followed her out of the bedroom to the kitchen, where she occupied herself preparing coffee. "What would you like for breakfast?" she asked. "We've got some leftover petits fours."

"Ugh," Andrew grunted. "Too sweet." *Just like you,* he added internally. *Sweet and delicious and gone before the taste has faded.*

"How about English muffins, then?" she offered. "I've also got some grapefruit."

"Fine." He felt uncomfortably idle, standing to one side while she bustled around the kitchen. "Anything you want me to do?" he asked.

"Just sit," she said, beckoning toward the dining table.

He obeyed. He balanced one ankle across the other knee and jiggled his bare foot nervously. Was it his imagination, or were he and Kimberly acting as stilted as they had when he'd arrived at her office two days ago? Was she already suffering from remorse, wondering how in high hell she and Andrew had let down their guard so totally last night?

She sliced a grapefruit in two and carried the halves to the table. Setting one half in front of him, she leaned over and kissed the crown of his head. The gesture seemed natural, but he suspected that it was simply her way of putting them both at ease.

She returned to the kitchen and busied herself with the toaster. Neither of them spoke until their breakfast was on the table and Kimberly took a seat facing Andrew. She helped herself to a muffin half, buttered it and set down her knife. Before biting into the muffin she gave Andrew a critical glance. "Why do I have the distinct feeling that you're closing up on me?" she asked.

He chewed on his muffin, swallowed, then washed down the crumbs with a bracing gulp of coffee. "I'm not closing up on you," he countered.

"You're entertaining doubts about last night, is that it?"

He drummed his fingers against the table as he collected his thoughts. He couldn't read her expression—it seemed a bit accusing, a bit wounded, a bit . . . mocking, perhaps. He took another sip of coffee before responding to her charge. "We both had a lot to drink last night."

"We weren't drunk," she said forcefully.

"Look. Your divorce is very recent. You're lonely. You're on the rebound—"

"The rebound?" she exclaimed, her knife clattering against her plate. "Andrew, I was separated from Todd for an entire year before our divorce became final. And even before that Todd and I were hardly having a romantic relationship."

"Then you must be very lonely," he emphasized. "You don't have to apologize for it, Kim. It's a normal reaction to look to a friend for comfort and companionship—"

"What the hell do you think I am?" she erupted. "Comfort? Companionship? Do you honestly think I'm that superficial?"

"No, of course not," he hastened to assure her. Then he fell silent. He hadn't meant to offend her. His analysis of why Kimberly had invited him to spend the night with her was the only one that made sense to him. She had said she liked him, and he liked her, too. But beyond that, what existed between them? Other than the fact that they had attended college together, that they had both endured the demise of their marriages? Other than the fact that, for one crazy afternoon, they had playacted at being spies together?

The doorbell rang. Kimberly's obvious anger at Andrew redirected itself toward her caller. "God help me if Whitney had the gall to come here instead of phoning..." she muttered as she stood and marched into the entry hall.

Andrew pushed back his chair and watched her until she was out of sight. He listened to her unbolt the door and open it. Then he heard an unfamiliar woman's voice. "Hello, Kimberly. I hope you all don't mind a little surprise visit."

"Mother." Kimberly's tone was impressively calm. Indeed, she sounded much calmer than Andrew felt, lounging at Kimberly's table with his chest exposed while the mother of the woman he'd spent the night with barged into the apartment. He sprang to his feet in time to greet the two women as they entered the living room together.

If her mother was any indication, Kimberly was destined to age beautifully. Mrs. Belmont was strikingly handsome, petite like her daughter, with fair coloring. Her blond hair was carefully coiffed, pinned into a bouffant knot at the nape of her neck. She wore an expensive-looking tailored suit of white silk, with a violet blouse beneath and a string of pearls around her swanlike neck. She held a white envelope purse in her hand. Her eyes, the same vivid blue shade as Kimberly's, settled on Andrew and narrowed.

"Mother, this is Andrew Collins," Kimberly smoothly introduced them. "Andrew, my mother."

He extended his hand. "How do you do, Mrs. Belmont?" he mumbled politely.

Without bothering to shake his hand, she pivoted on the heels of her pumps to confront Kimberly. "What, may I ask, is the meaning of this?" Her drawl was much more pronounced than her daughter's.

Kimberly laughed. "For heaven's sake, Mother—if you don't know the meaning of this, then Father has my sympathy."

Mrs. Belmont's cheeks paled slightly at her daughter's impertinent remark. Her eyes sharpened on Andrew again, and he fumbled with the buttons on his shirt. "Need I remind you that your divorce—" she seemed to have difficulty shaping her lips around the word "—became final a mere five days ago."

"Oh? Who's counting?" Kimberly responded blithely. She strode into the kitchen and pulled a mug from a cabinet. "Have some coffee, Mother. You look as if you could use a cup. I haven't got any cream, so you'll have to make do with milk." Ignoring her mother's disdainful inspection of Andrew, she asked, "What brings you to town, anyway?"

"Your father's name has been bandied about in reference to a federal judgeship," Mrs. Belmont informed her, her gaze remaining on Andrew. "We flew up so that he could introduce himself to the right people. It's quite an honor, you know." Without comment she accepted the coffee Kimberly had fixed for her and sipped it. "What did you say your name was?" she asked Andrew.

"Andrew Collins."

"I see," Mrs. Belmont said, although Andrew could hardly guess precisely what it was she saw. Other than his chest, which was no longer in view as he finished closing his shirt and tucked the tails inside the waist of his slacks.

"Andrew is an old friend of mine," Kimberly elaborated.

"I should hope so," Mrs. Belmont sniffed. "How is Todd?"

"Beats me," Kimberly said with a flippancy Andrew suspected was reserved only for her mother. "Why don't you go drop in on him unannounced, too?"

"Kimberly." Mrs. Belmont gave her daughter a grave stare. "Need I remind you of your position?"

"My position, Mother, is that of a single woman. Surely a single woman is allowed to share breakfast with a gentleman in her home."

"A gentleman," Mrs. Belmont retorted, lowering her gaze to Andrew's bare feet, "wears shoes when he comes to call."

"Perhaps I ought to leave you two to talk alone," Andrew suggested discreetly, starting toward the bedroom.

Kimberly snagged his arm and held him in place beside her. "Don't be silly, Andrew," she remonstrated. "I'm sure that anything my mother has to say at this point will concern you. You may as well hang around and listen." She turned to her mother with a winsome smile. "Why don't you be courteous, Mother? Why don't you ask Andrew about himself? Ask him the right questions and he'll go on forever, isn't that so?"

Mrs. Belmont pursed her lips in disapproval. "Do you work for that senator of Kimberly's?" she inquired.

"No. I'm a college professor," he told her.

She sniffed again, as if college professors were the dregs of society. "Here at Georgetown?"

"At Amherst College," he replied.

"Amherst College. That's one of those northern schools, isn't it?"

"Yes, Mother. Like Barnard," Kimberly interjected.

"I wish I could say I was surprised. I suppose I am." Mrs. Belmont shook her head and sighed. "This all seems so tawdry." Her acute blue eyes flitted back and forth between Kimberly and Andrew. "How long has this been going on?"

"Breakfast? About twenty minutes," Kimberly replied. "We slept late," she added with the sole purpose of riling her mother.

Mrs. Belmont did her best to remain composed. "Does Todd know about it?"

"About what? That his former wife is an independent adult with her own life to lead? If he hasn't figured that out by now, more's the pity. Where's Father?" Kimberly inquired.

"He chose to stay at the hotel. Thank heavens for that. If he saw you behaving so brazenly, Kimberly—"

"Brazenly?" Rather than exploding with rage, as Andrew would have expected, she smiled demurely. "If I know Father, the sum total of his reaction would be to warn me that the people considering him for a judgeship had better not find out that his daughter had a man at her house at nine-thirty on a Sunday morning. Father always has his own best interests at heart." She released Andrew to cross the living room and drew the drapes open. "What a lovely day it's shaping up to be."

Her mother glowered at her. "Don't be sassy, Kimberly. It's disgraceful enough that you got a divorce, but now this...."

Kimberly turned to confront her mother. She easily met Mrs. Belmont's ferocious gaze. "What was disgraceful was that I married a man I was totally unsuited for," she said, her voice underlined with an uncharacteristic grittiness. "What was disgraceful was that I did the right thing, the proper thing. I followed your advice, Mother, and it was without a doubt the biggest mistake of my life. With your permission, I'd just as soon make my own mistakes from here on in."

"Well, you're certainly doing your best in that department," Mrs. Belmont muttered.

Andrew had been silent throughout their argument, but he had absorbed Kimberly's every word, her every motion, the defiant tilt of her chin and her proud bearing. As awkward as he felt, she appeared perfectly poised, completely unruffled. He was awed by her performance.

He couldn't stand by in silence while her mother reviled her so mercilessly. Even though Kimberly apparently didn't require Andrew's assistance in this showdown, he was a gentleman—bare feet notwithstanding—and he couldn't prevent himself from speaking up on her behalf. "Mrs. Belmont, Kimberly and I are good friends of long standing. We've known each other for years, and—"

"That's all right, Andrew," Kimberly said smoothly. "You aren't obliged to trot out my respectability for my mother. She should have given up on expecting me to behave properly by now."

"But there's nothing improper about—about—"

"About our having an affair, Andrew," she supplied for him. "You're absolutely right. Whether or not Mother agrees with us is beyond our control." She walked back to her mother and kissed her cheek. "I do love you, Mother, but you are truly being a pain right now. Why don't you go back to the hotel, and we'll meet for lunch."

Mrs. Belmont appeared nonplussed for a moment, unsure of whether to accept or reject her daughter's placating kiss. "Will he be joining us?" she asked tautly, shooting Andrew a hostile look.

He answered for himself. "No. I have to catch a plane back to Hartford."

"But it was so thoughtful of you to invite him," Kimberly cooed, deliberately misunderstanding her mother. "What hotel are you and Father staying at?"

"The Four Seasons," Mrs. Belmont answered limply. She apparently realized that she had been outmaneuvered by her daughter, and she conceded with as much grace as she could muster. "Come at one."

"I'll get there when I can," Kimberly remarked, clearly refusing to accede to even that most innocuous order. She took her mother's coffee mug, set it on the table and guided the older woman toward the front door. "So long, Mother."

Mrs. Belmont hesitated on the threshold. "Please don't let M.C. find out about this, Kimberly," she whispered, eyeing Andrew one last time. "She looks up to you so."

"I won't mention it unless it comes up" was all Kimberly would promise. "So long." She nudged her mother outside, kissed her cheek again and shut the door. Then she returned to the living room.

Andrew remained mute as he tried to unscramble his thoughts. He struggled to remember what he and Kimberly had been quarreling about before Mrs. Belmont's arrival, but he came up blank. All he could think of was how marvelously Kimberly had comported herself in what had to be considered a humiliating situation.

Did cheerleaders really possess such backbone? Had cutesy Kimberly really held her own against such a powerful adversary? It was one thing to take on a stranger like Wilding, but quite another to take on one's own mother. If anything about Kimberly commanded respect, it was her abundance of feistiness and courage.

"Who's M.C.?" he asked.

"My niece. She's eleven years old now. Much to my mother's horror, she's shown an interest in learning the facts of life." Kimberly moved past him to the kitchen to rinse her mother's mug in the sink.

He drifted to the counter and studied Kimberly. She seemed as collected with him as she'd been with her mother, as detached. Evidently she remembered their earlier argument better than he did. Or else she was angry with him for having been present in her apartment at the worst possible time. "I'm sorry," he said.

"About what?" Her voice was crisp and contained.

"About your having to go through that."

"Go through what? Andrew, I've been through far worse with my mother. There's nothing to be sorry about."

"You handled yourself splendidly," he noted, eager to make amends, although he still wasn't certain of why she was angry with him. "You were fantastic."

"Was I?" she asked frostily.

"Your mother seems like a tough cookie. You didn't let her rattle you. *I* was rattled, Kim, but you weren't."

"Goodie for me," she grumbled.

"I'm not kidding, Kim," he persisted. He had to make her see how dazzling she had been. "You've bowled me over. I thought you were spectacular yesterday, but today, after this . . . I never realized you had such guts."

"Yes, well, that's your problem, Andrew," she snapped, giving the clean mug a vicious shake before setting it in the drying rack. "You never realized a lot of things about me. You think I'm just a softheaded, softhearted twit, right? A cockeyed optimist, too brainless to comprehend the seriousness of the world."

"I didn't say—"

"You don't have to say it, Andrew," she cut him off. "You've always thought that of me. You've always looked down at me and judged me. Now you're doing it again."

She had a point. But he wouldn't let her astute observation derail him. "I'm judging you positively," he asserted.

"Spare me, Andrew. You're in no position to judge me at all. You think I'm just a poor, lonely divorcée looking for comfort. You think I'm the sort to kowtow to my mother. I'm sorry to disillusion you."

"I'm delighted to be disillusioned," he asserted, wishing that she'd recognize how sincere he was.

"Oh, you are not," she refuted him testily. "You like things neat and orderly, Andrew. You like to cling to your own narrow perception of things. I didn't put on that show with my mother to improve your opinion of me. I did it because that's the way I am with her. Always. With or without witnesses."

"Is there anything wrong with my being impressed by you?" he asked, bewildered.

"There's something wrong with my feeling that I have to prove myself to you, that you're so damned surprised whenever I do something that doesn't match with your condescending attitude toward me."

Her fury dumbfounded him. He grasped at a logical explanation for it. "Maybe you're still sore about your mother—"

. "No. I'm sore about you," she corrected him in a clipped voice as she stormed past him to gather up the breakfast dishes. "Why don't you just leave?"

"Leave? Now?" A half-hour ago he was sure that the night he'd spent with Kimberly was some sort of accident, best forgotten. But now he was determined to prove to her— and himself—that it wasn't an accident, that whatever was irking her, they ought to work it out. Now it was his turn to prove himself to her. "You really want me to leave?"

"That's what I just said, isn't it?"

"What if Whitney calls?" he asked, desperate to find a way to stay with her.

"I'll give him your telephone number at the motel," she replied. "I'll tell him the truth. Far be it from me to want to make you put up any longer with my asinine games."

"Kimberly—"

He noticed tears taking shape along her eyelashes, but she didn't relent. "Go, Andrew. Please. Go be a stuffy intellectual at Amherst. Surely you don't need a dumb blonde in your life."

"You aren't a dumb blonde." He inhaled for strength and reached across the counter to grip her shoulder. He wanted to shake her until her teeth rattled if that was what it took to get her to see sense. But he didn't dare. Instead he softened his hold on her, massaging the flesh of her upper arm with his fingertips. "Listen to what I'm saying, Kim," he murmured. "I'm complimenting you."

She eyed him wearily. "You're squinting at me, Andrew."

He knew his eyes were wide open; she was speaking figuratively. And maybe she was right. Revering her for behaving in a manner he would take for granted with any other woman was condescending.

When he had awakened that morning, he had believed that the previous night had been a dream. Perhaps Kimberly believed the same thing. Perhaps, in the brutal light of day, she also viewed their night together as an aberration, a reckless episode, not a realistic beginning to anything significant. They were too different from each other, too poorly matched. They both ached for company, for intimacy, and while they had temporarily found those things in each other's arms, it wasn't fair for either of them to expect something lasting from it.

Of course he couldn't love her. He was already losing her—he had already lost her. She was once again the blond goddess, utterly beautiful, utterly baffling.

"All right," he acquiesced. "I'll leave."

Look what we've got for you:

...A FREE compact Harlequin umbrella
...plus a sampler set of 4 terrific
Harlequin American Romance
novels, specially selected by our editors.

...PLUS a surprise mystery gift
that will delight you.

All this just for trying our Reader Service!

With your trial, you'll get SNEAK PREVIEWS
to 4 new Harlequin American Romance novels a
month— before they're available in stores—with
9% off retail on any books you keep (just $2.49
each)— and FREE home delivery besides.

Plus There's More!

You'll also get our newsletter, packed with news of your favorite authors and upcoming books—FREE! And as a valued reader, we'll be sending you additional free gifts from time to time—as a token of our appreciation.

THERE IS NO CATCH. You're not required to buy a single book, ever. You may cancel Reader Service privileges anytime, if you want. The free gifts are yours anyway. It's a super sweet deal if ever there was one. Try us and see!

et 4 FREE full-length Harlequin American Romance novels.

this handy
compact
umbrella

a surprise
free gift

▼ PLUS LOTS MORE! MAIL THIS CARD TODAY ▼

Harlequin's Best-Ever "Get Acquainted" Offer

Yes, I'll try the Harlequin Reader Service under the terms outlined on the opposite page. Send me 4 free Harlequin American Romance novels, a free compact umbrella and a free mystery gift.

154 CIA NA8C

PLACE STICKER
FOR 6 FREE GIFTS
HERE

NAME _____

ADDRESS _____ APT. _____

CITY _____

STATE _____ ZIP CODE _____

Gift offer limited to new subscribers, one per household. Terms and prices subject to change.

PRINTED IN U.S.A.

Don't forget...

...Return this card today to receive your 4 free books, free compact umbrella and free mystery gift.

...You will receive books before they're available in stores and at a discount off retail prices.

...No obligation. Keep only the books you want, cancel anytime.

If offer card is missing, write to: Harlequin Reader Service, 901 Fuhrmann Blvd., P.O. Box 1394, Buffalo, NY 14240-1394.

Chapter Seven

"There's somebody downstairs to see you," Helen informed Kimberly through the intercom. "I just got a call from the guard at the Constitution Avenue entrance. He says some man down there wants to see you, but he can't get through the metal detector without setting off the alarm."

Some man wants to see you. Andrew, Kimberly instantly hoped, although she knew it couldn't be he. Wishful thinking. Just because she wanted to see him didn't mean he would ever want to see her again.

She had been too harsh with him last Sunday, dismissing him too quickly, too reflexively. Yet that had seemed the best way to protect herself at the time. She had loved a man once, and he had wounded her terribly. She wasn't going to let that happen again. Especially not with Andrew, someone who could wound her much worse. She knew intuitively that he could. Like a wild animal, when a man had been wounded himself he was more likely to wound others. And Andrew had suffered the worst of wounds.

She knew she would have to confront him sooner or later—sooner, she sternly reproached herself. Before leaving for his home state a couple of days ago, the senator had spent two hours in conference with Kimberly and Whitney so they could fill him in on everything they had learned about John Wilding and L.A.R.C. Discovering the driver of the black Cadillac had been easy enough. The diplomatic license plate had been issued to the Salvadoran Embassy. The driver, a garrulous secretary had informed Kimberly, had been a general in that country's army, a man who, according to the secretary, was at odds with the current government and aspired toward a leadership position himself. Just the sort of strongman someone like Wilding was looking for to squelch his manufactured revolution.

Officially the C.I.A. claimed to know nothing of Wilding's visit with the Salvadoran army officer. But individuals were willing to speak privately against Wilding. Nobody liked a megalomaniac, no matter how loudly he touted himself as a patriot with America's best interests at heart.

"I want to meet this nervy young Professor Collins," the senator had declared. "I want to know everything he has to tell us. If we're going to take on his case, we've got to do so armed with all the information he can give us."

"Kim will set it up," Whitney had assured the senator. "She and the nervy young professor are close."

About as close as San Salvador is to Washington, Kimberly muttered beneath her breath. Even announcing that Andrew wasn't at her apartment when Whitney had called Sunday morning hadn't dispelled his conviction that she and Andrew were "very dear friends." "I've got a racquetball game in fifteen minutes, so I'll just give you the scoop and you can pass it along to him when he gets back," Whitney had said before filling Kimberly in on his latest findings—that Wilding was a loner who operated L.A.R.C. by himself, boasting to a few associates that once El Salvador fell apart he would be its new hero, the only man with enough knowledge and foresight to put it back together again. Whitney had also learned that Andrew wasn't the sole academic L.A.R.C. had commissioned to do research for him. Andrew was the sole academic who had willingly stepped forward to expose Wilding, however.

Kimberly had derived a vague pleasure from knowing that morning that Whitney wasn't the only member of the senator's staff hot on Wilding's trail. Yet she wouldn't be able to find out about the black Cadillac until the following day, when she got to her office. So she had only thanked Whitney for the information. As soon as he had hung up, she had tried to reach Andrew at his hotel in Crystal City. But he'd already checked out, the desk clerk told her.

As gutsy as Andrew had considered her in her face-off with her mother, she hadn't yet found the courage to telephone him at Amherst. Instead she had taken the cowardly route and typed him a letter—a rather formal one—identifying the Salvadoran general for him and asking him if he would be so good as to return to Washington for a meeting with the senator. She had made no reference to the night she had spent with Andrew—or the morning after. What could she have written? "I thought I loved you, Andrew, but that's probably because I'm basically old-fashioned about sex, and I couldn't have allowed myself to sleep with you unless I was first convinced that I loved you. You are brilliant—I've always thought so—and I can't deny your contention that I'm lonely and on the rebound. It was easier for me to think that I loved you than to rationalize what happened between us the honest way."

She couldn't confess such things to him. She was having enough difficulty confessing them to herself. But for all of Andrew's annoying traits, for all his arrogance and eggheadedness, he was a remarkably perceptive man. The night they had spent together was unspeakably lovely, but how could that one night negate the fifteen years Andrew and Kimberly had known each other?

She couldn't truly be in love with him. It wasn't possible. It didn't make sense.

"Kimberly? Are you still there?" Helen's voice scratched through the intercom box.

"Oh," she said, snapping back into the present. "Sorry, Helen. Did the man downstairs give his name?"

"The guard said his name was Seth Stone. He's got a sweet young thing in tow, too. It sounds like major May-December stuff, given the way the guard was talking. Who is this guy, anyway?"

"Seth!" Kim had been so obsessed with thoughts of Andrew that she'd all but forgotten about Seth's scheduled visit to Washington with Laura's daughter. She laughed at the absurdity of Helen's remark about Seth's relationship with Rita. Like the secretary at the embassy, the senator's receptionist was a blabbermouth. "Please tell the guard I'll be right down," Kimberly requested.

She lifted her white blazer from the back of her chair and slipped it on over her flowered aqua-hued shirtwaist dress. Then she clicked off the word processor, grabbed her purse and left her office. Under other circumstances she would be delighted to see her old college friend, and she resolved to be cheerful with Seth even if he wound up making her think only of Andrew, that other friend from their college days.

Stepping from the elevator into the vaulted lobby of the modern Senate office building, she spotted a tall, lanky man in pleated gray trousers and a gaudy Hawaiian-print shirt, bickering with the uniformed guard by the door. Even if she hadn't recognized Seth, his bizarre mirror sunglasses, which he had worn when she'd seen him at Julianne's reunion over a month ago, would have given him away. Standing beside him was a slight teenage girl clad in an oversize white T-shirt, baggy knee-length shorts featuring a pattern as loud as that on Seth's shirt and leather sneakers. The girl's hair was dark and cropped short to expose her ears, which were adorned with dangling triangular earrings. She, too, sported a pair of mirror sunglasses.

Regardless of her troubling weekend with Andrew, Kimberly was thrilled to see Seth. She raced across the lobby.

"Seth!" she hollered in welcome. "What sort of trouble have you all gotten yourself into?"

He and the guard both turned to her. Seth appeared highly indignant, the guard cool and complacent. "Look at this," Seth complained, gesturing toward the table beside the metal detector. Across the top were strewn assorted metal objects: keys, coins, a nail clipper, a New York City subway token, a kazoo. "He's cleaned me out, Kim. I keep telling him, all I've got left metal-wise are my fillings and my fly. So what should I do, pull out my teeth or drop my drawers?"

The girl beside him giggled. "I think you should drop your drawers, Seth," she egged him on. "I think you've got a cute—"

"I know what you think, and keep your fresh mouth shut," he snarled at his companion, although he was laughing. "Help me out, Kim. Am I gonna wind up in jail or something?"

Kimberly's gaze traveled from Seth to the girl. "You must be Rita," she said warmly. "I'm Kimberly Belmont, your mother's friend."

"Yeah," Rita said, tucking her chin against her chest bashfully. "Hi."

Kimberly planted her hands on her hips, affecting a maternal pose. "What I'd like to know, young lady, is why you want Seth to drop his drawers. This doesn't seem at all appropriate for the daughter of the bride-to-be."

Rita shrugged and grinned mischievously. "Well, Seth, like, he isn't exactly inhibited, you know? Like the first time he stayed at our place, you know what he did?"

"She doesn't want to know," Seth muttered in warning. He turned helplessly to Kimberly. "Are you going to vouch for me, or are you going to stand there and watch me be utterly humiliated by this power-hungry Rambo clone?"

"Rambo clone?" Kimberly turned to the guard and guffawed. "William is very sweet," she objected. "And his gun is just for show. Isn't that right, William?"

The guard only smiled noncommittally.

"Sweet, huh." Seth sounded dubious. "If he's so sweet, how come he's hassling me about the fact that I don't wear pants with Talon zippers?"

"All right," she relented. "I'll vouch for you." She turned to the guard again. "Seth is a very strange man, William, but he's virtually harmless."

"Virtually?" the guard and Andrew echoed in unison.

"Seth isn't virtual," Rita piped up, comically misunderstanding the word. "He and Ma are kissie-kissie all the time, you know?"

"Speaking of kissers, you're going to get a pow in yours," Seth grumbled.

"Yeah?" Rita skipped through the metal detector and grinned defiantly. "Come and get me."

"Why don't we leave, instead?" Kimberly tactfully suggested. "I'm not planning to get any more work done this morning, anyway. If you'd like, I can show you all some of the sights."

Rita agreeably marched back through the metal detector as, mumbling beneath his breath, Seth gathered his belongings from the table and shoved them back into his pockets. "So help me, if I'm missing any money, I'm going to sue the federal government," he alerted the guard before accompanying Rita and Kimberly through the door and outside.

"What sights are we going to see?" Rita asked. "You know who I want to see? That senator, you know, the fox, from Massachusetts."

"Kennedy or Kerry?" Kimberly asked. "They're both foxes. So was Tsongas, for that matter. Massachusetts specializes in good-looking senators."

"She's neat, Seth," Rita appraised Kimberly. Addressing her directly, she added, "You were prettier on TV, though."

"Was I?" Kimberly frowned. "When did you ever see me on television?"

"*Evening Potpourri*," Seth reminded her, naming the television show all *The Dream*'s founders had appeared on at their reunion in March.

"Oh, Lord, yes," Kimberly recalled with a laugh. "How embarrassing that was. I sounded like a birdbrain."

"What's with you ladies?" Seth argued. "Laura thought she sounded bad, too. I thought you sounded great. We all sounded great. I sounded the best, of course...."

"Of course," Kimberly concurred somberly.

"And you sounded drawlingly Georgian, and Laura sounded like the bleeding heart she is, and Julianne sounded like an editor, and Troy sounded like a draft resister, and Andrew sounded like a pompous windbag."

Kimberly winced, then covered with a feeble smile. She would have to prepare herself for the likelihood that Seth would want to talk about their mutual friends from their college days. She would have to inure herself to any mention of Andrew. She didn't want to let on that merely hearing his name could put her nerves into a tailspin.

"So can we see this Kennedy dude?" Rita persevered. "I've ridden in a limousine twice, but I've never met a Kennedy."

"You've got to have something to look forward to in life," Seth dryly pointed out.

"I don't know if he's in town," Kimberly commented. "But if you'd like, I can get you passes into the Senate gallery for this afternoon—even though nothing much happens on a Friday afternoon. In the meantime, would you like to go to the Air and Space Museum? Or we could visit the I. M. Pei wing of the National Gallery. Or the First Ladies' gowns, if you'd rather. What have you seen so far?''

"The bar at L'Enfant Plaza," Seth grunted.

Kimberly eyed Rita, then clicked her tongue at Seth. "Have you been plying Rita with liquor?"

"Cokes. She downed three of them last night, chugalug, bottoms up like a regular sailor. She's got a crush on one of the mixologists.''

"He was a bartender," Rita corrected Seth. Kimberly laughed.

"What we really want to see," Seth informed her, "is the route Laura and I marched in November of '69.''

"That's what *you* want to see," Rita interjected, but she obediently followed Seth as he headed west toward the grass-covered Mall across the street from the Capitol.

"Where were you during the big march?" Seth asked Kimberly.

"Who remembers?" She frowned as she thought back to that period of her youth. "We were sophomores then, right? I was probably in the library, reading up on de Tocqueville."

"Who's that?" Rita asked. "Is he a fox, too?"

"Rita is demented," Seth confided to Kimberly, deliberately loud enough for Rita to hear him. "All she talks about is foxy guys."

"It happens to be a subject of great interest to many of us," Kimberly said, grinning at Rita. Then she slung her arm around Seth's waist and gave him a hug. "I was so pleased to hear about you and Laura, Seth. I think it's wonderful."

"I thought it was wonderful until I realized that Rita was part of the package," Seth groused, though he was clearly kidding. "Adolescent girls are absolute horror shows."

"Grown-up men are weird," Rita countered.

"And Seth is the weirdest of all," Kimberly confirmed. She shifted her hand to the crook of his elbow and peered up at him. "Your hair is getting long," she noted.

"Yeah. Laura likes it this way," he said, raking his hand through the shaggy dark blond locks. "She's reforming me, Kim. Turning me into a hippie again."

"You were supposed to reform her," Rita criticized him, glancing at Kimberly and then imitating her, slipping her hand through the bend of his other elbow. "You're falling down on the job, Seth."

"Go ahead, say it," he goaded her. "I'm a regular flame."

"What's a flame?" Kimberly asked.

"It's something like a slime, only less virtual," Seth replied. "Now that, if I'm not mistaken, is the National Archives," he said, pointing to a pillared building across the street. "As I recall, there was a street theater troupe with camouflage paint on their faces gathered there, doing t'ai chi. Do you know what t'ai chi is, Rita?"

"Uh-uh."

"It's an Eastern form of body movement," he told her. "Very spiritual. And here—" he indicated the stretch of roadway ahead of them "—is where we all stepped aside so a group from the Vietnam Veterans Against the War could parade through. One of them was blind, seated in a wheelchair with black flags attached to it."

"That sounds depressing," Kimberly reflected.

"It wasn't. It was incredibly moving."

"I think it sounds depressing, too," Rita sided with Kimberly. "How about let's go look at those dresses?"

"Listen up, Rita," Seth lectured her. "What we're doing here is more important than dresses. The Moratorium March is living, breathing history."

"Yeah," she scoffed sarcastically.

Seth ignored her. "Somewhere along here is the Department of Justice, isn't it?" he asked Kimberly. "We called it the Department of Injustice. There was a secondary demonstration there after the big one. That one was advertised as including gas."

"Gas?" Rita asked, her interest perking up. "Like, for cars?"

"Like tear gas," Andrew instructed her. "All along the route everyone kept saying, 'Hey, you gonna go to the demonstration at the Department of Injustice afterward? They're gonna be using gas at that one.'"

"Seth, that's sick," Kimberly protested. "Why would anyone knowingly go to a demonstration where tear gas was going to be used?"

Seth shrugged. "To be able to tell their grandchildren about it someday. 'I got gassed at the November Moratorium.' What do you think, Rita? Are you going to make your mother a grandma one of these days?"

"What for?" she responded. "I bet Ma didn't go to that demonstration, not if it had tear gas. She would never do anything that wasn't healthy."

"You're right," Seth agreed. "Neither of us went. We had to catch our bus back to Columbia. Now here—" he paused and gazed around him with a nostalgic smile "—this was the best part of the whole day. Out of the blue, all of a sudden, a whole bunch of us—total strangers—joined hands and started singing. 'Give Peace A Chance' and 'All You Need Is Love.' The classics. That was when I learned that Laura couldn't carry a tune."

"Yeah?" Rita surveyed their surroundings. "You were with my ma the whole time?"

"The whole time," Seth confirmed. "Maybe fate was trying to tell us that we were meant for each other."

"You sure took your time figuring it out," Rita carped. "If it wasn't for me, Ma still wouldn't have figured it out."

Seth turned sharply toward her. "What's that supposed to mean?"

"It means, if I hadn't pointed out to her that you were a pretty awesome dude, she probably wouldn't have noticed."

"You think I'm a pretty awesome dude, Rita?" Seth asked, obviously flattered.

"You're foxier than Kennedy," she praised him. "And that's saying a lot. How about these dresses, Kimberly? Are they radical or what?"

Kimberly floundered for a moment, puzzled by Rita's question. "They're fairly conservative, actually," she told the girl.

" 'Radical' means cool," Seth translated. "Rita's taught me a whole lot about the English language. I tell you what, Rita—why don't you go look at the dresses, and Kim and I can hang out and talk like grown-ups?"

"You want to lose me? Sure, Seth," Rita complied. "I know how to make myself scarce."

"Not that I've noticed," he muttered as they approached the branch of the Smithsonian that contained the display of the First Ladies' gowns.

A long line of visitors snaked beyond the display and into the museum's entry. Rita darted to the line, and Seth and Kimberly shared a bench in the echoing foyer in full view of the original star-spangled banner. Seth pulled off his sunglasses, waved reassuringly at Rita and then turned his attention fully to Kimberly. "How are you doing, Kim?" he asked, taking her hand and giving it an affectionate squeeze. "Laura told me about your divorce. That's a tough one, pal. I'm really sorry."

"Thanks, but I'm fine," Kimberly said.

"So what comes next? Are you going to play the field for a while? Live the swinging singles life?"

Kimberly grinned. Seth had always shot straight from the hip. She should have expected such a grilling from him. "I don't know," she answered. "I may just join a nunnery. Swinging singly is surely much more your style than mine."

"Not anymore," Seth said, pretending to look dejected. "It's Monogamy City for me now. Time to climb off the old single swing. I bet my hair turns gray within six months of tying the knot."

Did marriage make men's hair turn gray? Kimberly wondered, picturing the silver strands that wove through Andrew's dark hair. He had been married, and now he was going gray.

Damn, but she couldn't let herself keep dwelling on thoughts of him. "I was married for fifteen years and it didn't change the color of my hair," she told Seth. "I suspect that if anything makes a person go gray, it's the ending of a marriage, not the starting of one."

"Well, look at the bright side," Seth consoled her. "At least you don't have to deal with in-laws anymore."

Kimberly had never had much trouble getting along with Todd's parents—certainly no more trouble than she had getting along with her own. Both her parents and Todd's were cut from the same pattern, after all. Wealthy, Southern, traditional. "Are you having a hard time dealing with Laura's mother?" she asked Seth.

He rolled his hazel eyes in dismay. "'A hard time' is putting it mildly."

"Laura said her mother adored you."

"She does. That's the problem. Before I even had a chance to say hello to the woman, she had me in a strangulating bear hug. She thinks I've rescued her old-maid daughter from a fate worse than death." He shook his head. "Rita adores me, too. It's freaky, being surrounded by so many adoring women."

"Oh? I should think you'd be used to that, after your swinging single days," Kimberly teased him.

"Correction—so many adoring women from the same family. We're talking three generations of Brodies."

"You love it," Kimberly guessed.

Andrew conceded with an enthusiastic nod. "I love it. Laura's done wonders for me, Kim. And I've done wonders for her, too."

"Oh? What wonders have you done for her, Seth?"

He smiled reflectively. "You know Laura—she's too generous for her own good. She's so busy taking care of humanity that she forgets to take care of herself. I've finally convinced her that it's okay to stop worrying about everyone else for a little while and to let someone else take care of her. Namely me."

"I'm almost afraid to ask how you're going to take care of her," Kimberly joked.

Seth accepted her teasing good-naturedly. "I'm making her quit her job. The lady's burned out and she needs a break. She needs to be pampered, to have some fun. Admit it, Kim, aren't I fun?"

"No argument there," Kimberly agreed.

"I don't know if Laura told you," he went on, "but we're planning a big bash to celebrate the wedding in May. We're going to invite the whole *Dream* gang. These reunions are far-out, Kim. If it weren't for the last reunion, Laura and I would have never gotten together. Who knows what great love affair will arise out of the next one?"

Not the Kimberly-Andrew love affair, she answered internally. As much as she'd been looking forward to attending Laura and Seth's wedding at Laura's mother's house, the notion now filled her with apprehension. If she went to their big bash, she would have to see Andrew.

She wanted to see him, but she was afraid to. If she saw him, he might be his usual cutting, condescending self, and she couldn't bear that thought. But if he wasn't, if he was instead gentle and vulnerable, as he had been on Saturday night, then she might once again believe that she loved him. And she couldn't bear that thought, either.

She was going to have to see him, whether or not she wanted to. He would have to come back to Washington to meet with the senator. Even if she managed to escape from the city limits on a last-minute vacation when Andrew came back to town, she couldn't avoid him forever. She knew he would want to attend Seth and Laura's wedding, just as she would want to.

She would be forced to see him, and he would be arrogant toward her. And she would loathe him.

"Seth," she murmured solemnly. "What do you think of me?"

Her question clearly surprised him. He smiled. "I think you're gorgeous. If I weren't so madly in love with Laura, I'd ask you to marry me."

"You're really psyched on getting married, aren't you?" she asked.

"What can I say?" He shrugged and offered an easy smile. "I'm just an old softie, a romantic fool. Everybody ought to be a romantic fool at least once in his life."

"No more than once," Kimberly mused. She'd been a romantic fool with Todd, and that had been quite enough. She simply wouldn't allow herself to be a romantic fool with Andrew, as well.

Rita emerged from the gown display looking dissatisfied. "Yuck," she announced. "Ugly, ugly, ugly. How come none of them wore minis?"

"They wore those dresses to inaugural balls, Rita," Kimberly explained, happy for the distraction Rita provided. "Formal dances."

"Yeah, but they're so ugly. If I were a First Lady, I'd want to wear something awesome."

"That's what we need," Seth decided, greeting Rita's comment with enthusiasm. "Someone awesome for president. A burned-out hippie. A Grateful Dead-head. Someone who, if the Soviets got restive, would say, 'Let's do a number and meditate.' And if the economy was in the pits, he'd say, 'Score me some blotter and we'll get some visions on it.'"

"Are you announcing your candidacy?" Kimberly teased him. "If you are, I'll be your speech writer."

"And then what would poor Senator Howie do?" Seth posed.

"Run the country while you were in never-never land," Kimberly answered.

"Yeah, well, I'm starving," Rita declared, twirling her sunglasses between her thumb and forefinger and eyeing the door. "Is there a McDonald's around here or something?"

"She's a real gourmet," Seth joked, rising from the bench. "Her favorite food is anything loaded with cholesterol."

"Zit fuel," Rita elaborated.

"You all are my guests for lunch," said Kimberly, trying not to grimace at Rita's terminology. "So you may as well take advantage of me and pick someplace expensive."

"She's neat, Seth," Rita decided before prancing out of the museum.

"PROFESSOR COLLINS?"

Andrew glanced up from his desk to see Chip Wilton peering around the edge of his office door. Tall, with fresh-scrubbed good looks, Chip was clad in a red Izod shirt, beige corduroys and deck shoes without socks. He appeared to be the embodiment of Kimberly's description of an Amherst College man—except for the fact that he wasn't wearing a rugby shirt. The balmy spring weather called for short sleeves.

"Come on in, Chip," Andrew said, beckoning him inside the small, tidy room. Office space was at a premium at the college, and Andrew had to make do with a room barely larger than a walk-in closet. Countless books crowded the metal shelves lining one wall, and Andrew's desk, typing table and swivel chair took up most of the floor space. He'd managed to cheer up the office with a few posters on the walls: one of Martin Luther King; one of F.D.R.; one, a relic of his college days, depicting an impressionistic tree silhouetted against a yellow background, its limbs covered with the words "War is unhealthy for children and other living things." The poster was admittedly corny, perhaps as corny as "Smile—it increases your face power." But Andrew had saved it all these years. It made him think of Troy Bennett, one of his closest friends in college, who had fled the country to avoid having to serve in what had arguably been the nation's most unhealthy war.

Andrew folded the letter he had been reading and out of some obsessive neatness inserted it back into the envelope. Then he smiled at Chip and nodded toward the folding metal chair across the desk from him. A junior economics major, Chip was one of Andrew's most promising students. Andrew would always be willing to make time for kids like Chip.

"I know this isn't your scheduled office hour," Chip apologized for his intrusion. "But I saw your door open, and—"

"No problem," Andrew assured Chip. He was relieved that Chip had interrupted him. Andrew honestly didn't want to be reading that particular letter right now. Leaning back in his chair, he gritted his teeth at the squeak the chair's hinge invariably produced and adjusted his eyeglasses. "What's on your mind?"

Chip's expression was earnest and mildly uneasy. He sat, balanced his spiral notebook on his knees and took a deep breath. "Well...I don't know if you remember, but we've talked once or twice about the possibility of my going to grad school for a doctorate after I finish up here...." He trailed off uncertainly.

"I do remember."

"Yes, well..." The boy smiled sheepishly. "I think I may be having a change of heart."

"That's allowed," Andrew remarked. "You don't have to go to grad school immediately after college. Sometimes it's a wise idea to take a year off and unwind."

"That wasn't what I was thinking," Chip continued. "The truth is, I think I want to go to business school, instead."

"Business school," Andrew said, exerting himself to sound noncommittal.

"I've been giving this a great deal of thought, Professor Collins," he continued. "I've talked at length with my friends about it—not just my friends here at Amherst, but a lot of my friends from home when I was there over spring break. Business school seems so much more sensible in this day and age—"

"This day and age," Andrew echoed scornfully. Why was it that the best and the brightest in "this day and age" all wanted to go to business school?

He knew too well the answer to that: they wanted the bucks. They wanted to go into investment banking and pocket millions. They wanted to wear Brooks Brothers suits, own VCRs and work in offices more elegant than Andrew's. Then, when they were thirty, they wanted to marry corporate lawyers, start families, name their children Melissa and Zachary. They wanted to become "involved" fathers—or mothers—and spend "quality time" with their children without missing a day's work or a day's pay. They wanted to commute to their Wall Street offices from Darien and Greenwich and spend their weekends at "the cottage'' in East Hampton or on Martha's Vineyard, sailing "the boat,'' drinking Beefeater's martinis and vintage wines. They wanted to live the life Andrew and his compatriots used to thumb their noses at.

"Tell me, Chip,'' he proposed. "Do you think it's *sensible*, or do you think it's *practical*?''

"Both, I suppose,'' Chip acknowledged. "I love school and I love research, but where does it all lead?''

To this, Andrew almost replied. To a fulfilling, intellectually stimulating position at a low wage where one could help mold young minds, where one could think great thoughts. And, if one was lucky, where one could get tenure. "As you said, you love research,'' Andrew observed. "Business school offers few opportunities for research.''

"Yes, but it offers a degree that's worth something on the market,'' Chip countered.

"Are you sure you aren't just succumbing to peer pressure?'' Andrew asked, aware of the irony in his question. In his era, when the older generation worried about their offspring succumbing to peer pressure, they had in mind such evils as drug abuse and dropping out. Nowadays, when a youngster succumbed to peer pressure, chances were he'd wind up with a blond secretary and an office overlooking the Hudson River.

An image of Kimberly flitted across Andrew's mind. Not that she was a secretary, but she was blond, blond and beautiful, the sort of prize men who graduated from business schools tended to expect. Women like Kimberly weren't supposed to be included in the life of an assistant professor.

Don't even think about her, he chided himself, knowing that it was impossible not to think about her when her letter was lying right before him on his desk. Ever since pulling the envelope from his campus mailbox after his last class twenty minutes ago, he had been holed up in his office, reading it, reading it again, reliving every minute he'd spent with her.

"If you came here to receive my blessings," he said, abruptly remembering Chip in his office, "then you probably already know that you're going to be disappointed. I think you're an ideal candidate for an academic career—and I think you'd find it incredibly rewarding. But if you're looking to be *practical*, then go to business school."

"I plan to visit Harvard and Wharton this summer," Chip went on, brushing off Andrew's obvious condemnation of his choice. "Possibly Stanford, too. And I've heard a few good things about Northwestern's program. I was wondering if you had any other recommendations."

"Besides scrapping the idea? No," Andrew told him. "I know plenty about graduate programs, but not business schools. I've heard that as a rule, Harvard and Stanford B-School graduates are offered phenomenal starting salaries. If that's what you're interested in," he added pointedly.

Chip appeared slightly deflated. "You don't know anybody teaching at any of those schools, then? Anybody you could suggest that I should contact?"

"No," Andrew muttered wryly. "I don't travel in those circles."

"Well, I'll give it some more thought," Chip promised before standing. "I appreciate your opinions, Professor Collins—"

"No, you don't," Andrew mocked him with gentle resignation. "You wish I had said, 'Hey, that's swell, Chip. Business school! Go for it!'"

Chip smiled. "Yeah, I guess I was hoping you would."

"That's the way it goes, kid." He watched as Chip headed for the door, then called after him, "By the way, I haven't finished grading all the papers, but your paper on Cuba's economic dependency on the Soviet Union was outstanding."

"Thank you, Professor Collins," Chip said, his smile brightening as he sauntered out of the office.

"The kids today," Andrew mumbled under his breath. Not only did they all want to go to business school, but they all insisted on calling him "Professor Collins." When he had attended college, the students were far less respectful. They had called their favorite professors by their first names and their least favorites by their last names, without any title attached. The only exception Andrew could think of was that pompous poli-sci professor who had spent at least half the semester boasting about how he'd flunked all his students who had participated in the Columbia riots in 1968. As Andrew recalled, he and Troy had dubbed that teacher "Dr. Barfbag."

Left in solitude, Andrew couldn't keep himself from pulling out Kimberly's letter and reading it yet another time. "Dear Andrew, Would you please be so good as to return to Washington for a meeting with Senator Milford..."

The stuff she'd found out about the general intrigued him. The general's name was familiar to him. Several of the farmers he'd interviewed in El Salvador had mentioned him as the leader of one of the roving bands of army men who regularly terrorized the peasants. That Andrew and Kimberly had actually witnessed a meeting between the general and Wilding was exciting.

It was exciting to have made such a connection between the two. Even more exciting had been Andrew and Kimberly's trip to Fairfax, their snooping, their moments of fear, their exhilaration. Their touching. Andrew's hands around her waist, his arm across her chest, the pounding of her heart against his limb....

He cursed as a blaze of emotion seared through him. He wasn't used to feeling so strongly about anything anymore—or, more accurately, about *anybody*. His job, yes, he felt strongly about that. His job, his health and his politics. But not a person. Not a woman.

The emotion was hard to define, but he had pretty well narrowed it down to rage. Rage at Kimberly for shutting him out. Damn it, so he'd fumbled. So he'd expressed himself poorly. So, in the course of revising his view of her, he had let her see that his view had been in need of revision. Was that reason enough for her to show him the door?

Rage, yes. But even more than rage, guilt. Guilt at having fallen for her beauty, at having been sucked in by her undeniable charm. Guilt at having experienced with her a pleasure he'd never known with a woman before, not even with Marjorie.

He had spent the past five days trying to ignore the truth. But he was a scholar, inherently unable to turn his back on the facts. In this case, the fact was that not once in what he had considered a nearly perfect marriage had he ever felt anything quite as strong as what he'd felt in Kimberly's arms. They were such graceful arms, he reflected, her skin so soft, her hands so delicate, and her fingernails... Marjorie used to bite her fingernails down to the cuticle. But not Kimberly. Her fingernails were oval, smoothly filed. He still hadn't forgotten the sensation of them scraping tenderly across his skin.

Nor had he forgotten the smell of her, the delectable curves of her body, the golden silk of her hair dipping against his jaw. Or her almost superfluously feminine underwear. Underwear! Andrew had never been a fetishist, but Kimberly, in that dainty bra and panties...

Rage again. Rage that he could have been so receptive to her, only to have her turn her back on him. And guilt that he could have been so receptive to someone like her in the first place.

"Would you please be so good as to return to Washington for a meeting with Senator Milford," he read. Not for a meeting with her, not for the time they needed to work things out. Evidently she felt that nothing needed working out. The working out had already been accomplished as far as she was concerned. She had worked him out of her life.

"Hey, Andy—how about lunch?" Bob McIntyre called through the open door.

Andrew again folded the letter and stuffed it into the envelope. Then he lifted his gaze to the man filling the doorway. Bob was smaller than average in build—no more than five-seven, with a slim frame. Yet owing to his status in the department, he seemed to cut a powerful, looming figure.

"Hello, Bob," Andrew said smoothly, hoping that he had concealed the edginess he currently felt in his mentor's presence.

"Lunch?" Bob repeated.

He ought to accept Bob's invitation. He ought to be congenial and collegial, as one was supposed to be in order to win tenure. Yet he couldn't picture himself chatting amicably over a sandwich with the man who had hooked him up with the C.I.A., the man responsible for getting Andrew entangled with John Wilding and L.A.R.C.—and, indirectly, with Kimberly.

"Thanks, but I can't," he declined. "I've got some errands to run."

"You're a busy man," Bob joked. "I hear you were down in D.C. last weekend. More research for that El Salvador study?"

How did you guess? Andrew grunted silently. "Visiting a college friend," he said aloud. He wasn't ready to discuss the L.A.R.C. situation with Bob yet. He wasn't even certain precisely what the situation was. And he wouldn't learn what it was unless he would be so good as to return to Washington for a meeting with Senator Milford.

"Well, I won't keep you. Maybe we can have lunch next week." Bob smiled and vanished from the doorway.

Restless, Andrew gathered up Kimberly's letter and the student papers he still had to grade, slipped them inside his briefcase and left his office. He strolled across the campus, trying to let the warm April sun relax him, trying to appreciate the fragrance of sprouting grass and budding leaves and the uninterrupted blue of the Berkshire sky above him. He waved at students who shouted greetings his way and sidestepped a game of catch between two baseball-mitted students on the lawn.

Given the mild weather, Andrew had walked to the college that morning instead of driving his car. His apartment was slightly more than a mile away. Ordinarily he enjoyed his stroll home through the heart of Amherst's business district, which was adjacent to the campus. The town had evolved a great deal in the five years Andrew had lived there; new shops, restaurants, theaters and clubs were thriving, endowing the neighborhood with the same sort of liveliness Andrew had felt in Georgetown.

He didn't enjoy the stroll today, not only because it reminded him of Georgetown, but because, even if it hadn't reminded him of Georgetown, he was too immersed in thoughts of Kimberly to enjoy much of anything. He would have to go back to Washington—no question about that—but what would happen when he got there? Would the blond goddess snub him again? Would she perform her magic on him, make him feel irresistibly comfortable with her and able to confide in her and then accuse him of some hideous crime and boot him out?

Or would she once again be the woman he had known in college, pretty and bubbly, the ebullient cheerleader who thought Andrew was squinting at her?

He hadn't come to any resolutions by the time he had reached his place. He unlocked his apartment door, stared into the starkly neat living room, then tossed his briefcase inside and left the house again. His ten-year-old red Volvo was parked in the paved lot behind the house. He climbed in, started the engine and coasted down the driveway.

He wasn't sure where to go. He had never been one for cruising—driving aimlessly seemed wasteful to him, especially since he'd lived through two oil crises in the past decade and a half. He shifted into idle at the corner of his block and struggled to decide on a destination.

Donna's apartment. He hadn't seen Donna since his return from Washington, although he'd spoken with her once. She had been curious to hear what he'd learned about L.A.R.C., but Andrew hadn't wanted to see her until he came to terms with his feelings for Kimberly.

He still hadn't come to terms with them, but he couldn't put off seeing Donna indefinitely. He headed north toward the University of Massachusetts campus and reached Donna's apartment building before he had any concept of what he was doing there, what he would say to her or, for that matter, whether she was even at home.

She was, and through the intercom she sounded delighted by Andrew's unscheduled visit. "I'll buzz you in," she said. "Come on up."

He entered and climbed the stairs. The building was about twelve years old, brightly lit, with apartments much larger than Andrew's, at lower rents. However, he liked his own place better. It had more character. Also, ever since Marjorie had died, Andrew had preferred to live in a small place. At first he had felt as though large apartments emphasized his aloneness, making him too acutely conscious of Marjorie's absence. Now it was merely a habit. He was used to compact living.

Donna had her front door open for him when he arrived at her floor. He stepped inside, closed the door and searched the vacant living room. "Hello? Donna?"

"In here," she shouted from the bedroom.

He walked through the living room to the bedroom. Donna was seated crosslegged on the floor, dressed in a pair of old dungarees and a baggy sweatshirt, surrounded by cardboard cartons from the neighborhood supermarket. One of her bookcases was almost empty, its contents packed into two of the cartons. "What's going on?" he asked.

She smiled and shoved her hair back from her angular face. Then she got to her feet and surveyed the mess around her. "I decided to get a head start on packing. By the way, can I ask a big favor of you? What I was thinking was, I could pack up my books for the post office and leave them in your apartment. Then I could call you as soon as I find a place in Fullerton and you could address them and mail them to me. Would you mind doing that?"

"Not at all," he told her. As she picked her way across the room to him, he assessed her lanky body, her haphazard grooming, her puppy-dog appeal. He felt nothing resembling Kimberly's effect on him last weekend. No surge of longing, no aching desire either to make love to her or to bare his soul to her. No misery at the thought that he would be losing her to a teaching job in Fullerton. He felt friendly toward Donna, that was all. Friendly and safe. "I take it you've decided to accept the job at Cal-State," he remarked.

"Yeah. I got another rejection letter this week, from the University of Southern Mississippi. It seems that nobody but Cal-State Fullerton wants me A.B.D.," she explained, referring to her "all-but-dissertation" academic status. "Thanks, Andy. I know it's going to be a pain getting all these heavy cartons to the post office, but—"

"Don't pack them so full, and then they won't be so heavy," Andrew suggested.

Donna grinned at his pragmatic suggestion and kissed his cheek. "You're a sweetheart," she said before piling the empty cartons along one wall, out of the way. "So tell me, how did your visit to Washington go?"

"I'm not sure," he said. "I have to go back. Senator Milford wants to meet me." *There,* he added silently. *I've admitted it. I've said it out loud. I have to go back.*

"That must make you feel pretty important—a command performance for a U.S. senator." She resumed the chore of packing her books into cartons. "Your namesake Andy Warhol said everyone's supposed to be famous for fifteen minutes. Maybe meeting with a senator is going to be your big moment in the sun." She dusted her hands off on her thighs and lifted her gaze to him. Her smile was quizzical. "Why the long face? Don't you want your allotted fifteen minutes?"

Andrew shrugged. "If I'm going to fly all the way down to D.C., I'd better get more than fifteen minutes with the man." He managed a chuckle. "Actually, fame is the last thing I want out of this. I'd rather just keep the meeting as quiet as possible." He found a clear space on her desk and rested his hips against it, thinking that the room's clutter would be easier to take sitting down. "If I've got a long face, it's probably because one of my smartest students just told me he wants to go to business school."

"He sounds smart, all right," Donna commented. "Business school is the safest route to go these days."

Andrew contemplated her observation. He had always thought that winning tenure was the safest route. Tenure was safe—but winning tenure entailed minding one's own business and not ruffling the feathers of one's colleagues by meeting with senators in Washington.

It was too late for Andrew to opt for safety. He had already set things in motion. By returning to the capital to see Senator Milford, he was probably risking his career, his future, everything that still mattered to him.

Including Kimberly. She still mattered to him, even if only as a source of rage and guilt. By returning to the capital, he was probably risking his friendship with her—if it was a friendship. Whatever the hell it was, he was risking it.

On the other hand, if he didn't return to Washington, whatever he had with her was already doomed.

He had to go.

Chapter Eight

"So the phone rang—this was about nine-thirty, Saturday night—and it was Seth. He said, 'They're about to lock me up, Kim, but I demanded my one telephone call first. Do you know any good lawyers?'"

"Oh, no!" Julianne dissolved in laughter. She was laughing so hard she had to hold her cordial glass with both hands in order not to spill any of her crème de menthe. She fell back against the sofa cushions as her shoulders shook. "First the metal detector and now this! What was he arrested for?"

"He said they were charging him with drunk driving."

Julianne's laughter waned, and her clear blue eyes widened with dismay. "Drunk driving? With Rita in the car? Kim, that's serious."

"He was innocent," Kimberly defended Seth. She tucked her feet beneath her and nestled deeper into the plush upholstery of the sofa, twisting to face Julianne. They had already eaten dinner and were now relaxing in the comfortable living room of Julianne's Manhattan apartment, sipping after-dinner cordials and listening to a tape of Joni Mitchell songs. Although in her youth Kimberly had derived malicious pleasure from shocking her parents by serenading them with Rolling Stones rock and roll, she honestly preferred the gentler acoustic music of her era—Joni Mitchell, James Taylor, Simon and Garfunkel. Her parents probably would have approved of such musicians, so Kimberly had kept her taste a secret from them.

Julianne had an excellent collection of late-sixties folk music. She and Kimberly had dined to the accompaniment of Crosby, Stills and Nash. Once that tape had expended itself, Julianne had put on one of her Joni Mitchell tapes, and the singer's sweet, distilled soprano floated in the air around Julianne and Kimberly as they caught up on each other's lives. The senator, Whitney Brannigan and Lee Pappelli, the senator's chief aide, weren't due to arrive in New York City until the following morning for a meeting with the mayor and a scheduled speech before a convention of electronics manufacturers, but Kimberly had traveled up ahead of time in order to visit Julianne.

"Anyway," she related, "according to Seth, he had rented a car to take Rita to see Mount Vernon. On their way back to the city, they stopped for dinner at a place in Arlington that makes the best Peking Duck outside China. Then they drove back into Washington. He was cruising on a street in Southwest that has two lanes of traffic in each direction, with a dotted white line separating the lanes. A few cars were parked along the curb and they jutted out into the right lane. But he had to make a right turn to get back to L'Enfant Plaza. So he was weaving in and out of the right lane, sometimes straddling the dotted line, because of the parked cars. A policeman thought he was driving erratically and pulled him over."

"Didn't he explain what he was doing?" Julianne asked.

"You know Seth. His explanations usually require explanations." Kimberly took a sip of the sweet, minty liqueur in her glass and set it on the coffee table. She raked her hair back from her face with her fingers and chuckled.

"He told me the policeman asked him to touch his nose with his eyes closed, and he did that just fine. Then the policeman asked him to walk a straight line, heel to toe, and he passed that test, too. But *then* the policeman asked him to do a pirouette on his left foot and walk *backward*, heel to toe. At that point Seth said something like, 'Who the heck do you think I am, Mikhail Baryshnikov?' Only I don't think he used the word 'heck.'"

"I'm sure he didn't," Julianne concurred with a smile.

"So the policeman asked Seth if he'd been drinking, and Seth, true to form, said, 'All I've had is some Coke.' Not surprisingly, the policeman misunderstood him and decided to frisk him."

"Good Lord!" Julianne was overcome with fresh laughter. "Couldn't he have just taken a Breathalyzer test and gotten it over with?"

"He refused to. He said he wouldn't take one without a lawyer present. Naturally the cop ran him in."

"What did you do? Did you find a lawyer for him?"

"At nine-thirty on a Saturday night?" Kimberly snorted. "Washington may be overrun with lawyers, Julianne, but most of them have better things to do on Saturday night than bail out an obstreperous former hippie. I went down to the station house myself." She reached for her glass and took another sip. "What a scene! They had Seth locked into a holding cell with three dissolute street drunks who smelled like sewers, and Seth was attempting to teach them the words to 'Alice's Restaurant' while he accompanied them on his kazoo. It was an absolute scream."

"I wish I could have seen it," Julianne said wistfully. "I wish Laura could have seen it. Maybe she'd rethink her decision to marry him."

"I bet it would only have made her love him more," Kimberly argued, eliciting a nod of agreement from Julianne. "I found Rita perched on the desk of the night sergeant, wearing her mirror sunglasses and describing how cute Seth's backside is."

"What?"

"You didn't hear about that?" Kimberly grinned. "It seems that the first time Seth stayed the night at Laura's apartment, before they were a couple, he slept on the living room couch. In the buff. His blanket fell off, and guess who found him sprawled out in all his glory the following morning?"

"You're kidding!" Julianne's guffaw temporarily drowned out the stereo. "That probably made Laura love him more, too. They're so much in love, Kimberly—it's incredible. You should see them together. They're so affectionate, so adoring, it's just marvelous. I wish they could have come to dinner tonight, too, but Laura was busy with a group therapy session she runs for pregnant high school students and Seth had a meeting with a couple of investors to pitch his new movie." She stretched her long legs, propping her feet up on the coffee table, and sighed. "Well? How did you spring Seth from the slammer?"

Kimberly shrugged. "He sprang himself. It was all an interesting adventure to him—something he can make use of the next time he writes a socially relevant screenplay. But by the time I showed up, the whole thing had pretty much played itself out. He blew into the balloon, passed with flying colors and thanked the police officers for an edifying experience."

"It sounds like his little sojourn to the capital was eventful, to say the least," Julianne concluded.

"I believe he had the time of his life. It doesn't take much to make good old Stoned happy—an hour in jail, a chance to holler 'Up against the wall!' and a stroll down memory lane." She glanced at the tall, conservatively attired woman sharing the sofa with her. "You didn't march in the November Moratorium, did you?"

Julianne shook her head. "I spent the day on a street corner on Upper Broadway, collecting signatures for an antiwar petition. How about you?"

Kimberly scowled. "I worked on a research paper about de Tocqueville. Aren't I a drip? Seth thinks I won't have anything to tell my grandchildren."

She sighed, suddenly pensive. She used to dream of telling her grandchildren juicy stories about her youth. But how would she ever have grandchildren if she didn't have a child?

She had become obsessed lately with thoughts of motherhood. Her longing to bear a child was nothing new; the problems with her marriage might not have come to a head if it hadn't been for her implacable desire for children. But ever since spending the previous weekend with Rita and Seth, viewing the relationship blossoming between the soon-to-be stepdaughter and stepfather and sensing the genuine affection that existed just beneath its playfully antagonistic veneer, Kimberly hadn't been able to get the notion of having a child out of her mind.

No, her obsession predated Rita's visit to Washington. It had arisen from her conversations with Andrew. When she wasn't busy fuming about his supercilious attitude—and even when she *was* fuming, sometimes—she meditated on the story he had told her about his wife's passing. It was tragic enough to lose one's wife at such a young age, but even more tragic was losing one's wife at a moment when all one's hopes and plans centered around conceiving a child. As irrational as it seemed, Kimberly imagined that hearing his wife's dire diagnosis wouldn't have been quite as painful for Andrew if it hadn't come as a result of the woman's miscarriage. In a sense he had suffered two losses at once.

She knew he had endured something terrible. She knew that he had been through hell...and she knew that, for a few brief hours, she had touched him, carried him away from his grief, enabled him to experience the rewards of opening himself up to joy again. Why couldn't he have admitted it? Why couldn't he have accepted that Kimberly was someone who could make him happy?

He couldn't admit it and he couldn't accept it because he still didn't think very highly of her. In his eyes she was still a brainless cheerleader. Nothing more.

She was tired of dwelling on thoughts of Andrew and the weekend they'd spent together. With a determined shrug she focused on Julianne. "How's work? How are things at *Dream*?"

"Hectic," Julianne reported, although her placid smile belied her claim. That was the way Julianne was—even-keeled, mellow, unflappable. Undoubtedly her life was as full of ups and downs as Kimberly's, but one would never guess by looking at her. "We've decided to devote a full edition of the magazine to the topic of changes in the American family. I told you about the article we have on Laura's work with unwed mothers, didn't I?"

Kimberly nodded.

"The article is terrific," Julianne continued. "Instead of running it right away, I thought it would be interesting to publish it with a few complementary pieces that are still in the works. One is an analysis of demographic trends, another one deals with current welfare policy, and then the story on Laura offers the human side of the issue. All we need now is some solid art. The reporter I assigned to Laura's story took scads of photos, but they aren't good enough. Susan's an excellent writer, but she's pretty much a hack when it comes to photography."

"Why didn't you assign someone else to do the photos?" Kimberly asked.

"Laura's suggestion. She was concerned about imposing on her clients with not one but two strangers in tow. So I let Susan do the photos. They're okay, but..." She wrinkled her nose. "They aren't great. I'm not sure what to do about it, though. Laura's going to be meeting with her teenage mothers for only a month and a half more before she moves out to California with Seth. If I want better art, I suppose I'll have to move quickly on it."

Kimberly eyed her friend speculatively. Julianne's calm attitude might reveal little to most people, but Kimberly had known her long enough to discern that something significant lay beneath Julianne's uncertainty about hiring another photographer. "Why haven't you moved on it yet?" she probed. "You must know enough talented photographers to fill a NYNEX telephone book. Why don't you just commission one and get on with it?"

Julianne eyed Kimberly and smiled hesitantly. "I already know the photographer I want for the job."

"Troy Bennett," Kimberly guessed, naming their college classmate, the man who had filled the pages of *The Dream* with his striking, powerful photographs. She knew as well as Julianne how superbly Troy would be able to capture on film the moods and feelings of struggling young mothers. His portraits expressed far more than merely a catalogue of a subject's physical characteristics. His pictures literally told stories.

"He's not available," Julianne said swiftly.

"Have you already asked him?" Kimberly leaned forward to keep the sofa cushions from swallowing her up. "I know he's got his photography studio up in Montreal, Julianne, but if you paid him enough, covered expenses and all, he might do it."

Julianne shook her head. "He wouldn't," she said laconically. Before Kimberly could question her further, Julianne smoothly redirected the conversation to Kimberly. "Once I finish this Broken Families in America issue, I'm going to expect a hot scoop for the magazine from you and Andrew on his involvement with the C.I.A. So don't you dare leak the story to anyone else." She took a sip of her cordial, then asked, "When is Andrew supposed to arrive in New York to meet with Senator Milford?"

"Tomorrow at three," Kimberly reported, hoping that her voice didn't betray her turbulent emotions when it came to Andrew. "The senator's spending the morning at Gracie Mansion, having lunch with the mayor there, and then he has a few hours free in the afternoon before he has to deliver his speech to the electronics folks. That's when Andrew's been sandwiched in."

"He must have been pleased that you could set up the meeting here in the city so he wouldn't have to travel all the way to Washington again."

"'Pleased' is an understatement," Kimberly muttered, her facade cracking. "I doubt he'll ever want to return to Washington."

"Why?"

Kimberly circled the rim of her glass with her finger as she ruminated. She usually had no difficulty confiding in Julianne; they had known each other since their sophomore year at Barnard, and unlike the other founders of *The Dream*, Kimberly and Julianne had maintained close contact in the fifteen years since they'd graduated from college. During the course of those years Kimberly had never hesitated to tell Julianne about anything that was bothering her, particularly in matters of the heart. Julianne had absorbed Kimberly's tirades about Todd, about the problems in their marriage and the hardships of her separation and divorce. Julianne was easy to talk to; she never stood in judgment of Kimberly, never lapsed into pity, but always offered sympathy and sound advice.

Yet telling Julianne about Andrew seemed risky. Julianne had seen for herself the tension and animosity that marked Kimberly's relationship with Andrew in college. If Kimberly revealed that Andrew had spent the night with her, Julianne might berate her for her lack of common sense. Worse yet, Julianne might laugh at her.

"I slept with him," Kimberly blurted out before she could stop herself.

Julianne choked on her drink. "You did what?"

Kimberly averted her gaze. "When Andrew was in Washington I slept with him."

Julianne took a moment to collect herself. She lowered her glass carefully to the table and turned her gaze to Kimberly. "And?" she said expectantly.

"And it was a mistake," Kimberly lamely summed up.

"Why?" Julianne pressed her. "Wasn't he good in bed?"

"Don't be crass," Kimberly scolded her.

Julianne smiled hesitantly. "I'm sorry, but you've taken me by surprise. I mean, you and Andrew Collins, archenemies... Why was it a mistake?"

"You just said it yourself, Julianne. We were archenemies."

"Are you still?"

Kimberly pondered the question. As angry as she was with Andrew, and as hurt, she couldn't consider him her enemy. "The whole thing was silly," she said, trying to justify what had occurred. "We'd both had a lot to drink and we were talking too much, and one thing led to another."

"Oh, come off it," Julianne scoffed. "You aren't the sort of person who drifts into something like that. Neither is he.

People don't wind up making love by accident—certainly not people like you and Andrew."

Kimberly conceded with a slight nod. "I think . . . I think it was more that I was feeling lonely, rebounding from the divorce, and he was there," she said, relying on his explanation for her behavior. "We had spent a lot of time together and we were getting along . . ."

"You were getting along, so just for the hell of it you made love. Come on, Kim!" Julianne's tone was laced with sarcasm. "You've got more control over yourself than that. If you slept with Andrew, it was because you wanted to sleep with him. With *him* in particular, not with anyone who just happened to be handy."

"I know," Kimberly admitted in a small voice. "And yes, he was good in bed. It was wonderful, Julianne, but . . . but I've never slept with anyone I didn't love before." She didn't bother to add that she'd never slept with anyone but her husband. Numbers didn't matter. All that mattered was that she had always believed that love and sex were irrevocably intertwined.

"Do you love Andrew?"

"No!" Kimberly said vehemently.

Julianne measured her heated denial and sighed. Then she reached across the sofa to pat Kimberly's arm reassuringly. "You aren't the first woman who's made love without being in love, Kim. You don't have to act as if it's the end of the world."

"Have you ever slept with someone you didn't love?" Kimberly shot back.

Julianne smiled. "It's your situation we're talking about, not mine. Do you feel guilty? Did you hurt Andrew's feelings?"

"I don't know. No," Kimberly decided. "He's much stronger than I am about these things. He's a man, after all."

"A man," Julianne repeated. "Not an ogre. He's a very sweet man, and he's not constructed of steel. If you're feeling bad because you might have hurt him, then you'll feel a lot better if you make up with him."

"It isn't that," Kimberly asserted. She closed her eyes and let Joni Mitchell's soothing music spill over her. The ballad was unfortunately melancholy and soulful, and it didn't improve her spirits. "He was the one who hurt me," she confessed. "The morning after he said things that implied... Julianne, he's never thought much of me. I'm sick of men treating me like I'm an idiot, like I haven't got a functioning mind. Todd always talked down to me, and Andrew does, too. I don't want to be insulted anymore. I don't want to be hurt."

"Nobody wants to be hurt," Julianne said quietly. "But it comes with the territory." She stood and crossed to the dining table, where she'd left the bottle of crème de menthe. "What are you going to say to Andrew when you see him tomorrow?" she asked.

"I'm going to say, 'Andrew, I'd like you to meet Senator Milford. Senator, this is Professor Andrew Collins.' Then I'm going to leave the room."

Julianne stared at her from across the room. She laughed. "That's about the worst strategy I've ever heard."

"What's wrong with it?"

"It's called running away, Kim. And if I know Andrew, he's not going to let you get away with it."

"Why not? He's got a girlfriend up in Amherst. Probably some whiz kid who loves discussing logarithms with him over dinner."

"He's an economist, not a mathematician," Julianne pointed out.

"All right. The gross national product."

"Are you jealous?"

"Of course I'm jealous," Kimberly retorted. "He respects her more than he respects me."

"How do you know that?" Julianne posed. When Kimberly failed to speak, she returned to the sofa and refilled their glasses. "I've always gotten along better with Andrew than you have," she observed. "I can't say I know him inside and out, but I honestly don't think he's the type to take advantage of a woman, especially a woman who's recovering from a painful divorce. Don't forget, he's a widower. He's endured his share of pain, too. Whatever happened when he was in Washington, whatever he did, I can't believe that he deliberately wanted to hurt you." She sipped from her replenished glass, then added, "Talk to him tomorrow, Kim. Work it out, or it's going to fester inside you forever."

"Why are you always so damned sensible?" Kimberly complained.

"Good midwestern breeding," Julianne joked. "All that manure-scented air I inhaled as a child. Drink up, Kim."

AT A QUARTER TO THREE, Lee rang Kimberly's room to announce that he and the senator had returned from their luncheon with the mayor. "Come on up," Lee requested. "The senator wants you to background him a little more on the professor. He gets so edgy when he has to face someone who's smarter than he is."

"Don't we all?" she grunted before hanging up. She ran her brush briskly through her hair, straightened the jacket of her cream-colored suit, adjusted the collar of her royal-blue blouse and left her room for the senator's suite.

Whitney was already in the sitting room with Lee and the senator when Kimberly entered. A fresh pot of coffee stood on a room-service tray and a side table held a few bottles of liquor. The senator had loosened his tie and removed his shoes. His dense gray hair was neatly combed, however, and he seemed refreshed.

"How did your meeting with the mayor go?" she asked politely.

"Not badly," he replied, helping himself to a cup of coffee. "The man tends to go on and on, and he's awfully full of himself. But, then, I suppose we politicians always are. I've looked over everything you and Whitney have ferreted out about this L.A.R.C. proprietary," the senator continued. "It's all very juicy, but let's face it. I can't make an issue out of a bunch of off-the-record innuendos. Does this friend of yours have the—" he checked himself before using one of his off-color phrases in Kimberly's presence "—brass to follow through if I start something with the committee?"

"Andrew is very brassy," Kimberly said emotionlessly. "You can see how far he wants to go with it when you meet him."

The hotel concierge telephoned to inform the senator that Professor Collins was in the lobby and had identified himself to the hotel guard's satisfaction. "Send him up," Lee said.

Kimberly paced nervously to the window and peered out at Central Park. A hard rain descended from the swollen gray clouds overhead. The expanse of grass and trees to the north of the hotel appeared blurred and soggy.

At the light rap on the door she jumped, then spun around in time to see Whitney answer. "Hi, there," he hailed Andrew familiarly. "How's life treating you at that bastion of intellectual excellence?"

Kimberly recognized that with his robust greeting, Whitney was merely trying to put both the senator and Andrew at ease. Yet Andrew didn't appear particularly relaxed. Dressed in a tweedy tan blazer, dark brown corduroy slacks, a white shirt and a brown tie, he clutched his leather briefcase and smiled woodenly as he stepped inside the room. His gaze moved from Whitney, whose hand he dutifully shook, to Lee, to the senator, and finally to Kimberly, where it lingered.

Perhaps she was imagining things, but his square jaw seemed to grow visibly stiffer as his eyes coursed over her. She prayed that he would smile and reveal that uncharacteristic dimple of his, but he didn't oblige. Instead he turned back to the senator, who was padding in his socks over the thick carpet toward him. "Andrew Collins? Thanks so much for coming all the way down from Massachusetts."

"Thank you for having me," Andrew responded, accepting the senator's beefy handshake. "It's an honor."

"An honor, is it?" The senator chuckled. "I like you already. Can I get you something to drink? I've got coffee and booze."

"Coffee, thank you," Andrew said, permitting himself the slightest hint of a smile at the senator's down-to-earth manner.

The senator looked to Lee, who looked to Kimberly. With an inaudible sigh she strode to the cart and fixed a cup of coffee for Andrew. She understood that fixing coffee was her responsibility because she had the least seniority of anyone in the room, but she bristled at the knowledge that Andrew would interpret her action as a sign of her feminine subservience.

She exerted herself to present Andrew with a smile as she handed him the cup. "I hope your drive down wasn't too tiring," she said coolly.

"The weather could have been better," he remarked, just as formally.

Stifling the urge to wince, she lowered her eyes to his hand as he took the cup. She suffered a fleeting memory of the way his fingers had felt on her body, so gentle in their caresses, and took an abrupt step back from him. "Perhaps you'd like to meet with the senator in private," she said, not only because she was eager to get away from Andrew but because she knew he was concerned about protecting his research from inquisitive eavesdroppers. "You'll be able to speak more freely with him if we all aren't around."

"Thank you," he murmured. She caught a glimpse of his dimple and felt her innards unclench slightly.

"Why don't we retire to my bedroom?" the senator suggested, leading the way to an inner door. As his suggestion registered, he issued a hearty laugh. "Don't worry, Andrew—you're perfectly safe with me. I'm a happily married man."

Grinning affably, Andrew followed the senator through the door. The door closed.

"Is it just me, or are things getting chilly in here?" Whitney asked Kimberly, shooting her a wily grin.

"It's just you," Kimberly said curtly. "I'll be down in my room if anybody needs me." She marched out of the suite and slammed the door shut behind her.

Locked inside her own room, she groaned. She tried to recall Julianne's counsel about talking to Andrew and getting her feelings off her chest. The recommendation had sounded so logical last night, but Kimberly knew it wouldn't be easy to talk to Andrew. Especially since she had no idea what she would say.

To distract herself, she slumped in the chair by the desk and leafed through her notes for the senator's speech. She didn't need to read the speech; she'd fussed with it all morning, and by now she practically had the thing memorized. She knew its cadences, its stresses. She knew exactly how the senator would sound when he spoke the words she'd written for him.

She wished she had a speech writer for herself, someone who could compose a magnificent oratory for her to deliver to Andrew. "I am distressed by the way things ended between us a week and a half ago. I am distressed by the way I feel about you. I am distressed by the way I seem not to know whether I am coming or going, whether we are friends or enemies, whether you love me or loathe me, desire me or despise me. I am distressed by the way you explain away my emotions." That sounded magnificent, full of rhythm and punch, the phrases carrying a music all their own. She knew the senator could make a speech like that soar. If only he could recite it on Kimberly's behalf....

She tried not to be so conscious of the passage of time, but each tick of her watch seemed to resonate inside her. One hour, an hour and a half, two. What on earth could Andrew be telling the senator for two hours?

Her room phone rang. Inhaling deeply, she walked to the night table and lifted the receiver. "Hello?"

"Kim? Whitney here. Lover boy is all done with the big man. He's on his way down to your room."

"Oh." She thought it rather presumptuous that Andrew would head directly for her room without first asking if he was welcome. Moreover, she wondered how he had learned her room number. From Whitney, probably. Andrew was apparently still playing Kimberly's game, permitting Whitney to think they were an item.

She thanked Whitney for the warning, hung up and threw back her shoulders. Trying to remember the speech she had mentally written for herself, she came up blank. A quick glance in her mirror informed her that her hair was mussed and her lipstick bitten off. But before she could repair her appearance, she heard Andrew's knock.

She glimpsed through the peephole to ascertain that it was he, then opened the door to admit him.

"Hello," he said.

She opened her mouth and then shut it. As if in a stupor, she watched him close the door behind him and set down his briefcase. Then he pulled off his eyeglasses and massaged his nose, a gesture of weariness. "Was it rough?" she asked, suddenly solicitous.

"Rough?" He smiled wryly. "No. Your boss is a nice guy."

"Then why do you look as if you just completed a marathon?" She mulled over what she'd said, then grinned. "I reckon two-plus hours is a long time to be shut up in a bedroom with another man."

Apparently hearing the word "bedroom" gave Andrew pause. He slipped his eyeglasses on and gazed around Kimberly's room, which was markedly smaller and less elegant than the senator's suite. His eyes came to rest on the double bed with its quilted brown cover, and one corner of his mouth skewed upward, shaping something that was a cross between a smile and a grimace. "Kimberly—"

"He wants you to testify, doesn't he?" she said briskly, trying to ignore the disappointment she felt at hearing Andrew use her full name. "Whitney's told me that the senator has discussed setting up hearings on the issue, and the senator's also made some mention of the idea to me. He wants you to testify before the Intelligence Committee. Right?"

Andrew didn't answer. He only stared at Kimberly, his expression unreadable, his eyes half-hidden behind the glare the bedside lamp created on the lenses of his glasses. His lips softened, and then he looked toward the bed again. "How are you?" he asked.

Despite the fact that he was standing only inches from the bed, he hardly sounded passionate. Rather, his tone was polite and reserved. She didn't want courtesy from him, but that seemed to be the level on which he intended to deal with her. "Are you going to testify?" she asked, bypassing his innocuous question. Maybe she should have taken him up on his gambit, answering him in a way that would introduce a more intimate note into their conversation. But as soon as she spoke, she realized that the opportunity for personal dialogue was gone.

"I don't know," Andrew replied.

"It's important," she stressed. "If you want to uncover this nefarious Wilding character—"

"Kim, I don't know," he replied tersely. "I have to give it some thought."

She sensed him sealing himself up, recoiling, retreating. She wouldn't allow him to slip away from her. Julianne was right; Kimberly and Andrew had to talk. Lifting her face to his, she suggested, "Let's have dinner together and discuss it. I'll put it on the senator's tab. The least he owes you is a good meal for having come all this way."

Andrew contemplated her invitation. "I've got to make a call first."

Kimberly pointed to the telephone and crossed the room to the window, affording him a measure of privacy. Still, she couldn't help but overhear his end of the call. He requested an outside line, dialed the numbers and waited. "Hello, Edith. It's Andrew," he said. "I've got to beg off for dinner tonight. I'll be eating in town.... No, thanks anyway. Maybe next time. Take care now." He hung up.

"You didn't have to break a date," she remarked, hoping she didn't sound querulous. She already knew that Andrew had a girlfriend, but she couldn't prevent herself from suffering a pang of jealousy at listening to his conversation with another woman.

"It wasn't a date," Andrew told her. "Edith is my mother-in-law." He checked himself. "My former mother-in-law," he clarified. "She and Marjorie's father live in White Plains. They invited me to stop at their place for dinner on the way back to Amherst. But we hadn't made a definite plan."

That Andrew felt he owed Kimberly such an extensive explanation placated her. She smiled weakly, gathered her purse from the bureau and preceded him from the room.

They rode the elevator downstairs in silence and strolled through the teeming lobby to the hotel's restaurant. Kimberly identified herself to the maître d', who promptly seated them at a cozy table against the wall. Within a minute a waiter approached, pencil at the ready, and asked if they wanted drinks.

"No," Kimberly said hurriedly. She wasn't going to let them use alcohol as an excuse for their behavior with each other this time.

Still without speaking, they buried themselves in their menus until the waiter returned to take their orders. Once he was gone they had no choice but to confront each other. "Why don't you want to testify before the committee?" she asked, figuring that the best way to begin was to concentrate on business.

Andrew pondered the question for a moment before answering. "You know I want to keep this thing as quiet as possible. It's endangering my status at Amherst. To go public in such a big way would be foolhardy—to say nothing of embarrassing."

"Embarrassing? What's embarrassing about it?"

"It's embarrassing that I got hoodwinked," he explained. "It's embarrassing for someone like me to find out I was working for the C.I.A. And I know it's going to embarrass Bob McIntyre—my mentor at Amherst. If there's any way I can spare him a major humiliation—"

"Andrew, testifying before the committee isn't like appearing on Johnny Carson. The whole matter can be handled discreetly."

He laughed caustically. "Tell me about it. I know what these Senate hearings are like. I watched nearly every minute of the Watergate hearings on television. I watched as James McCord and Alexander Butterworth entered living rooms all across the country. I watched John Dean become a celebrity simply by testifying. How could he not become a celebrity? The journalists outnumbered the participants by about ten to one. It was a circus, Kim."

"That was the Ethics Committee. And that was a very different situation. The Intelligence Committee never holds open hearings, Andrew. No journalists will be present."

He frowned, evidently unpersuaded.

Giving him time to reflect, she scanned the dining room. At the doorway, she spotted Lee and Whitney awaiting a table. Whitney caught her eye and inquired with a few gestures of his hand and some mouthed words whether he and Lee could join her and Andrew for dinner. She shook her head.

Andrew noticed her movement and glanced over his shoulder to see whom she was communicating with. "Lee and Whitney," she whispered. "I don't want them sitting with us."

Andrew smiled wryly. "Of course not. It's much more fun playing games with Whitney, isn't it."

Kimberly's anxiety boiled over into pure fury. "Will you shut up about that, Andrew? Will you just do me a favor and forget the whole thing? If you think that's all that's going on here, all we've got between us—''

"No," he said quickly. "No, I don't think that."

"Then what in high heaven do you think?"

He was spared from responding by the arrival of the waiter with their salads. Once they were alone again, Kimberly fixed Andrew with a brutal stare. He met it unflinchingly. "I think...I think you were a bit too rash with me the last time we were together."

"I surely was," she muttered, trying to dissipate her anger by stabbing a tomato wedge with her fork. "I was most definitely too rash with you. I should never have allowed you to stay—"

"That wasn't what I was talking about," Andrew corrected her, his voice low and intense. "You were rash when you threw me out the next morning."

"You deserved to be thrown out," she snapped. "Impugning me that way, claiming that I was some lonely lady who didn't know her own mind...."

"Ah, Kimberly." He sighed. "Kim. I've—" He mulled over his words, then boldly plowed ahead. "I've missed you."

She didn't dare to interpret his confession as a positive sign. "What did you miss about me? The fact that I crammed pastry down your throat?"

"Among other things." His eyes drifted past her, focusing on the wall. "I haven't stopped thinking about you since I left Washington, Kim. I honestly don't think we're right for each other. But...but the night we spent together felt right. It felt better than right—it felt good. I haven't felt that good in a long, long time." His words spent, he returned his gaze to her and smiled hesitantly.

His unexpected declaration stunned her. She set down her fork and studied him, searching his face for a clue to what she was supposed to think, what she was supposed to say. When Andrew opened his soul to her so completely, she knew she was correct to love him. When he let down his guard and allowed her to see the man he truly was, she had no choice but to let down her guard, as well.

"It did feel good," she whispered shyly.

"Then what went wrong?" he asked. "Why did we blow it the next morning?"

"You're so smart, you ought to know," she countered.

"I know...I know I insulted you. I didn't mean to, Kim, but whatever I said obviously rubbed you the wrong way."

"You said you didn't believe I could love you," she reminded him.

"Did I?"

"Not in so many words, but yes. That's what came across."

He lowered his eyes to his salad, fidgeted with his fork, then let his hand come to rest on the table. "It's the truth. I don't believe you love me."

"Why not?"

"Because..." He sighed again. "You're so beautiful, Kim, so—so precious. You're like a fragile piece of china, delicate and fine—"

She laughed nervously. It felt wonderful to laugh in Andrew's presence, so wonderful her nervousness vanished and her laughter became genuine. "Fragile? Oh, sure, I can break. But trust me, Andrew. I'm not some sort of object you ought to put on a shelf and stare at. I'm no more china than you're steel," she concluded, recalling what Julianne had said about Andrew the night before. "We're both just flesh and blood. And on those rare occasions when you deign to get off your high horse, yes, I sure as hell believe that I love you."

Her announcement startled them both. She hadn't intended to tell him she loved him, and he clearly hadn't expected to hear her express such a feeling. But now the words had been spoken, and they hung in the air between her and Andrew like a solid link, a tangible connection.

"Stay," she murmured, her eyes riveted to his, her hand reaching across the table to him. "Spend the night with me."

"I can't," he said. He didn't pull his hand from hers as her fingers curved gently around it, but his gaze broke away, dropping to his salad again, as if he could no longer bear to look directly at her.

How could he refuse her? How could he refuse them both? After she had publicly acknowledged her love for him, how could he turn away? "Why not?" she asked, her voice resonant with dismay.

"I have to teach a class tomorrow morning."

That was a feeble excuse, and they both knew it. "You could stay for a while, at least—"

"No, Kim. No. I can't."

"Why not?"

He willfully pulled his hand out from under hers and fumbled with his napkin. "You know what will happen if I testify before the committee, don't you?"

She scowled, nonplussed. Why had he decided to reintroduce that subject? "What will happen?" she pressed him, trying to stifle her impatience.

"I'll probably lose my job. The department will let me ride out the last year of my contract and then they'll drop me."

"Maybe they won't," Kimberly disputed him. "Maybe they'll admire your courage and—"

"That's not the way things work in academia," he cut her off. "They'll think I'm an upstart, rocking the boat, putting one of their esteemed colleagues into an untenable position. I'll lose my job," he said with finality. His gaze rose to hers again. "I've lost too much in my life already, Kim. I'm not a kid anymore. I'm too old to go through anything like that again."

She tried to discern the meaning beneath his words. "What does that have to do with us?" she asked softly.

His poignant smile contradicted the somber glow of his eyes as he stared at her. "I don't want to have to lose you, too."

"*Have* to lose me? What makes you so sure you'd lose me? I just told you I love you, Andrew." Saying it reinforced her certainty that she did.

He warred with his thoughts for several minutes, then relented. "I'm not sure. I just don't know."

"Then take a chance," she implored him. "Take a chance and find out."

His smile grew warmer, and she noticed his delectable dimple taking shape at the corner of his mouth.

Chapter Nine

The waiter tactfully refrained from commenting when Kimberly refused their dinner order and signed the check. She figured that if she and Andrew were hungry later they could always order room service. She thought briefly about the waste of the dinner they had canceled, the millions of starving people in the world, and the danger of running up an extravagant bill when one was a public servant. Then she blithely shrugged off those considerations. She doubted that the senator would care, but if he did, she would reimburse his travel fund.

She didn't want to worry about such practical matters. Nor did she want to worry about Andrew's uncertainty regarding her. He had never been reckless, even in their college days, when recklessness was considered the height of fashion. He had always been a cautious man, analyzing every detail to death. That he was reluctant to accept what was obviously developing between him and Kimberly wasn't surprising.

She forgave him his apprehension; as he had said, he'd lost enough in his life. But so had she. And she was sure of her love for him, positive of it. She knew that in time he would be sure of it, too.

Their ride upstairs was as silent as the trip downstairs had been, but the only tension between them now was the electric anticipation of what lay ahead once they reached her room. Her pulse accelerated as she unlocked her door. Before she could close it, Andrew gave her an adorable smile and slung the Do Not Disturb sign over the outer doorknob. "I've always wanted to do that," he confessed.

"Do what?"

"Use a Do Not Disturb sign—for something besides sleeping." He wrapped his arms around her and kissed her brow. "Would I be shattering your illusions if I told you I've never made love in a hotel room before?"

Kimberly laughed airily. She wondered what Andrew would think if he learned about her own inexperience. Hotel rooms were the least of it.

Her laughter ebbed as he fingered the top button of her blouse and eased it through the slit in the cloth. His hands moved efficiently down the front of her blouse, unbuttoning it and tugging it free of the waistband of her skirt. "Is making love in a hotel room one of your fantasies?" she asked, loosening his tie.

He abandoned her blouse to remove his jacket and open his shirt. His smile faded as she reached out to stroke his bare skin. "When I fantasize, Kim, it's about beautiful blond women with dazzling blue eyes."

"And razor-sharp minds?" she inquired, only half joking.

"Minds like yours," he whispered before covering her mouth with his.

His kiss seemed to last an eternity. As her tongue danced with his, her entire body responded, her fingers fisting against the soft wisps of hair covering his chest, her scalp tingling, her hips growing heavy with yearning. The only thing that made ending the kiss endurable for her was the understanding that there would be more to come.

It took them little time to finish undressing. They tumbled onto the bed, their lips fusing again, their fingers interlocked as Andrew's naked body pressed along hers. She wanted to touch him, to stroke the smooth skin of his back and sides, to strum across the surface of his chest again, but his firm clasp wouldn't allow any exploration. She comprehended that he was deliberately pinning her hands to the mattress in order to prolong their lovemaking, and she knew that she would ultimately thank him for setting a leisurely pace. But her frustration was almost palpable, her desire for him a swelling ache deep inside her.

"Underwear, too," he mumbled, lifting his face and gasping for breath. "I've fantasized about your underwear."

"You have?" she exclaimed. "You like ladies' underwear?"

"Not underwear in the general sense," he explained before bowing to graze her throat. "Only yours, Kim. It's so pretty."

"You seemed in an awfully big hurry to tear it off me just now," she playfully reminded him.

"Maybe I ought to put it on you again," he mused.

"Don't you dare."

As if there were any question that he would want her dressed at that moment. His mouth had already shifted downward to taste her breast, and her voice disintegrated into a sigh of pleasure as his lips tightened around her nipple and sucked. At last he released her hands, and she curled her fingers helplessly into his thick dark hair, holding his head to her. Her toes slid along the hard muscle of his calf and he groaned.

"You," he whispered hoarsely, nibbling a meandering path down to her stomach. "The hell with your underwear. I fantasize about you." His lips drifted lower, skirting the golden thatch of hair to browse along the skin of her inner thigh, then rising again and finding her.

A momentary panic seized Kimberly. Once more Andrew was introducing her to something new; once more her ignorance abashed her. And once more the sensations he aroused within her vanquished her panic and her bashfulness, leaving in their wake a maelstrom of thundering emotion.

She heard an unfamiliar sound tearing from her throat as he cupped his hands beneath her hips and deepened his kiss. A distant moan of passion, of glorious torment as her body slipped away from her, submitting fully to the force of his tender assault. She soared to a crest, swept up in a throbbing current, losing consciousness of who she was, where she was, everything she had ever known before.

When Andrew rose onto her she clung to his sturdy shoulders, struggling to regain her bearings. But before her mind could clarify itself, he was in her, filling her, giving her no respite from the storm. Her body moved with his, enveloping him, carrying him with her this time. They reached the peak together, surrendered, hurled themselves into ecstasy.

For a long time afterward, the only reality Kimberly was aware of was Andrew's motionless weight upon her, his chest crushing down on hers with his every ragged breath, his head sharing her pillow, his lips brushing her earlobe. Eventually he raised himself and peered down at her. His thumb glided across her cheek, capturing a tear. Until that moment Kimberly hadn't realized that she was crying.

"Are you all right?" he asked, his voice a husky rumble.

She nodded, then lifted away from the pillow to kiss him. Her arms snaked around his neck and pulled him back down to her. "You're wonderful, Andrew," she whispered.

"I think you deserve at least half the credit."

"No." Her arms tightened on him. "It's all your doing. I'm sure of that."

She couldn't see his face, but she could sense his pleasure. She hadn't spoken to boost his ego, but simply because what she'd said was the truth. He was wonderful.

Closing her eyes, she twirled her fingers through his hair and reminisced about the long, desolate stretch of days between their last meeting and now, when her only contact with him had been a brief, awkward telephone call during which Kimberly had informed him that the senator would be willing to meet with him during an upcoming trip to New York. She had arranged to have Helen, the senator's receptionist, call Andrew to finalize the appointment.

One cold, strained telephone call. And days of recriminations, days of anguish and anger. Why couldn't it have been this way, instead? Why couldn't they have stayed this close, sharing themselves this intimately even when four hundred miles stood between them? "I've missed you, too," she revealed, massaging the muscles at the base of his neck.

"It was nice of Milford to provide us with this little love nest halfway between D.C. and Massachusetts," he teased. "How did you talk him into it?"

She snorted. "I didn't talk him into reserving me a room with this in mind," she pointed out. "He's giving another series of speeches in Chicago tomorrow, and he brought some of us along with him so we could fly from New York together. It made more sense than flying back to Washington and taking off from there. Not that I'm complaining, as things worked out."

Andrew nipped her shoulder before pulling away and rolling onto his side. His gaze ran the length of her body and then lifted to her face. "Have you lost weight?" he asked.

She let out a startled laugh. The fact was, her appetite had been markedly smaller than normal lately, a direct result of her emotional turmoil. But the two pounds she'd lost were hardly noticeable. "How can you tell? You're not even wearing your eyeglasses."

He smiled enigmatically. "I memorized you last time. I memorized the way you looked, the way you felt...."

She was inordinately flattered by his words. "Should I gain the weight back?" she asked. "Do I look better this way or that way?"

"Both," he answered tactfully. "You weren't overweight before. You aren't underweight now. Either way you're perfect."

"How do you think I'd look if I were pregnant?" she asked whimsically.

Andrew was obviously startled. His eyebrows dipped in a frown of consternation as he scrutinized her. "What are you getting at?"

"What do you think I'm getting at?" she returned, shifting onto her side to face him and grinning at his bewildered expression. "Pregnant. With my stomach popped out and funny blue veins rippling up my legs." His stunned silence prompted her to continue. "Why do you look so shocked, Andrew? We talked about this when you were in Washington, remember? You assured me that I wasn't too old to have a baby."

He took his time digesting her words. Finally he spoke. "Um—can we back up a few steps here?" He inhaled steadily, then added, "I thought we were speaking hypothetically then."

"I wasn't," Kimberly maintained. "I want a child so badly, Andrew. I'm supposed to be among the first generation of Superwomen, having it all. And that's what I want."

"Kimberly." His tone was stern and somewhat tense. "Couldn't we have discussed this first?"

Suddenly the reason for his stricken appearance dawned on her. She burst into laughter. "Oh, Andrew, do you think—do you think I tricked you into something just now? Do you think I schemed to seduce you in order to get pregnant? Oh, my!"

Her thrilling giggles thawed him, and he settled against the pillow again. "Okay," he murmured sheepishly. "I admit I should have taken a little more responsibility here and made sure you were using something. When I'm with you, I guess I get carried away. I didn't think to ask."

"There's nothing to ask," Kimberly assured him. "If I'm pregnant now, there's a big drug company we'll have to sue." She leaned forward to kiss him. "I don't know if you heard, but Seth was in Washington last week with Laura's daughter. She's turned out so well, Andrew. She's kind of weird, but she's thirteen, after all, and you have to expect some weirdness at that age. But she's a terrific kid. I would have loved to spend some more time with her than I did. Laura's done a magnificent job raising her. All by herself, too. I'm envious."

"You could have a child by yourself," Andrew noted. "Isn't that all the rage among Superwomen these days?"

"Oh, I couldn't," Kimberly disagreed. "I'm not nearly as strong as Laura is. And don't forget, when she had Rita, she was living on a commune, with lots of adults for help and companionship and no full-time job outside the home. Besides—" she grinned mischievously "—can you imagine what my mother would say if I became pregnant out of wedlock? The poor woman still hasn't come to terms with the fact that I could have a strange man in my apartment at nine-thirty in the morning."

"Barefoot, too," Andrew recalled with a tenuous smile.

Kimberly sighed wistfully. "I've always been a closet square, Andrew. I'm afraid I'm just old-fashioned enough to think I ought to get married before I become a mother."

He brushed a wavy strand of hair back from her face, then let his hand drift to her shoulder and down her graceful arm to clasp her hand. "Is this a proposal?"

She tried to interpret his cryptic smile and the solemn amber radiance of his eyes. His question hadn't been asked in rancor or revulsion. She recognized that she could hardly ask Andrew to marry her when he wasn't even ready to admit that he loved her, but the fact that he wasn't running for his life at the mere idea heartened her immensely. "It's a thought," she said.

He slid his hand to the center of her back and pulled her closer to himself. His mouth met hers, and he kissed her profoundly. As if by instinct, her legs tangled with his and her arms drew him onto her again, and every thought burned away in the immediacy of her passion for Andrew.

THE WINDSHIELD WIPERS swept rhythmically across his vision, clicking in a counterpoint to the progressive rock music blaring from his radio. A four-hour drive through a downpour late at night wasn't Andrew's notion of a good time. But he didn't complain. It was a small price to pay for the evening he had spent with Kimberly.

He felt invigorated, almost hyperactive. Sex had a way of keying up his nervous system, fueling his soul. There had been times, after making love with Marjorie, when he had been tempted to abandon her and take a five-mile jog to unwind.

He didn't want to jog right now; driving would suffice. And he certainly didn't want to think about Marjorie. He wanted to think only of the breathtaking blond woman he had kissed goodbye less than thirty minutes ago, the alluring woman he had left standing in her pale blue bathrobe, pushing the room-service cart out into the hallway and then watching until Andrew disappeared into the elevator. He wanted to think only of Kimberly.

Yet as soon as a memory of Marjorie flitted across his mind, he couldn't fight off the inevitable wave of emotion that crashed over him. Tonight the wave carried not grief, as it often did, but guilt, the same guilt that had been plaguing him ever since the last time he had been with Kimberly. The same guilt and the same fear.

He had nothing to feel guilty about, he lectured himself. If Marjorie could speak to him from beyond the grave, she would probably tell him to go for it, to chase Kimberly and enjoy her and put the past behind him.

However, she would undoubtedly question Andrew's taste. *Her? You want a pretty little snippet like her? All that pale hair and those big kootchie-kootchie eyes? Well, whatever turns you on, lover....*

Guilt was supposed to have been one of those emotions that was trashed back in the late sixties. It had been reserved for the adults of an earlier time, people who had spent the best years of their lives polluting the environment and supporting the arms race. But not for young folks like Andrew, who were determined to live by their principles and who held fast to their inalienable right to pursue happiness—even if principles and happiness sometimes lay at cross-purposes.

He had no reason to feel guilty about wanting Kimberly. But the fear...the fear that he might lose her was harder to vanquish. He could pursue Kimberly and he could enjoy her, but could he really keep her? Could a four-eyed high-brow like him truly possess the love of a woman as ravishing as Kimberly? Regardless of her profession of love for him and her oblique introduction of the subject of marriage, Andrew couldn't shake off the doubt that gnawed at him.

He knew that she hadn't yet recovered completely from the heartache of her divorce. But in time she would. And when she did, hundreds of far more suitable men would be pounding on her door. Classically handsome, cultured, rich men. She could find among them one with good genes—not merely a bootlegger among his ancestors, but also twenty-twenty vision and nary a trace of gray hair—and she could mate with him and have herself the child she longed for, a child as beautiful and well-bred as she herself was.

Andrew wouldn't deny that a strong bond existed between Kimberly and him. He wouldn't deny that he was very close to falling in love with Kimberly—if he hadn't already fallen. And he couldn't stand the possibility of again losing someone he loved. Kimberly had told him to take a chance and he wanted to. But he was scared.

If only things were different, if only Kimberly weren't quite so irresistible, if only they lived closer to each other so they could take this thing one step at a time....

He cursed. "If only" was a habit he thought he had broken long ago. He had resorted to the phrase too many times after Marjorie had become sick. If only she hadn't had the miscarriage, if only they hadn't tried to conceive, if only he hadn't married her, if only he hadn't met her in the first place. If only he were an ostrich with his head in the sand.

It was pointless to torture oneself with "if onlys." What happened happened. Marjorie died. Andrew finished his Ph.D. and landed a position at Amherst. Kimberly entered his heart. What happened between Kimberly and him from here on in was still within his control.

What happened with his job, too. Protecting himself emotionally was one thing; protecting himself professionally was another.

What should he do about Senator Milford's request that he testify before the Intelligence Committee? Kimberly had probably been correct when she'd assured him that the hearing would be closed and that Andrew's face wouldn't be splashed across every television screen in the country simply because he had gone public with the information that a lunatic in the C.I.A. wanted to destroy the economy of El Salvador. But still, the entire nation didn't have to know about it to put an end to Andrew's career at Amherst. Only Bob McIntyre and his cronies in the economics department had to know. If Andrew testified, there was no way he could keep it a secret from them.

Senator Milford had seemed like a good man. He had quickly put Andrew at ease with his relaxed demeanor. Seated cross-legged on his bed, he had loosened Andrew up by chatting at length about his dealings with the C.I.A., sounding not like a politician polishing his image but like a human being with a genuine concern for the way the government functioned.

If Kimberly's mother had met Milford, she wouldn't have considered him a gentleman. Not only because of his liberal bent, but because he hadn't been wearing shoes.

Damn. Andrew probably should have kept his mouth shut about the whole L.A.R.C. affair. He probably should have handed his notes to John Wilding, published a few papers and put the entire episode behind him.

"Coward," he muttered aloud, succumbing to a surge of self-contempt. At a younger age he wouldn't have been so careful. He would have met Wilding head-on, with fists raised. He would have issued a score of papers, not on the agronomy of El Salvador but on the dangerous excesses of a certain C.I.A. operative. If he lost his job in the process, he would have issued a score more papers on Amherst's capitulation to government pressure. He would have moved into a cheap efficiency apartment somewhere and survived on canned sardines—he'd been a graduate student, he knew how to live on next to nothing. Maybe he would have founded another underground newspaper.

Not that such a venture would succeed as it had fifteen years ago. College students nowadays dreamed of going to business school, not of overthrowing the power structure and shaping a more equitable society. Julianne had known full well what she was doing when she turned *The Dream* into a slick-format monthly magazine featuring articles with mass appeal.

The rain began to let up. "Here's a golden oldie," the late-night deejay babbled on the car radio, introducing the Rolling Stones classic, "You Can't Always Get What You Want."

"If that's a golden oldie, so am I," Andrew mused. He recalled the morning, several years back, when he had discovered a few strands of silver infiltrating his beard and had been forced to contend with the reality that he was aging. Three days later—three silver beard hairs later—he'd shaved his chin smooth. Without the beard he looked noticeably younger, but he still carried within himself the knowledge that he was growing old, that his body was giving him away. In time the hair on his head had begun to turn silver, as well. By now he ought to be used to the fact that he wasn't a kid anymore.

How odd that the Rolling Stones song, which had been written the year Andrew graduated from high school, was so much more pertinent today. In his youth he had been convinced that one *could* always get what one wanted. He had long since been disabused of that idea.

By the time he arrived at his home around one o'clock, the rain had ended. The night air was heavy with the fragrance of spring and wetness as he parked behind the massive brick house and strolled around to the front door to let himself inside. Before unlocking the door, he emptied his mailbox, one of four fastened to the wall alongside the door.

A gas bill, an advertisement for computer software and a stiff cream-colored envelope with his address handwritten across it. He refrained from opening it until he was inside his apartment and the door was bolted behind him. Then he dropped his briefcase beside his desk and slid his finger beneath the envelope flap.

Laura Brodie
and
Seth Stone
cordially invite you to share
in the celebration of their marriage
Sunday, the Seventeenth of May
Nineteen Hundred and Eighty-Seven
Two O'Clock p.m.
at the home of Arlene Brodie
King of Prussia, Pennsylvania

Enclosed in the fold of the invitation was an R.S.V.P. card and a map and printed directions to Arlene Brodie's house.

Andrew reread the invitation and smiled. Laura and Stoned. They were really going to do it.

He carried the invitation to the sofa and sank onto it. Marriage. He wondered whether Laura and Seth comprehended the amount of courage one needed to get married, to survive a marriage. When Andrew had married Marjorie, he had had no idea whatsoever. He'd had no inkling of how his commitment to Marjorie would sap his reserves of strength, of how enormous a price love could exact. With good fortune, neither Laura nor Seth would ever have to pay that price, but still...anything was possible. When love was involved, when one was committed, one couldn't conveniently walk away from the hardships.

Setting the invitation on the cushion next to him, he reached over the arm of the sofa to the neat stack of magazines on the end table and located the April edition of *Dream*. Julianne had dedicated her "Editor's Page" to the magazine's fifteenth anniversary. In her essay, she had written a history of the magazine's founding and evolution and a succinct description of what each of the founders was doing currently. The piece was illustrated with an amusing photograph of the six of them as undergraduates, clowning around on the Columbia campus in front of the building that had contained *The Dream*'s office.

Andrew had noticed the photo on display during the reunion Julianne had orchestrated in honor of the magazine's fifteenth birthday. He had laughed at it then, joking with the others about how vastly they'd all changed. Fifteen years of barbers and beauticians had altered them at least as much fifteen years of "real life."

He studied the photograph on the magazine page intently. Maybe they hadn't changed that much. Seth, although shorn of his wild sand-colored mane, was still the sort to wear bizarre T-shirts and wave his hand in a V-for-Victory salute, as he was doing in the picture. Laura appeared to have added a few pounds to her scrawny frame since college—a definite improvement, Andrew allowed—but she seemed at peace with herself in the photograph, her

Mona Lisa smile hinting at inner contentment. They made a good couple, he decided. They would be happy together.

His gaze shifted to Kimberly. In the photo she had waist-length hair that was pinned back from her face with barrettes. She looked like a professional model—too short, perhaps, but no less beautiful. Her lips curved in a radiant smile. Because her hands were hidden, Kimberly's engagement ring was invisible. But Andrew knew she had been wearing it that day. She had always worn it. He doubted that she had recognized at that time what her marriage would do to her, what misery she would experience because of it. Like Andrew, she had entered into it in ignorance.

He continued to stare at her face, comparing it to that of the mature woman he had left in New York City. She was just as lovely today, just as radiant, just as hopeful—hoping for a child now, if not for true love.

His forehead ached from his rigid expression, and he folded the magazine shut. Then he felt his brow and the bridge of his nose relax. He had been squinting at her, he realized.

He wanted Kimberly, wanted her immeasurably. If he were careless, if he let himself, he would undoubtedly grow to need her. But that wouldn't have to happen if he protected himself.

He would never stop wanting her. But he could keep himself from needing her.

Mick Jagger knew what he was talking about. You couldn't always get what you wanted, but if you tried sometimes . . . if you tried very hard, sometimes, if luck was with you, you just might get what you needed.

"ANY QUESTIONS?"

The hour was nearly up, and he scanned the class of attentive, bright-faced youngsters, waiting. He had just delivered one of his favorite lectures, concerning the repercussions of colonization on the impoverished nations of the Caribbean Basin. As he had outlined it, the stranglehold the Duvaliers, *père* and *fils*, had maintained on the downtrodden population of Haiti, rendering it the poorest nation in the hemisphere, wouldn't have been possible if the country hadn't been browbeaten by centuries of economic exploitation by Western powers.

A hand shot up and he smiled. "Duff?"

The young man grinned sheepishly. "I was wondering if you could talk a little about the final exam, Professor Collins," he requested.

"The final exam?" Andrew exclaimed, closing his folder of notes. "That's over a month away."

"I know," Duff conceded. "But, well, could you at least tell us what form it's going to take? What material is going to be on it? How heavily is it going to count in our final grades? I'm sure I'm not the only person here who wants to know." This assertion was greeted by a great deal of head bobbing from his classmates. Even Chip Wilton, who was seated in the front row, nodded vigorously.

Andrew groaned inwardly. His students were far too obsessed with grades. They were intelligent, they worked hard, but Andrew rarely sensed that their primary motive was the simple lust for knowledge.

In his own day grades hadn't mattered to him and his friends nearly as much. Of course, he himself had never had to worry about his grades; he could have coasted through college without exerting himself and managed to graduate with a respectable record. That he had exerted himself had resulted in his election to Phi Beta Kappa and the inclusion of summa cum laude on his diploma, but such honors hadn't been paramount in his decision to make the most of his college years. He had wanted to know things, to gather information, to deepen his perspective. He had wanted to leave Columbia a wiser man than he had been when he'd entered. He had known he was about to be thrust into a harsh world, and he had wanted to confront it armed with every intellectual weapon at his command.

To his current students the most important weapon was a high grade-point average. Such a weapon would unlock the doors to professional schools, to corporate offices. Heaven forbid that they should bother to learn anything that wasn't necessary for making a fat income once they left the ivory tower.

"I'm not going to discuss the final," he said resolutely. "It's much too premature."

"But you know what's going to be on it," Duff persisted.

Andrew chuckled sardonically. "Of course I do. I'm the teacher, remember?"

A few of the students joined his laughter. As the minute hand on the large wall clock swept across the twelve, they gathered their notebooks and rose from their desks, chattering softly among themselves. Andrew slipped his folder into his briefcase and watched his pupils file out of the classroom. When the last pair had departed, he switched off the light and exited.

He spotted Bob McIntyre at the end of the hallway, approaching. "Andy!" the wiry, energetic man shouted, increasing his pace. "Wait up."

Andrew complied. As the older man neared him, Andrew concentrated his vision on Bob's curly salt-and-pepper hair to avoid having to meet his colleague's gaze directly.

"How about lunch?" Bob asked. "I feel as though we haven't talked in ages."

"Well..." Andrew made a big show of checking his wristwatch, even though he knew it was noon. "I've got a few things to take care of—"

"Take care of them later," Bob insisted cheerfully. "It's time to take care of your stomach now."

Andrew relented with a sigh. He couldn't keep avoiding Bob indefinitely. Managing a faint smile, he accompanied Bob down the corridor to the stairs.

"If I didn't know better," Bob babbled, "I'd suspect that you've been trying to keep your distance from me lately. What's got you so tied up these days?"

"Things," Andrew answered with a vague shrug.

"Research things?" Bob pressed him. "Or something better? You know, my wife still wants to introduce you to that divorced cousin of hers. You ought to thank me for sparing you from a fate worse than death."

"Many thanks," Andrew obliged. "I don't need any matchmakers in my life at the moment."

"Glad to hear that." Bob's eyes coursed over Andrew. "Stay a bachelor much longer, pal, and we're going to be seeing you walking around in mismatched socks."

"I've always been very precise about my socks, Bob," Andrew claimed, figuring that he ought to maintain a spritely attitude with the man whose company he had come to dread.

"Let's eat off campus," Bob suggested as they emerged from the building into the noontime sun. "I've had enough of dealing with these jackass undergraduates for a while."

"So have I," Andrew concurred. "They're already pestering me about the final exam. Is it just my imagination, Bob, or do they get worse every year?"

"They get worse every year," Bob confirmed, ambling across the grass with Andrew. "If the seventies was the 'Me Decade,' the eighties must be the 'Brownnose Decade.'"

They headed for a chic eatery a few blocks north of the campus. Andrew liked the place; its glass walls lent it the atmosphere of a greenhouse and its food was fresh and reasonably priced. Although the restaurant was crowded, he and Bob didn't have to wait long for a table.

Once they had ordered, Bob embarked on a long-winded discourse about a reputed shake-up in the dean's office. Andrew did his best to remain calm. He used to enjoy listening to Bob explain the ins and outs of the college's bureaucracy. If they could spend their entire meal conversing on such safe topics, Andrew would be supremely pleased.

However, the arrival of their sandwiches dashed that hope. "So," Bob said before treating his hamburger to a blizzard of salt. "How's that El Salvador project coming along? When am I going to see your byline in some journals?"

Andrew squeezed a lemon wedge into his iced tea and stirred the drink, playing for time. He thought about his students, that meek, frightened herd dedicated to the proposition that security was all that counted in life. He thought, too, about Donna, whose preparations for her move to Fullerton were in high gear and who rambled constantly about how she was going to finish her dissertation, get tenure and live happily ever after in California. He thought, as well, about Seth and Laura, about their bravery in following their hearts, about how different they were from his students and Donna.

And he thought about Kimberly. He thought about the crystalline light of her eyes as she had gazed across a table at him in the Essex House's restaurant and said, "Take a chance."

She had been talking about something else at the time. She had issued her challenge in the context of their relationship. And Andrew still hadn't decided whether to accept the challenge.

But there was a limit to how many risks Andrew could shrink from. His soul was one thing. His integrity was quite another.

"When you put me in touch with the Latin-American Research Council," he began, resolving to confront Bob, "what did you know about it?"

Bob smiled quizzically. "What do you mean?"

"I mean," Andrew said emphatically, "did you know it was a proprietary of the C.I.A.?"

Bob hesitated before biting into his hamburger. Then he took a robust mouthful, chewed, swallowed and shrugged. "So?"

"So? Why didn't you tell me you were hooking me up with a C.I.A. agent?"

"I didn't know," Bob declared. "I may have had my suspicions, Andy, but who am I to lead you by the nose? You've got a good head on your shoulders. I figured you could handle whatever you had to handle."

"I *can* handle it," Andrew stressed. "But it would have been nice of you to share your suspicions with me. I might not have participated in anything with Wilding if I'd known."

"Wilding's a reasonable man," said Bob. "I've worked with him before."

"You have?" Andrew gaped at Bob. He hoped he didn't look as accusing as he felt.

Bob ate some more, then shrugged again. "A few years ago I worked up some projections he wanted on Syria's oil exports."

Andrew swore beneath his breath. The information Whitney had accumulated on John Wilding's activities in the Middle East—his plan to undermine Syria single-handedly—reverberated inside Andrew's skull. "Honest to God, Bob! Didn't it occur to you that if Wilding was acting within the limits of the law, he could have found out everything he wanted to know about Syria's future oil exports through legitimate C.I.A. channels? He didn't have to hire an academic to make projections for him. The C.I.A. has more than enough analysts on the payroll."

Bob appeared unperturbed. "I've already told you, I don't know whether the man's affiliated with the C.I.A. I didn't know then and I don't know now."

"I do know," Andrew muttered. "I went to the effort of investigating Wilding."

"Well." Bob dabbed his lips with his napkin, then leaned back in his chair and took a languorous sip of his lemonade. "All right, Andy. You went to the effort of investigating. I'm sure that if the C.I.A. actually told you Wilding was working for them, that's what they want you to believe."

"If he isn't working for the C.I.A., then it's even worse," Andrew argued. "The guy's a one-man army out to overthrow foreign governments."

Bob scoffed. "You've got a vivid imagination. Maybe you've been reading too many spy thrillers."

"I haven't read a spy thriller since high school," Andrew informed him dryly. "And my imagination isn't working overtime. Wilding himself told me he was working for the C.I.A."

"For what that's worth," Bob grunted.

"I didn't know whether to take him at face value, either," Andrew admitted. "So I dug deeper. I've got a contact in Congress, Bob. An aide to a senator on the Intelligence Committee. They found out that under the cover of the C.I.A., Wilding is trying to wreak economic havoc in El Salvador. That's what he tried to do with oil exports in

Syria, and now he's trying to do it again. It isn't right, Bob. You know it and I know it. This thing isn't right."

For the first time since the subject arose, Bob looked disturbed. He sat up straighter and eyed Andrew with piercing curiosity. "An aide to a senator?"

"I've been asked to testify before the committee," Andrew announced.

"Testify? About this?" Bob fidgeted with his straw wrapper, rolled it into a ball and tossed it into the ashtray. "What the hell is there to testify about?"

"Whether the C.I.A. condones this sort of surreptitious intervention in other countries."

"Now, Andrew," Bob said, abruptly conciliatory. "What's the good of testifying? Do you realize the damage you could do?"

"To whom?" Andrew shot back. "To me? Or to you?"

"To Amherst," Bob explained. "The school has a reputation to protect, for crying out loud. Do you think we're the only two college teachers who have ever done research for the C.I.A.? More faculty members at more universities than you can count are involved in this sort of activity. It isn't a sin. It does bring about negative publicity, however. The students get all riled up. The administration finds itself with egg on its face. And what for? Grandstanding about the situation doesn't help anybody."

Andrew contemplated Bob's argument. It probably wouldn't be such a terrible thing to rile up Amherst's student body, he mused. They were too complacent; a rowdy uprising would probably do his students a world of good.

On the other hand, would testifying before Senator Milford's committee change anything? Perhaps the C.I.A. would fire Wilding, but then what? Would they stop recruiting academic professionals for research? Would they stop disguising their activities behind proprietaries? Of course not.

As if he could sense that Andrew was wavering, Bob pressed his case. "Look, Andy. What exactly do you want? The same thing I want. To work at Amherst, a school where we're left alone, where we're given a great deal of freedom to teach the way we see fit, and the chance to work with gifted young minds. We sure as hell aren't here for the money—you don't need me to tell you that our salaries are barely adequate. We're here for the intellectual stimulation and the freedom. So what's to be gained by humiliating the college?

"If Wilding is as dangerous as you seem to think he is, then it's the C.I.A's responsibility to take care of him, not yours, not mine. And, for that matter, not the Senate's. I'll grant that I didn't inquire as deeply as you did about Wilding's intentions. But so what? I gave him solid data. I earned the stipend he gave me. And I've got a clear conscience. You should have a clear conscience, too." He paused to catch his breath, then smiled, evidently certain that he had persuaded Andrew to see things his way. For added effect, he queried, "If a man buys a screwdriver and uses it to break into someone's house, is it the hardware store's fault?"

Andrew pondered Bob's analogy. "Is it the gun store owner's fault that people buy pistols from him and use them to shoot other people? Is the brokerage house implicated when one of its executives is charged with insider trading? Albert Einstein had enough dignity to be horrified when the results of his genius helped others to build an atom bomb."

"I hardly think you and I are in the same class as Albert Einstein," Bob remarked.

Andrew shook his head. "You know what they used to say when I was in school? 'If you aren't part of the solution, you're part of the problem.'"

"They also used to say, 'Never trust anybody over thirty.' You're over thirty, Andrew. It's time to grow up."

Andrew didn't need Bob to remind him of his age. But perhaps he did need Bob to remind him of what was at stake. If Andrew testified before the Intelligence Committee, Bob wouldn't be the only one embarrassed. The news that two of Amherst's esteemed faculty members had, however guilelessly, collaborated with the C.I.A. would tarnish the college in the public eye. If that happened, Andrew's tenure decision would no longer rest with Bob McIntyre or with the economics department. The highest levels of the school's administration would want a troublemaker like Andrew out.

"Don't do anything precipitous," Bob counseled Andrew. "Take your time. Think things through. I'm sorry I put you in touch with Wilding. I thought you'd benefit from the association. I thought you'd be flattered."

"I was," Andrew acknowledged.

"Then think about it," Bob concluded before signaling the waitress for the check.

Andrew would indeed think about it. After parting ways with Bob and returning to his office cubicle, he slumped in his desk chair, removed his eyeglasses and rested his head in his hands. Bob had made some valid points. To spill the beans before a Senate committee might help to purge Andrew of his resentment and anger, but would it really change anything? Senator Milford already had enough information to demand that the C.I.A. get rid of Wilding and keep a tighter rein on its other operatives. It wasn't necessary for Andrew to beat his breast in public.

He'd done enough. He owed it to Amherst to keep quiet from here on in. Bob's final words implied everything Andrew needed to know about what would happen to him if he didn't keep quiet.

There was a limit to how many chances a person could take. Andrew couldn't risk everything—his career *and* his emotions—at the same time. Opening his heart to love again was dangerous enough. He didn't have to imperil himself professionally, too.

He wanted his job. He wanted peace in his life, and security and continuity. The days when a person could score points toward salvation by lambasting the C.I.A. were long gone.

It was definitely time to grow up.

Chapter Ten

Kimberly's rented Buick swallowed up the miles of the Massachusetts Turnpike. Andrew had told her that the drive from Boston would take her about two hours, but she didn't mind. The weather was mild, the trees lining the highway lush with foliage. The cartoonish Pilgrim's hat that appeared on all the road signs, symbolizing the turnpike, appealed to her.

She and Andrew had spoken three times in the week since she'd seen him in New York—once when she'd called to say hello from Chicago, once when he had called her after she had returned to Washington and then again the next day, when she had found out that she was going to be traveling to Massachusetts. "The senator's got to be in Boston Thursday to confer with the head of the American Society for the Prevention of Cruelty to Animals over some pending legislation," she had informed Andrew excitedly, "and I've talked him into letting me hitch a ride. Exactly how far is Amherst from Boston?"

"Too far for me to meet you there," Andrew had answered. "I've got classes to teach."

"I was thinking, maybe I could stick around at the A.S.P.C.A. long enough for the senator to think I've earned my keep, and then bolt and visit you. I'd love to see Amherst. I'd love to see you, too."

"I'd love to have you," he swore. "If you don't mind driving all that way, and sitting through my afternoon class..."

"I think I could stomach it," she joked. "Expect me around two-thirty."

Reviewing their conversation in her mind as she drove, she decided that Andrew had sounded delighted by her impulsive plan. She comprehended that he still wasn't ready to make a commitment to her. But as long as he wasn't backing off from her, she was hardly about to complain.

She had on a pair of crisp white slacks and a yellow knit jersey; a dress and a pair of shorts were packed in the overnight bag she had stowed on the back seat. She wished she could have made a long weekend of her visit and returned to Washington on Sunday. But a surprise party had been scheduled for the following night in honor of one of the senator's long-time aides, who was retiring. Kimberly couldn't miss it.

Maybe she could talk Andrew into returning to Washington with her. Falling in love with someone who lived so far away from her was inconvenient, to say the least.

The traffic jam caused by a jackknifed truck just outside Boston slowed her pace, as did a bottleneck in Worcester. It took her close to fifteen minutes to find a parking space near the college—Andrew had warned her that her car would be ticketed if she parked in one of the campus lots without an appropriate sticker. Yet even as she raced across the campus to his office, she had a chance to glimpse the lovely scenery. Amherst was as different from Columbia as the bucolic Berkshires were from gritty Harlem. The clean, well-maintained grounds, with their towering trees, manicured lawns and stately buildings, could definitely serve as the setting for an Andy Hardy movie.

She was panting slightly when she reached his office. "Am I late for your class?" she asked as he swung open the door in response to her knock.

He smiled, a warm, dimpled smile that would have made her breathless even if she hadn't just run half a mile at breakneck speed. "I wish all my students were as concerned about getting to my classes on time," he remarked, drawing her into his arms and kicking the door shut behind them.

His kiss was slow and sweet. She sighed happily, then pulled back to view him. "Why don't your eyeglasses ever steam up when we kiss?" she asked.

"Believe me, it's not because you aren't a very steamy lady," he complimented her in a hoarse voice. Then he cleared his throat and turned toward his desk. "However, since you mentioned it, we are running late. Did you bring any paper with you to take notes on? I intend to quiz you after class."

She laughed, watching as he slipped a folder into his briefcase. "I shall inscribe your every word on my heart," she promised melodramatically. As soon as he joined her at the door, she smoothed out the collar of his oxford shirt. "It won't do, Professor, to arrive at class looking like you've just checked out of an orgy."

"I'm always rumpled," Andrew told her. "It's the official professorial style. My students wouldn't take me seriously if my shirts were ironed." He clearly enjoyed the sensation of her cool, slender fingers against his neck, but after a moment he pulled her hands from him and opened the door. "We'd better get moving—the class meets in another building."

Again Kimberly found herself dashing across the campus. Andrew seemed to have forgotten that she was a good eight inches shorter than he. She had a difficult time keeping up with his brisk, loose-limbed gait.

The classroom he led her to was already nearly filled with attentive young men and women when Kimberly and Andrew entered. He nodded her toward a vacant desk at the rear of the room, and she felt the curious stares of his students following her as she took her seat. In answer to their unspoken questions he announced, "A friend of mine is visiting today. Kimberly Belmont is the head speech writer for Senator Howard Milford. If you'd like, I'll try to end a little early so you can ask her some questions."

Kimberly's jaw dropped in astonishment. How dare Andrew put her on the spot like that? Her chagrin gradually dissipated as she took note of the excitement his announcement had generated. Of course college students would love to question a senator's speech writer. In their place she'd be agog, too, just as eager as they were to learn what life was like in the corridors of government power.

She settled back in her seat, feeling her cheeks cool as the students directed their attention back to Andrew. He opened his folder of notes and proceeded to lecture on sugar price supports and their effect on the economies of foreign countries. She would never have imagined that so much could be said on such an esoteric subject. More than that, she never would have imagined that she would be so interested in it. Perhaps it was just Andrew's riveting presentation that made the subject seem fascinating. Losing track of time, she absorbed his talk, accumulating all sorts of intriguing information about the international value of empty calories.

When Andrew concluded his lecture, his eyes met hers and he grinned. Then he addressed his students. "All right, boys and girls. I think I'll turn the class over to Ms. Belmont now, and she can fill you in on the inside story of how sugar tariffs are enacted.''

Kimberly's cheeks colored slightly as en masse the students twisted in their seats to gawk at her. Andrew beckoned her to the front of the room, and forcing a modest smile, she inhaled and strolled forward to stand at the chipped wooden lectern. He moved out of her way, taking his place by the window and lounging against the sill.

''I'm afraid I'm more used to writing speeches than giving them,'' she began apologetically. ''And as far as sugar tariffs go, all I can tell you is that they're generally introduced into law by senators from the South, not by my boss.''

A hand shot up, and before she could acknowledge the student, he spoke. ''How did you get your job?'' he asked.

Kimberly ought to have expected such a question, not only because her job conveyed a certain glamour but because students of the eighties were allegedly obsessed with the mechanics of obtaining equally glamorous jobs once they finished their schooling. ''I began my career with a public relations firm in Washington,'' she related. ''A few years ago, Senator Milford received an information packet I had prepared on behalf of a client. The senator was impressed with what I'd put together, and he offered me a position as a speech writer on his staff.''

''What about connections?'' another student called out. ''Don't you have to know the right people if you want to wind up in a prestigious job like yours?''

Kimberly shook her head. ''There's something to be said for networking, but that's not the way I got my job.''

''She got it through talent and hard work,'' Andrew piped up on her behalf. ''I know all of you have read every bestselling book ever written on the subject of how to become president of the corporate world in five years or less, and those books always exhort you to use your connections and grease palms. But believe it or not, a lot of people wind up in high places through something as basic as ability.''

"Thank you, Andrew," she said, tossing him a smile. Obviously Andrew had finally come to terms with the fact that Kimberly was not a mental midget.

"Do you ever get a chance to influence legislation?" a young woman seated at the back of the room called out.

Kimberly contemplated the question. "I can't say that I have a direct influence," she admitted. "But sometimes I'm lucky enough to introduce new issues to the senator," she added, thinking about the Intelligence Committee hearings the senator planned to set up as a result of Andrew's experience with the C.I.A. "You've got to remember, our form of government doesn't follow straight lines and clear paths. It's hard to say specifically where one person's influence ends and the next person's begins."

"Forgive me for being forward," a fellow seated a few feet from her spoke up, "but you're an attractive woman. Isn't it true that a lot of congressmen set up little love nests for their pretty female employees?"

Kimberly fought valiantly against the surge of anger that threatened her in response to the boy's offensive question. Stifling the impulse to tell the leering young fellow that she would never forgive him, she said calmly, "I don't suppose you'd have asked that if I worked for a woman senator. Frankly, I don't believe it deserves an answer."

The class fell silent for a moment; apparently nobody wanted to risk raising her hackles again. Finally, a young woman broke the stillness. "First, Ms. Belmont, I'd like to thank you for putting creeps like him in his place." This comment brought cheers from the other women in the room, as well as a few of the men. "I'm a theater major," the student went on, "and I'm curious—as a speech writer, would it help to have experience in the theater?"

Kimberly laughed. "I reckon it wouldn't hurt. Most politicians are indeed actors, aren't they?"

Her audience broke into laughter again, evidence that the mood of the class was once again upbeat, and Andrew took that as his cue to relieve Kimberly. He crossed to the lectern and announced to the students, "We've run out of time for today, gang, so let Ms. Belmont off the hook. Remember to read the assigned articles on G.A.T.T. for next Tuesday. They're on reserve at the library." With that he dropped his folder into his briefcase, a sign that the class was dismissed.

"Why did you do that to me?" Kimberly muttered beneath her breath once the last few students had departed from the room.

"Do what?" Andrew asked ingenuously.

"Put me on display that way."

"I knew the kids would be interested in what you do," he justified himself.

"Yes, but you could have given me some warning," she reproached him. "You didn't have to spring it on me by surprise."

Andrew took his time clasping his briefcase shut. Then he turned fully to her. "You're right, Kim. I could have warned you," he granted. "But . . . I guess I was curious to see how well you would think on your feet."

"Damn it, Andrew!" She suffered another surge of anger, not the standard annoyance she had felt earlier at his student's patently sexist insinuation, but a deep, personal anger at the realization that Andrew had been testing her. "I don't have to prove anything to you. It ought to be obvious by now that if I couldn't think on my feet I wouldn't be where I was today."

"I know," he murmured contritely. "You're right, Kim. I just . . ." He cupped his hands about her upper arms and gave her a crooked smile. "I'm still a bit amazed by you. I'm still coming to terms with the fact that I was very mistaken about you fifteen years ago. It's such a kick for me to see how spectacular you can be in situations like this." He kissed her forehead tenderly. "I'm sorry."

As irked as she was, his candor touched her. She slung her arms around his waist and gave him a hug. "It's about time you started getting used to who I am," she complained.

"I know, Kim." He slid his hands to the nape of her neck, and his lips grazed her hair. "I love you."

Her heart froze in her chest for a moment, and the air seemed to grow still around her. Had he actually said what she thought? Had he really spoken those three magic words? She tried to fight off her disbelief, tried to bring her crazed nerves under control. "What?" she mumbled into his chest.

"You heard me."

"You mean, you love me because I held my own at that impromptu news conference you just threw for me?" she pressed him.

He drew back to gaze at her. "I mean that I love you because you can hold your own with me. When I'm a jerk you call me on it. You're honest, and true to yourself." He touched his lips to hers. "That's why." He kissed her lips once more, then grinned. "At the risk of igniting your wrath again, I kind of like that kid's idea about love nests. If you're interested, I've got a tiny apartment about a mile from here in dire need of some feathering."

"Andrew Collins, you're very fresh," she scolded him, but she was too thrilled to mean it.

He slipped his hand around hers and escorted her from the room. "I made dinner reservations for seven o'clock. That gives us plenty of time."

As if dinner mattered, Kimberly mused silently. The last time she'd been with Andrew, they'd made do without a fancy meal at a restaurant. And this time would be better. This time Andrew was finally ready to acknowledge that he loved her.

As they left the building, he informed her that he had left his car home and walked to campus that morning, which meant that they could drive to his house together. Trying to remember where she had parked her car, she made a wrong turn at the town green, then backtracked and located the rented Buick on the next block. A strange blend of anxiety and euphoria rendered her too jittery to drive, and she handed Andrew the keys and asked that he drive them home.

The broad brick colonial he took her to was set back from the street and surrounded by a lush, recently mowed lawn, with a blossoming apple tree and a thriving red maple standing on either side of the front walk. Andrew steered up a paved driveway that led to a small lot at the rear of the house. He lifted Kimberly's suitcase from the back seat, took her hand again and ushered her around the building to the front door. Not bothering to check his mailbox, he escorted her inside.

He had already mentioned that his apartment was small, and he hadn't exaggerated. She didn't mind its size, though. She liked Andrew's neatness, the array of books lining every inch of shelf space, the orderliness of his desk and the homely warmth of his other furnishings. Andrew was a man who didn't exert himself to make his living quarters decorator perfect, and Kimberly considered that a refreshing change from the rigidly impeccable taste of the people she had grown up with, people who were far too compulsive about appearances.

She followed Andrew down a short hall, which contained a closet and a bathroom, and into his bedroom. It, too, was clean and orderly, the furniture not distinctive but sturdy and serviceable. The open window admitted a cool breeze into the room, causing the curtains to flutter.

"I love you, too," Kimberly whispered, curling her arms around him and holding him close.

"I know. You've already told me."

"Does it bother you to hear it more than once?"

"Not from you," Andrew assured her. "Please feel free to say it as often as you wish."

If she had wanted to say it again, she wouldn't have been able to. Andrew's penetrating kiss swamped her, rendering her certain that she would be hard-pressed to utter a coherent sentence, let alone the most important sentence in the world. So she told him without words that she loved him, gripping his broad back and parrying the daring lunges of his tongue. By the time he broke from her, she doubted that he needed any further proof, verbal or otherwise, of her love for him.

It took them little time to undress and fall together onto the bed. Andrew's mouth conquered hers with another devastating kiss. Then he let his head drop to the pillow to catch his breath, as his fingers spun lazily through her hair. The pause gave her an opportunity to recover, to savor all over again what he had told her. "I don't mind hearing it more than once, either," she prompted him.

He grinned. "I love you," he obeyed. Then his smile grew wistful. "I'm sure you've noticed by now, Kim, but I'm not a very romantic person."

"What's your idea of a romantic person?" she asked, raising herself up on her elbow and peering down at him.

The movement of the drapes created faint, dancing shadows across the dynamic features of his face—his brow and jaw, his sharp nose, his surprisingly sensuous mouth, his eyes even clearer and more penetrating without his eyeglasses than with them. He shrugged. "Someone who doesn't have difficulty saying 'I love you,'" he replied. "Someone who sends you long-stemmed roses and gives you perfume on your birthday—"

"Flowers and perfume are meaningless," she assured him. "I was married to one of those romantic types, Andrew, and I don't recommend it."

"What's your idea of a romantic person, then?"

She kissed his jutting chin, then settled on the mattress beside him. "A man who waits until he's absolutely sure before he uses the word 'love.' A man wise enough to make certain he knows his own mind before he shoots off his mouth."

Andrew mulled over her definition, and his smile faded. "There can be such a thing as too much wisdom," he muttered, a subtle self-criticism. "The last time I saw you, Kim... I wanted to tell you how I felt. But then, after I left..." He faltered, focusing on a memory. "I felt so guilty."

"Guilty?" she exclaimed, startled by his admission. "Why?" At his prolonged silence, she shored up her courage and asked, "Because of your wife?"

"Partly."

Kimberly wasn't terribly surprised by that. Given how much he had loved his wife, it must have been hard for him to admit that he could find himself in love with another woman. Irrational though it was, he might have felt disloyal to his wife, his first love. "I wish you had told me," she murmured. "We should talk about these things, Andrew. We shouldn't keep them from each other."

"I wasn't deliberately keeping anything from you, Kim," he swore. "It wasn't thoughts of Marjorie that had me so confused. It was more..." He reflected, collecting his thoughts, and then sighed. "It was more that I felt as if I had no right to want you as much as I do."

She recalled the astonishment she had experienced every other time she and Andrew had talked this freely with each other. By now, especially since he had told her he loved her, she ought to have grown accustomed to his willingness to open up to her. Yet his statement still came as a revelation. "Love has nothing to do with rights, Andrew."

"Now that's a romantic thought," he teased her. Then he grew solemn again. "I do want you, Kim. Very much. And I don't want to lose you."

"You won't," she swore before bending to kiss him.

He pulled her onto himself, his hands skimming down her back and his legs sandwiching hers. His arousal was as immediate as hers, as intense and consuming. She rocked her body against his, fully aware of the blissful torment she was causing him with her motions. His helpless moan as her teeth nipped his lower lip only fed her desire even more.

His fingers rounded her bottom to stroke her thighs. They parted and he arched up into her. His forceful thrusts sent shock waves through her flesh, inundating her with glorious sensations, rapidly driving her and him both to their moment of consummate satisfaction.

Whenever they had made love in the past, Andrew had always proceeded much more slowly, with great tenderness and patience. But this time, such preliminaries had been all but superfluous. This time, he had given Kimberly more than his lovemaking; he had given her his love. The single word, spoken in his rumbling baritone, was like an aphrodisiac. She didn't need anything else.

"You're incredible," he groaned, refusing to let her slide from him as his body softened beneath her. His arms bound her to him, holding her comfortably in place. "The most incredible woman in the world."

"Why, you romantic old fool," she joked before nuzzling the warm crook of his neck.

"I'm serious," he insisted. "You do things to me . . ."

"Andrew." She lifted her face from his shoulder and met his shimmering gaze. "I think—I think you ought to know something about me."

Her solemn expression seemed to unnerve him. He gave her an inquisitive scrutiny, then sank deeper into the pillow and smiled. "Forget about suing the big drug company," he declared. "Maybe it's a blessing in disguise."

There was nothing facetious in his tone. Nor was there a hint of dismay as he gave voice to his erroneous deduction that Kimberly was pregnant. One more sign that he loved her, she thought with a contented sigh. "No, it's nothing like that," she reassured him, gingerly pushing a dark lock of hair back from his brow. "It's—I'm kind of embarrassed to admit it, Andrew, but—well, I'm not very experienced."

"Experienced at what?"

"At *this*, you fool," she said, punching his shoulder playfully. "At sex."

He pondered her confession, then grinned wickedly. "Well, sweetheart, you've sure got good instincts."

She leaned back to punch him again, but he trapped her wrist in his strong fingers and pulled her down to him again. "Don't make fun of me, Andrew," she said. "I thought you ought to know this about me. I was a virgin when I got married."

"The last of a dying breed," he quipped.

"Andrew!" She laughed in spite of herself. "I just told you something very important about myself."

"You obviously think it's more important than I do," he countered, embracing her more snugly. "You were with your husband for, what, fourteen years? I'd hardly call that inexperience."

"It was," she insisted. Then she reconsidered. "I take back what I said. It isn't sex I'm inexperienced in. It's making love. You're the one who does incredible things, Andrew.''

''I've got good instincts,'' he remarked.

''Andrew. I'm trying to compliment you, and—''

''And I'm very, very complimented,'' he whispered, at last accepting her words as she intended them. ''The truth is, Kim, it's all a matter of inspiration. And you, lovely woman, are inspiring beyond description.'' His lips met hers, and his body, decisively putting an end to the conversation.

''How was Boston?'' he asked.

They were seated at a table in the Lord Jeffrey Amherst, a charming inn not far from the campus. The dining room's decor was colonial, with dark, heavy furnishings, thick rugs, and waiters garbed in costumes that suggested the historical period of the town's founding. Kimberly had donned her dress for their dinner out, and Andrew was wearing a tie and a tailored jacket. He looked dashingly handsome, not the least bit rumpled.

She sipped her wine and shrugged. ''I can't say that I saw much of the city,'' she allowed. ''We arrived at around nine-thirty, went straight to the A.S.P.C.A. headquarters, took a tour of the facilities and talked shop.''

''What kind of shop?'' Andrew inquired. ''Or is that privileged information?''

''It has to do with a bill regulating research using animals,'' she told him.

Andrew scowled, obviously disgruntled. ''Don't tell me Milford is going to capitulate to those idiots.''

''What idiots?''

''The idiots who want to stop all medical research that requires testing on live animals.'' He shook his head scornfully. ''Don't these people realize that without animal tests, doctors are never going to be able to conquer certain diseases?"

Like cancer, Kimberly mutely supplied. Given that Andrew had lost his wife to cancer, it was no surprise that he supported all attempts to discover a cure for the disease. A great deal of medical research using animals was performed in pursuit of that elusive cure. "The senator doesn't want to put a stop to all animal tests," she explained. "However, there are a few research centers performing horrible, pointless tests and treating their animals inhumanely. If those researchers aren't controlled, Congress won't have to outlaw animal tests—the public outcry will put a stop to the research. The purpose of the new regulations is to end the inhumane testing in order to restore public confidence in the field of animal testing as a whole."

Mollified, Andrew subsided in his chair. A waiter brought them their salads and a basket of warm popovers. Andrew passed the basket to Kimberly, then helped himself to one of the popovers. He broke it open, releasing a puff of steam, and spread some butter onto its eggy crust. "I guess I shouldn't have used the word 'idiots,'" he conceded. "But I have no patience for people who want to curtail research efforts. I'm a professor, after all. Research is what I do. You can't learn anything by sitting back and waiting for knowledge to drop into your lap. It just doesn't work that way."

"I know that," Kimberly agreed. "On the other hand, if you were doing your research on—on El Salvador, for instance, and a source didn't want to tell you what he knew, you wouldn't resort to torturing him, would you? There's a right way and a wrong way to gather information."

Andrew fell silent. He bit into his popover, swallowed, reached for his goblet and took a long drink of wine. His eyes shifted from Kimberly to focus on the enormous brick fireplace built into the wall across the dining room from their table.

Kimberly recognized that Andrew was applying what she'd said about animal testing to his entanglement with John Wilding and L.A.R.C. She'd deliberately referred to El Salvador in the hope that he'd make that connection. What John Wilding had done, in the name of research, was to try to gather information the wrong way, by misrepresenting himself to Andrew. What the agent was planning to do with that information was far worse than the way he'd obtained the information, of course. But surely, after having been misled by Wilding, Andrew had to acknowledge that research wasn't always performed in the purest and most noble fashion.

She and Andrew hadn't discussed the problem of his unintentional involvement with the C.I.A. since they'd seen each other in New York. She had avoided broaching the subject during their telephone conversations, figuring that he needed the freedom to reach a decision, without any interference from her, about testifying before the senator's committee. There was no reason for her to try to pressure him into testifying; if he gave the idea the careful consideration he gave to most things, he would have no choice but to conclude that testifying was the right thing to do.

Nine days had passed since he had met the senator in New York. Andrew had had enough time to think about the issue. And since it was hanging between him and Kimberly now, she decided to question him about his plans. "Have you made up your mind whether to honor the senator's request that you appear before the Intelligence Committee?"

Andrew meditated for a moment, running his fingers along the rim of his goblet. "Exactly what does he expect to accomplish by holding a hearing?"

"It won't be a hearing," Kimberly clarified. "It will be a closed session. And what he hopes to accomplish is to find out exactly what Wilding was up to, whether there are other operatives like him engaged in efforts to undermine foreign governments and whether the C.I.A. officially condones such activities."

Andrew digested her answer. "Does Milford really need me there to accomplish that?"

"You're a first-hand witness, Andrew. Nobody else has had the courage to come forward and speak out against Wilding. Of course he needs you."

"Kimberly." Andrew paused, then took a bracing gulp of wine. "If I thought he couldn't do it without me, I would testify. But... Look. I'm an economist. I've done a cost-benefit analysis on the situation, and I can't help but think that the cost of my testifying is far greater than the benefit Milford would accrue from it."

"It isn't just for the senator's benefit," Kimberly argued. "It's for the benefit of the country. Ideally, it's for the benefit of the C.I.A., too. They're just like the medical researchers, Andrew. A few bad apples can destroy their public support and prevent them from doing the work they've got to do. If the Intelligence Committee can root out the troublemakers, everyone will benefit."

Andrew whispered an oath. He seemed exasperated, although Kimberly couldn't guess why. "All right," he muttered. "I had the courage to come forward and speak out. I gave your boss everything I had on Wilding. Everything. Even the data I was going to use for my articles. He can share them with his damned committee if that's what he wants. But he doesn't need me there in person."

"If he didn't need you there, he wouldn't have asked you to do it," Kimberly pointed out, refusing to allow Andrew's foul temper to discourage her. "When you decided to share your data with the senator, you made a commitment to him. Now you've got to follow through on it." Afraid that she was coming across as too preachy, she softened her tone before adding, "He understands that it's a hardship for you to appear, but—"

"A hardship?" Andrew snorted. "It's my job, Kim. Not his. *Mine.*"

"Andrew," she cajoled, "I really think you're blowing things out of proportion when you say you think your job is at risk because of this."

His frown intensified. "If that's what you think, then you're wrong. I've already discussed the matter with Bob McIntyre."

"Who?"

"Bob McIntyre. My alleged mentor. The generous full professor who did me a whopping big favor by putting me in touch with Wilding in the first place."

"You did? You spoke with him?" Despite Andrew's obvious anger, she considered his having confronted his mentor a hopeful sign. Surely facing the man who had such a large say in Andrew's professional future must have been more difficult than facing a session of a Senate committee would be. If Andrew had survived that, he could survive anything. "What happened?" she questioned him.

The waiter arrived with their entrées, and Andrew waited until he and Kimberly were alone again before replying. "He let me know that if I testified, it would count in a big way against me because it would reflect badly on the college."

"He's crazy," Kimberly asserted. "I think it would reflect much more badly on the college if you *didn't* testify."

"Not that you're particularly impartial about whether I testify," Andrew grumbled. "If I do, it will make your boss look good, and it's your job to make him look good. But that's beside the point." He cut off her protest before it could take shape. "If I testify, people are going to learn that Amherst College faculty members do research for the C.I.A. That's not the sort of news university administrations want to publicize. It taints their image as objective bastions of truth with a capital *T*. If I testify about L.A.R.C., it's going to hurt Amherst's image."

"Poor, poor Amherst," Kimberly cooed sarcastically. "We don't want to hurt its pretty little image now, do we."

"I don't care about Amherst's image. I care about my job," Andrew claimed. "I've worked too hard to get this far. It's difficult enough completing a Ph.D. under the best of circumstances, but I earned mine under the worst of circumstances. It's difficult enough getting any teaching job at all, but I busted my butt, and I managed to land an excellent teaching job."

"Sure, it's an excellent teaching job," she agreed. "But what are you committed to, your job or the truth? I thought professors were dedicated to seeking the truth."

"I sought the truth," Andrew maintained. "And I found it and I passed it along to your boss. But I'm not going to be forced out of my job, Kim. My work is all I have."

"You have me," she reminded him in a low voice.

He fell back in his seat and angled his head, appraising her in a new light. A cryptic smile crossed his lips. "Am I supposed to sacrifice my job to make your boss look good simply because I love you?" he posed. "That sounds like blackmail to me."

"It isn't just my boss," she shot back, stung by his accusation. "It's a matter of principle, Andrew. If you aren't willing to put your job on the line, then you're a coward."

"Don't hand me that crap," he retorted caustically. "If anyone should understand what it means to be committed to one's work it's you. You told me yourself that one of the reasons your marriage broke up was that you didn't want to give up your job.''

That was true enough. But at that time her job was all she'd had. Her marriage had been loveless by then. Her career had been her entire life.

And teaching was Andrew's entire life. Not Kimberly, not the love he had so recently admitted to. Only teaching.

Her soul grew brittle inside her, then cracked, then splintered into a million pieces. Perhaps Andrew loved her, but not enough. Not as much as she loved him. Not enough to believe that he needed nothing else.

She gazed forlornly at the plate in front of her, the thick pink slab of roast beef, the baby peas, stuffed potato and parsley garnish. ''I'm not hungry,'' she whispered.

Andrew groped for her hand and covered it with his. ''I'm sorry if you're disappointed, Kim, but—''

''Disappointed?'' Her head jerked up and she stared at him. She couldn't very well tell him that he had just shattered her heart. She had too much pride to say that. ''Yes, I'm disappointed,'' she conceded bitterly. ''I thought you had more guts than you've just shown me.''

He appeared wounded, but he refrained from responding until he had composed himself. ''I'm not a kid anymore,'' he said quietly. ''It's easy enough to be gutsy when you're a kid. It's easy enough to stick your neck out when you're young, when you believe you're invincible. But I'm not that young. I want to remain in one piece.''

''That's your choice,'' she said coolly. ''Let's go.''

Another dinner uneaten, Kimberly mused miserably as Andrew settled the bill. They left the restaurant wrapped in a silence so icy that even the balmy, starlit night couldn't thaw it. When Andrew unlocked the passenger door of his Volvo for her, she slumped on the seat and stared straight ahead, stubbornly refusing to look at him. He closed the door behind her, stalked around the car to the driver's side and climbed in. He inserted the key in the ignition, then hesitated and turned to her. "How bad is this thing, Kim?" he asked, slipping his hand beneath her chin and urging her around to face him. "Do you hate me?"

"No," she said with a sigh. "I don't hate you, Andrew. I just—" She felt tears accumulating along the fringe of her lashes and batted her eyes. She didn't hate Andrew, but she wasn't sure she loved him, either. When she had fallen in love with him, she had done so with the conviction that he was the strongest, bravest man she had ever known. He had been strong enough to overcome a crushing grief, strong enough to fight for what he had, strong enough to devote his life to seeking the truth and righting wrongs. Strong enough to return her love.

He was only human, however. His strength had limits. She wished those limits had revealed themselves in some other way, in some other context. But they hadn't. He had fallen short of her ideals exactly where she had expected him to be strongest. In his principles. In his morality. He was opting for safety over righteousness, and she questioned whether her feelings for him could recover from the shock.

Aware that he was waiting for her to speak, she fought against the waver in her voice and said, "I think I ought to go back to Washington tonight." She clung to the logistics, afraid to verbalize her despair. "I can drive back to Boston and catch the next shuttle flight down. I think they run pretty late into the night."

Andrew assessed her decision and exhaled. His hand fell from her face and he turned resolutely toward the steering wheel. His lips set in a grim line, he drove through downtown Amherst to his home.

Neither of them spoke as she packed her overnight bag. Andrew merely watched her from the doorway as she moved about his bedroom, gathering the slacks and shirt she'd worn for her drive to Amherst and tossing them into the small suitcase, rummaging through her purse for her car keys. His eyes were partially obscured by his eyeglasses, but his lips remained clamped shut, as if to keep his thoughts from slipping out.

At last she was ready to go. When she approached him, he caught her in his arms. "I do love you, Kim," he murmured.

Standing so close to him, she could see the sadness glimmering in his honey-brown eyes. She willfully averted her gaze. It hurt too much to look at him directly.

"You're only saying that to get me to stay," she charged.

He held her for a split second longer, then let his hands fall to his sides. "There's no way I can get you to stay if you want to go," he said in resignation. He stepped out of her path. "Goodbye, Kim."

"Goodbye," she mouthed, too disconsolate to speak the words aloud.

Later, when she was able to sort out her thoughts and regain control over her nerves, she would be able to convince herself that she was doing the right thing by leaving. Later—much later—when she had the chance to reflect objectively on what had happened, she would console herself with the fact that she couldn't possibly love a man who wasn't as committed to love and honor as she herself was, a man who had made the choice Andrew had.

And then, perhaps, she would be able to live with her own choice—leaving him.

Chapter Eleven

"Weddings depress me," said Troy.

Andrew carried two fresh bottles of beer outside to the small front porch. He handed one to Troy, then dropped onto the concrete step beside him and stared out at the silver semicircle of moon hanging just above the horizon in the sky. The night air held a slight chill, and when Andrew had gone into his apartment for the beers, he'd pulled on a plaid wool jacket over his cotton shirt. Troy was wearing a denim dungaree jacket with the collar turned up and heavy leather boots. But Andrew didn't suggest that they head indoors to warm up. He wanted to sit outside on the porch with Troy for a while longer, to gaze across the trimmed front lawn and listen to the shrill song of the crickets.

The rasp of a match scraping against flint caused him to turn to his friend. He watched as Troy lit a cigarette, shook the match dead and dropped it into the empty beer bottle at his feet. "You smoke too much," Andrew remarked.

"What else is new?" Troy dragged on his cigarette, exhaled, then sighed. "Don't get me wrong," he said, reverting to his initial comment. "I'm not saying the thought of Laura and Seth getting married is depressing. I like them both. I wish them the best. I'm sure their wedding is going to be a gas, and I'm honored that they want me to do the photos for them. But most of the weddings I go to are real bummers."

"In what way?" Andrew asked.

Troy shoved a shock of wavy black hair back from his brow, tipped the bottle Andrew had given him against his mouth and swallowed a long draught of beer. Then he lowered the bottle and shrugged. "Any time I've got to wear my tuxedo it's a bummer," he clarified. "Did you know I own a tuxedo? Me, Troy Bennett, the owner of a tux. With three—count 'em, three—ruffled white dress shirts to match."

"It's a requirement of your job to own a tux," Andrew pointed out rationally.

"Don't remind me," Troy snorted. "At least I don't have to wear the tux for Laura and Seth. They'd probably kick me off the premises if I did."

Andrew chuckled in agreement.

"But my tux isn't the depressing part. It's the groom's tux. His tux and the bride's fancy gown and the whole scene. The bride and the groom always come into my studio sometime before the wedding to meet me and write up an order. They look so normal then, you know? They're usually wearing jeans, or maybe some nice clothes from work if they come in on their lunch hour. But they look like real people. Then I arrive at the church or the hall where they're having the wedding, and the bride and groom look so—so artificial. The bride can't move in her dress, and she's got makeup slathered all over her face, and her hair is all done up and sprayed to the consistency of plaster of paris. And the groom is in his tux, looking queasy, maybe a little hung over from his bachelor party. They don't look anything like the human beings I met earlier at the studio. It's the most important day of their lives, and they look like aliens from another planet."

"It's called rituals, Troy," Andrew noted. "A wedding is a ritual, and certain customs must be observed."

"Right." Troy laughed sardonically. "One ritual is the dehumanization of the bride and groom. Another is the champagne toast—they always serve that sweet, cloying champagne that tastes like soda pop—and another is the cutting of the cake, during which I'm supposed to take pictures while man and wife smear each other's faces with whipped-cream frosting. And then there's the bride dancing with her father-in-law and the groom dancing with his mother-in-law—the groom is probably never going to have a civil conversation with his mother-in-law for the rest of his life, but there they are, waltzing around the dance floor while the band plays 'Sunrise, Sunset' from *Fiddler on the Roof*. They're supposed to look like they're enjoying themselves, and I'm supposed to immortalize this precious moment on film." He laughed again and shook his head.

"You're a misanthrope," Andrew chided him. "The only reason you don't like photographing weddings is that you'd rather be photographing fishermen in Nova Scotia." He sipped his beer, savoring its cold, sour foam on his tongue. "How come you didn't find a job in journalism when you went to Montreal? You would have liked that much better."

"I'm sure I would have," Troy concurred. "I applied for work at a few newspapers, but they were sensitive about hiring expatriates from the States, taking valuable jobs away from Canadians. Those of us who were able to make a go of it up there did it by starting our own businesses." He smoked for a while, then angled his head toward Andrew. "How about you? Do weddings depress you?"

"Not as a rule," Andrew replied. "Certainly not when the featured players are people I care a lot for, like Laura and Seth."

"It doesn't bother you, going to weddings? I mean, given what happened to your marriage and all...."

Andrew watched the glowing orange coal of Troy's cigarette as it arced through the darkness. He offered a bittersweet smile. "You would have hated my wedding, Troy. It was as typical as any. A service at church, then dinner at a banquet hall. I even wore a tux."

"Rented, I bet," Troy guessed. "At least you didn't have to go out and buy three ruffled shirts." He dropped his cigarette carefully into the neck of his empty bottle, and it emitted a tiny hiss as the hot ashes hit the residue of beer at the bottom. "Do you think Seth'll be wearing a tux?"

"Not if his life depended on it," Andrew answered. "He'll probably be wearing something outrageous."

"Maybe they'll have a granola wedding cake," Troy commented. "I admit I'm looking forward to the affair. It'll be good to see everybody again, even if it's for something as depressing as a wedding."

Andrew's expression became pinched and he turned away. It would be good seeing Seth and Laura and Julianne, just as it was good seeing Troy now. He was glad he had been able to talk Troy into coming to Massachusetts the night preceding the wedding so they could visit a bit beforehand and then drive down to Pennsylvania together for the ceremony.

However, it wouldn't be good seeing Kimberly. Andrew imagined that having to see her tomorrow at the wedding would be something akin to torture.

"What?" Troy probed, easily discerning his friend's altered mood.

"Nothing," Andrew fibbed.

Troy assessed him for a moment. "I'm sorry I made you dredge up memories of your wedding. You should have just told me to shut up."

"It has nothing to do with that," Andrew claimed, inadvertently admitting that there was an "it," a specific something that was troubling him.

"What does it have to do with?" Troy pressed him.

Andrew took another drink of his beer. He almost wished he smoked; if ever he could use a rush of nicotine, it was now. "Kim," he finally admitted, trying not to choke when he gave voice to her name.

"Kim Belmont?" Troy scowled in bewilderment. "The cheerleader? What about her?"

"She isn't a cheerleader," Andrew retorted, then took a deep breath and focused on the luminous half-moon until his temper subsided.

If he had learned anything in the past few weeks, it was that Kimberly was smarter, deeper and much more complicated than the word "cheerleader" connoted. She *was* a cheerleader—not a vacuous little girl waving pom-poms and doing splits in midair, but someone who exerted herself to inspire others to do their best, to do what was best for them. Her cheers didn't rhyme, they lacked tune and tempo, but she was a cheerleader nonetheless.

Except that Andrew had turned a deaf ear to her exuberant cheers. Except that he had chosen sanity over valor. He had let her down, disappointed her—and he had lost her. And it hurt like the devil.

In the more than two weeks since he had last seen her, he had frequently found himself questioning his decision not to appear before the Intelligence Committee. He still wasn't sure whether Kimberly had only been pretending to love him in order to get him to testify, thereby promoting her boss's career. But Andrew had met Senator Milford, and he didn't think the man was that conniving. In Andrew's heart, he didn't believe that Kimberly could be that conniving, either.

If he had believed that, he wouldn't feel so disconsolate about losing her.

Losing Marjorie had also hurt him terribly, but that loss had been an act of fate, beyond his control. Losing Kimberly had been an act of will. He had to take full responsibility for it. The knowledge that he had saved his career in the process offered meager solace.

"All right," Troy said, apparently growing impatient with Andrew's extended silence. "She's not a cheerleader. Why are you so broken up about her?"

Andrew opened his mouth to protest that he wasn't broken up, then shut it again. Who was he kidding? He was devastated about what had happened between Kimberly and him. And he wasn't going to win points for stoicism. Denying the truth didn't automatically make it untrue.

"It's a long story," he began hesitantly.

"I've got time."

Andrew drained his bottle and set it between his feet on the bottom step. "I love her," he revealed.

"Kimberly?" Troy exclaimed. "Are we talking about the same person? Southern belle Belmont?"

"That's the one," Andrew confirmed glumly.

"How the hell did you fall in love with her? I'll grant you, Andrew, she's a knockout. But you and she detested each other in college."

"We've—we've gotten to know each other since then," Andrew explained. He gave Troy a sketchy description of his involvement with the C.I.A., his decision to turn to Kimberly for help, the time they'd spent together in Washington and the relationship that had blossomed between them and flourished—until he'd stupidly spoiled everything. "It took me so long to come to terms with the fact that I loved her," he groaned. "I swore to myself, after Marjorie died, that I'd never let myself go through this sort of thing again,

I'd never lose a woman I loved that much.'' He cursed softly.

"Andrew, if she loves you, too, then she'll want to make up with you. She's probably hurting as much as you are," Troy observed with supreme sensibility.

Andrew shook his head dubiously. "She loved me when she thought I was some sort of spiritually chaste knight," he argued. "Once she realized that I wasn't as full of noble principles as she expected me to be, she fell out of love with me. If she's hurt, it's only because I let her down."

"That's life," Troy maintained. "People let each other down sometimes."

"Tell me about it," Andrew muttered. He watched as Troy groped in the breast pocket of his jacket for his cigarettes and matches. "Is it different in Canada? Are the women easier to deal with up there?"

Troy chuckled. "Womanhood is a biological condition, not a nationalistic one." His grin contained an undefined sadness. "You aren't the only man who's loved and lost, Andrew. It happens to the best of us."

"Yeah, but I'm two for two," Andrew grumbled. "And this time I should have known better. I should have done things differently. What happened was my own fault."

"So what do you want, a medal? We do what we have to do," Troy said pointedly. "Sometimes the decision hurts, but you weigh your choices and do the best you can, and you hope you haven't blown it. And if, years later, you realize that you have..." He lit his cigarette and shook the match slowly to extinguish it. "If you realize that you did blow it, then you just have to learn to live with your mistake. There's no going back, Andrew. You learn to live with it."

Andrew surmised that Troy was speaking from personal experience. But he didn't want to hear about Troy's heartbreak any more than he wanted to relive his own. Tomorrow they would be attending a wedding. It would be in poor taste, to say the least, if they arrived at Laura's mother's house morose and bitter, not ready to celebrate Laura and Seth's love, but, eager instead, to consign all love affairs to the trash heap.

Andrew turned to gaze at the moon again, wondering whether Kimberly was as anxious about having to see him as he was about having to see her, wondering whether, as Troy had suggested, she loved him enough to want to make up with him. Wondering whether she loved him enough to accept him for what he was, not for what she desired him to be.

"We've got a long drive ahead of us," Troy remarked, extinguishing his cigarette in the empty beer bottle. "And I've got a sleeping bag to unroll on top of that couch of yours. What do you say we hit the hay?"

"Sure."

They collected their bottles, entered the house and shut the door behind them.

"I'VE KNOWN LAURA since she was a little girl, and I join with you, her family and friends, in deriving pleasure from this very special occasion, this day of immeasurable happiness for her and Seth," said the short, balding man who stood before Laura and Seth at one end of the rolling backyard. Julianne had already informed Andrew that the municipal judge performing the wedding ceremony had gone to high school with Laura's father and had remained a friend of the family even after Laura's father had passed away. Andrew liked that. He thought it appropriate that when people got married, the person who joined them as husband and wife was someone with a strong personal connection to the couple.

He liked the judge, and the spacious backyard of Arlene Brodie's suburban brick house, with its hedge of redolent lilacs and its circular tulip and daffodil beds carved into the carpet of grass. He liked Arlene Brodie, a matronly woman in her early sixties with a stylish mane of dark curls and a face as open and smiling as her daughter's. She was seated in the front row of folding chairs, beaming at Laura and Seth. Laura's daughter, Rita, wore a hot-pink minidress, and she, too, smiled broadly while she stood proudly behind her mother as the judge continued his affectionate speech.

The widest smiles belonged to Laura and Seth themselves. Laura looked utterly wonderful in a lacy white peasant dress that fell to midcalf, a pair of white sandals and a laurel of daisies crowning her thick, loose hair. She held a bouquet bursting with daisies, ivy and baby's breath. True to form, Seth wore nothing as typical as a tuxedo. He had on his white linen suit, a navy blue shirt, a bright red bowtie and his red high-top sneakers. A crimson carnation adorned his lapel.

Andrew wished he could concentrate fully on the wedding ceremony. But he was painfully distracted by the petite blond woman who sat on the chair next to his, wearing a silk dress the same baby-blue color as her eyes and a delicate perfume that wafted into his nostrils every time he inhaled. Julianne sat on Kimberly's other side, and Troy was kneeling in front of the assembly, taking pictures.

Andrew and Troy had arrived at the Brodie house early, since Troy had wanted to take some prenuptial photos. "None of the standard wooden-Indian poses, please," he ordered Seth and Laura, nudging them toward the lilacs and snapping the shutter of his camera before they could settle into position in front of the backdrop of lavender blossoms. "Come on, Seth, pick her up and throw her around. Let's capture the true you on film."

"If he throws me around, I'll kick him," Laura warned before succumbing to laughter.

"Sounds like a match made in heaven. I don't suppose it occurred to you, Seth, that the groom is supposed to visit a barber before his big day."

"If I'd gone to a barber," Seth complained, raking his shaggy dirty-blond hair out of his eyes, "Laura would have called the whole thing off. She intends to turn me into a hippie."

"And you intend to turn me into a Hollywood wife," she countered, disheveling his hair in time for Troy to snap the photo. "Don't forget to take some pictures of Rita, too. And my mother. Okay?"

"Hostess!" Troy obliged, jogging across the lawn to commandeer Arlene Brodie, who was conferring with the hired bartender as he set up his wares on a portable table. "I've got a negative here that has 'Mrs. Brodie' written all over it."

Laura's mother laughed. "If it's got writing on it, Troy, it's going to make a lousy picture."

"The real question, Mrs. Brodie," Troy said as he snapped a candid shot of her beside the bartender, "is, if I take enough pictures of you standing here, will people think you're a lush years from now when they're flipping through the pages of the wedding album?"

Arlene Brodie dissolved in more laughter. Obviously she was quite taken with Troy's unorthodox approach to his assignment.

Andrew remained out of the way during the pre-wedding bustle, keeping himself occupied by helping the caterer set up the rented chairs and chatting with Laura and Seth when they weren't being dragged off by Arlene, Rita, the judge or

Troy to attend to business. At one point, when Troy shepherded the three Brodie women into the house for what he promised would be some "feminist shots," Andrew and Seth took a leisurely stroll along the perimeter of the yard. "How are you doing?" Andrew asked.

Seth dug his hands into the pockets of his loose-fitting trousers and grinned. "Hanging in there," he replied. "I still haven't recovered from Laura's ban on sunglasses at this gig, but...as she likes to remind me, being in love means being willing to compromise. On the trivia, of course. We don't have to compromise on the big stuff, thank God. We're already in complete agreement on that."

"She's looking terrific," Andrew commented, casting a glance toward the house, into which Laura had disappeared. "So are you. Even if you do seem a bit more flamboyant than normal," he added, eyeing Seth's appealingly bizarre outfit.

"Yeah. You look more like a groom than I do," Seth observed, studying Andrew's conservatively styled blue suit— the only suit he owned—and striped necktie.

"Are you scared?"

Seth's dancing hazel eyes met Andrew's, and he shrugged. "I gather that I'm *supposed* to be scared," he confessed. "But I'm not. I'm really sure of what Laura and I are doing, Andrew. If you think about it objectively, this doesn't look like the easiest marriage in the world. I've got a teenage stepdaughter to cope with. And I'm uprooting her and Laura and taking them to California, far from Arlene—the only family Laura's got. My parents are happy I'm getting married, but they think maybe I've bitten off more than I can chew, marrying a woman with a kid."

"What do you think?" Andrew asked.

Seth shrugged again. "I think you've got to follow your heart and go for it," he said. "The bottom line is, I love

Laura. And she loves me. We're good for each other. Laura needs me as much as I need her. She tells me to grow my hair and not to wear sunglasses at weddings, and I teach her how to play the kazoo and how to get the most out of a Porsche. Obviously we're made for each other.'' He smiled gently. ''Maybe we're taking a chance here, but if you can't take a chance on the woman you love, then what's the point of anything?''

He resumed his leisurely pace, Andrew falling into step beside him. ''We love each other, Andrew,'' he continued. ''We can handle the glitches. It really isn't much of a risk when you've got love on your side. There are my folks,'' he said, gesturing toward a man and a woman who had emerged from the house and waved to him. ''Ten dollars says my mother's going to sob so loudly during the ceremony she'll drown out the judge.'' Sure enough, as Seth loped across the lawn to greet his parents, his mother pulled a handkerchief from her purse and dabbed at her glistening eyes.

More guests appeared: Seth's brothers and their wives and children; other relatives; a couple of Laura's colleagues from work; a girl who was apparently a close friend of Rita's, given their boisterous embrace when they saw each other; the girl's parents and brother. Andrew wandered around the side of the house in time to see a familiar BMW pull up to the curb. He smothered the urge to flee and stood bravely on the slate walk as Julianne and Kimberly climbed out of the car.

''Andrew!'' Julianne hailed him, striding up the walk and giving him a warm hug. ''How are you?''

''Fine, Julianne, and you?'' he said reflexively. His eyes, however, fastened themselves to Kimberly, who seemed to be taking more time locking up her car than any reasonably dextrous person required.

"Kim is just as nervous as you are," Julianne whispered before sweeping into the house in search of Troy, Laura and Seth.

Andrew suspected that Julianne's ulterior motive in going inside was to leave Andrew and Kimberly alone to confront each other. He wondered when Kimberly had confided to Julianne about him, and what she had said.

Kimberly slipped her car keys into her purse, straightened up and threw back her shoulders. Her eyes were wide with an emotion he could define as either panic or hauteur. The high midday sun glanced off her hair, causing it to shimmer about her face like a golden halo.

Not a halo, Andrew silently corrected himself as she approached him. She wasn't an angel. She was a woman. An important distinction, that.

"Hello," he said, swallowing the catch in his throat, pretending that he didn't find her so dazzlingly beautiful.

"Hello," she responded, sounding calmer than he felt.

"Nice weather they've got for the big day," Andrew remarked. Then he winced inwardly. The weather? Couldn't he do better than that?

"Yes, they're really lucky," Kimberly agreed. "According to Laura, she and her mother were arguing up to the last minute about whether to rent one of those massive outdoor tents. Laura insisted that if it rained a huge tent wasn't going to do much good, anyway, and they'd have to move everyone into the living room. But it's much nicer having the party outdoors, isn't it?"

"Much nicer, yes," Andrew mumbled, feeling as if he were withering inside. Without exchanging another word, he and Kimberly walked together to the backyard and conveniently lost each other in the crowd of guests.

Now, as Seth and Laura, flanked by one of Seth's brothers as best man and Rita as maid of honor, exchanged rings, Andrew reflected on what Seth had confessed to him before the wedding. If you had love on your side, what was the risk? Why not take chances?

Because, Andrew answered internally. Because if one did a cost-benefit on it, the costs would in all likelihood outweigh the benefits.

If Andrew tried to repair his relationship with Kimberly, it would probably cost him his job, the one thing that had kept him going during his darkest hours, the one thing he had always been sure he could count on.

It would cost him the fear he would have to live with forever, the fear of losing Kimberly, the fear that she didn't love him enough, the fear that she was so beautiful that as soon as the rest of the male half of the world discovered she was available, she would have an army of attentive gentlemen from which to choose a partner. The persistent fear that she was still on the rebound, that Andrew was only a temporary cure for her loneliness.

And what were the benefits? He could think of only one: Kimberly herself. Having her as long as he could, loving her for as long as he had her.

Damn. What was wrong with him? Why did he have to reduce everything to an economics equation? At the rate he was going, he might as well just pull out his calculator, punch a few buttons and trust to the microchip wizardry to tell him what to do.

Seth's words echoed inside Andrew: *You've got to follow your heart and go for it. If you can't take a chance on the woman you love, then what's the point of anything?*

"By the power vested in me by the state of Pennsylvania," the judge intoned, "I now pronounce you husband and wife. You may kiss the bride," he informed Seth.

"It's about time!" Seth hooted, to the great amusement of his audience. He slung his arms around Laura, hoisted her high into the air and planted a resounding kiss on her lips.

If you can't take a chance, then what's the point? The hell with cost-benefit analyses, Andrew reproached himself. *The bottom line is, you love her.*

The three-piece combo set up on the patio broke into a rendition of Mendelssohn's wedding recessional. Their faces radiant with joy and promise, Seth and Laura skipped up the improvised aisle between the rows of chairs. They didn't break stride until they reached the patio, where they began a comical waltz to the classical music.

Around Andrew people were rising to their feet, stretching their legs and chattering. Andrew stood, as well, and turned to Kimberly, who was inspecting the wrinkles in her dress, as if to avoid having to look at him. "Let's talk," he murmured.

SHE HAD KNOWN that this would be an awkward day for her, and she had tried to prepare herself for it. Last night at Julianne's apartment she had downed glass after glass of white wine, until her head was buzzing. But the wine hadn't helped any more than Julianne's logical advice.

"Kimberly," Julianne had said, effecting her stern, I-am-the-boss-and-I-know-these-things manner. "If you love Andrew, can't you love his flaws as well as his strengths? The man's been through hell once in his life. He doesn't want to go through hell again. He wants some stability, something he can rely on. He loves his job and he doesn't want to risk it. What more can you expect from him?" At Kimberly's obdurate silence, Julianne had added, "He isn't a paragon, Kim. He's a human being."

"He's a chicken," Kimberly had countered. "He's a spineless coward. He brought me the matches, the kindling, the lighter fluid—and then, when I was about to start a fire, he ran for cover. What kind of human being is that?''

"A normal one, if you ask me," Julianne had argued. "It took incredible guts just to bring you the matches and the rest of it. If he doesn't feel like getting burned in the conflagration, can you blame him?''

"When I first knew him back in school, he wouldn't have minded getting burned," Kimberly had muttered. "He was just as brave as the rest of us. When the president of Columbia refused him an interview, Andrew hounded the man mercilessly until he got the story he wanted. When Troy was applying for his conscientious objector status, Andrew was the first to volunteer as a character witness at Troy's draft board hearing.''

"And when he knew you in school, he thought you were a pretty pom-pom girl," Julianne had reminded her.

"Maybe he still thinks I am," Kimberly had mumbled sadly.

"I'm sure he doesn't," Julianne had refuted her. "He's a smart, perceptive guy. Fifteen years is a long time, Kim, and you've both been through a lot. Neither of you is the same person you were back then. Certainly Andrew is aware of that.''

"I don't know." Kimberly had drained her glass and sighed. "What if he isn't?''

"He wouldn't be in love with you if he didn't recognize you for who you really are," Julianne had rationally pointed out. "He isn't blind. If you think he is . . . maybe it's your own insecurity that's eating you up." As Julianne's insightful words sank in, her eyes had met Kimberly's. "What's really bothering you, Kim? Are you upset because Andrew doesn't want to testify before your boss's committee, or are you upset because Andrew is refusing to do something *you've* asked him to do? Is it Senator Milford's hearing you're thinking of or your own ego?''

She'd had a valid point, one that Kimberly hadn't stopped meditating on. As soon as she'd seen Andrew, the notion had come into full focus. The Intelligence Committee hearing was important, but it couldn't be important enough to make her feel as despairing as she did about Andrew.

Maybe Julianne was right. Maybe Kimberly was ascribing personal motives to Andrew's decision, taking his rejection of her invitation to testify as a rejection of herself.

He said he wanted to talk. She wanted to talk, too. He looked miserable, and she loved him too much to allow herself to be the cause of his misery.

But the band was playing a soupy version of "Something in the Way She Moves," and before Kimberly could react to Andrew's suggestion, a strapping young man in a navy blazer and gray slacks gripped her hand and announced, "I'm Seth's cousin Larry and Seth says you're single. Care to dance?" Without giving her a chance to refuse, he dragged her to the patio.

She tossed Andrew a helpless smile, and he shrugged. Twisting her head in order to see him as Larry twirled her around the patio, she noticed Andrew guiding Julianne to the patio to join the dancers. He held Julianne a discreet distance from himself, and they talked and smiled as they danced. Kimberly tried to guess what they might be discussing. Was Julianne doling out some more of her commonsense advice to him?

The song wasn't that long, but it seemed to last forever. As soon as the band reached the final chord, Kimberly extricated herself from Larry's embrace, mumbled a hasty thank-you and wove among the dancers to Andrew. "All right," she said, gazing up into his gentle eyes and refusing herself the chance to evade him anymore. "Let's talk."

Andrew opened his mouth to speak. From the corner of her eye, Kimberly spotted another young man approaching her. *How many cousins does Seth have?* she wondered irritably. Slipping her hand through the bend of Andrew's elbow, she briskly urged him in the direction of the house before anyone else could waylay them—and before she lost her nerve.

They passed a linen-covered buffet table arrayed with hors d'oeuvres, chafing dishes and plates and entered the house through the back door. Inside the kitchen, a squad of uniformed waiters supplied by the caterer were swarming about, removing cookie sheets of canapés from the oven and loading doily-lined trays with stuffed mushrooms and pigs-in-blankets. Kimberly and Andrew exited the kitchen to find the living room also teeming with guests. Hoping that Mrs. Brodie wouldn't mind, Kimberly led Andrew toward the stairs leading to the second floor.

The upstairs hall was empty, and they stepped through an open doorway, entering a tidy guest bedroom. Kimberly smiled edgily and lowered herself onto the bed. Andrew sat beside her, but he made no move to put his arm around her or take her hand. That struck her as a bad sign—or else an extremely good sign. He was serious about talking, and he wasn't going to let their strong physical bond get in the way of their dialogue.

He didn't speak for several minutes. His gaze wandered from the open window to the bulletin board to his spread knees. "I've missed you," he finally said.

"I've missed you, too."

"Kimberly...Kim." He took a deep breath, then lifted his face to hers. His expression was inscrutable. "The last time we were together—"

"I'm sorry," she said in a timorous voice. Then the words tumbled out. "I shouldn't have run away from you, Andrew. That's what I did—I ran away. Just like the first time in Washington. I ran then and I ran again in Amherst. I was so busy thinking you were a coward, Andrew, but *I* was the coward, racing off like that. I should have given you a chance—"

"A chance to do what? To be more cowardly than you were?" He pulled off his eyeglasses, rubbed the bridge of his nose, then slipped the glasses back on and turned fully to her. "I've given a great deal of thought to my job, Kim. My work means a lot to me, you know that. But other things mean more to me than my work. They *have* to mean more. I haven't stopped thinking about this since we last saw each other, and I haven't stopped thinking about us. I'll—I'll testify for you."

"No," she said quickly.

He appeared startled. "What do you mean, no? Don't you want me to?"

Julianne's words resounded inside her skull, their truth overpowering her. "I don't want you to testify for *me*, Andrew. I want you to do it for *you*, because you yourself think it's the right thing to do—or else don't do it at all."

He gazed at her for a long moment, clearly puzzled. "Run that one by me again," he requested.

She smiled shyly, then busied herself smoothing out her skirt again. "I was wrong, Andrew, the way I tried to coerce you into doing it, as if you'd be doing it as a favor to me. If you testify, it has to be because you're committed to the idea of testifying. Not to satisfy me, but because you believe that some larger good will come from it." She sighed, then dared to meet his gaze. "I know how much your job means to you, Andrew. I don't want you to lose it."

"I don't want to lose it, either," he admitted. He rose from the bed and paced aimlessly. When he reached the window, he glanced out at the revelers in the yard below.

Then he turned back to Kimberly. "Do you know what my students dream of? They dream of going to business school. They dream of getting M.B.A.'s and earning lots of money and spending the rest of their lives in safety and security."

"There's nothing wrong with safety and security," Kimberly noted.

"Within reason, perhaps." He leaned against the windowsill, his eyes unwavering on her. "There's something wrong with safety and security when you make all your decisions with those questionable motives in mind. I..." He paused, mulling over his words, his angular jaw flexing as he gave shape to his thoughts. Then he continued. "I want safety and security. I want safety and security in my career, and I want them in my relationship with a woman. But I can't have them. Not without sacrificing something even more important."

She was unnerved by his having diverted the conversation to the personal issues that remained unresolved between them. She had thought that they were discussing his decision to testify, not his feelings for her.

But she wouldn't retreat from the emotional minefield into which Andrew had led them. If he was brave enough to introduce the subject, she would just as bravely meet him on that dangerous turf. "What is that important thing?"

"Love," he answered simply. "Love isn't always safe, Kim. It isn't always secure. But having it—even with all the risks... I'm beginning to think that maybe it's better to accept those risks than to avoid love altogether."

She wanted to rise from the bed, cross to him, fling her arms around him and hug him close. She wanted to tell him all over again, as often as he wanted to hear it, that she loved him.

But she didn't. He hadn't yet mentioned his love for her or hers for him. He was still speaking in generalities, and she thought it best to hold back. "Don't you think it's possible that love can sometimes be secure and safe?" she asked.

He shook his head solemnly. "No. And you don't believe it can, either, Kim. You know as well as I do that no matter how much you love a person, things don't necessarily work out. The man you loved and married wasn't the person you thought he was. The woman I loved and married died. There's no such thing as certainty."

"You're still a cynic," she chastised him, strangely deflated by his assertion. He claimed that he thought love might be worth the risks. So why couldn't he take an optimistic view of things? Why couldn't he also think that sometimes those risks were negligible?

"I'm a realist," he refuted her. Then his mouth softened, shaping a tenuous smile. "Okay, maybe there's a little bit of optimism inside me, too. Because every time I try to sort out my feelings, Kim, the realist in me says I should forget about everything between us, I should grab my tenure and live out a pleasant, trouble-free life in Amherst, teaching my students and taking home my pay.... And then that god-awful optimist in me tells me that I'd rather have you."

"Andrew—"

"He tells me that I should shore up my courage and face Milford's damned committee and get everyone into a lather at Amherst. He tells me that I should do what's right rather than what's safe, no matter what the cost. He tells me that if I don't do what's right, I'll wind up like my students— defeated by petty comforts and complacency."

"Why doesn't that optimist tell you that testifying before the senator's committee won't cost you your job?"

"Oh, he does," Andrew scoffed. "I tell him to shut up."

"He seems like a pretty talkative guy."

"Is he ever. Bombastic, pleonastic, irrelevant...." Andrew chuckled. "Once I took the muzzle off him—or maybe it was you who took the muzzle off him, Kim—I can't seem to get him to quiet down."

"Don't even try." At last she yielded to the urge to close the distance between her and Andrew. Hoisting herself off the bed, she marched across the room, placed her hands on his shoulders and rose on tiptoe to kiss him. "It's that bombastic, pleonastic, irrelevant optimist inside you that makes me love you so much."

Andrew's arms drew her to him, and he returned her kiss. His embrace loosened, but he didn't release her. "When I was talking to Seth just before the wedding, I asked him if he was scared. He told me he was too sure of what he and Laura were doing to be scared." His lips touched the smooth skin of her forehead and he sighed. "I wish I were as sure."

"You'll never lose me, Andrew."

"That's a promise you can't make," he said.

She knew he was speaking from his own mournful experience. Yet she wouldn't concede, not even to the capriciousness of fate. "As long as I've got any power over things, I can promise it. We love each other. That's all we have to be sure of."

"Right," he muttered doubtfully. He stroked his fingers through her silky hair and scowled. "I live in Massachusetts—and even if I lose my job, I've got one more year on my contract. You live in Washington, except when you're flying around the country with Milford. You aren't about to quit your job. So how does this thing work out?"

"Maybe—" she grinned impishly "—maybe your getting fired from Amherst would be the best solution."

"Of course," he grunted sarcastically. "Then I'll be an unemployed wretch. Or, if I'm lucky, I'll be able to snag a part-time job, teaching nights at a community college in some rural county thousands of miles from the nearest airport. Any other brainstorms?''

"Someone with a razor-sharp mind like mine always has brainstorms," Kimberly declared. "Here's one. Stop worrying about what you have no control over. That includes what Amherst decides to do to you, and it includes what Mother Nature decides to do to both of us. We'll get by, Andrew. We'll work it out. We'll be together when we can, and when we can't . . . we'll be together in spirit."

"What a cheerleader you are," he commented, smiling reluctantly. "You almost make it sound easy."

"It won't be easy, Andrew. But it can be done."

"How about when you get pregnant?"

Unsure that she had heard him correctly, she stared up at him, trying to make sense of his enigmatic smile. His eyes remained steadfast on her, his mouth still curved in that lopsided grin she adored. "Are you serious?" she questioned him.

"As serious as you are," he replied. "You're not the only one who wants a child, Kim."

"Then we'll work it out," she said with conviction.

It definitely wouldn't be easy. She knew that. But if Andrew wanted a child as much as she did—if he wanted one *half* as much—they would find a way to do it. He could arrange his teaching schedule to concentrate all his classes on Tuesdays, Wednesdays and Thursdays. Or she could reduce her work load on the Senate staff. Barry, the newcomer on the senator's speech-writing staff, was speedily learning the ropes. He could take over some of her responsibilities. Or she could take a maternity leave. Somehow, with two geniuses like Andrew and her working on it, they would come up with a solution.

The combo's music drifted up and through the open bedroom window. The band was playing Billy Joel's "Just the Way You Are.'' Kimberly imagined that the song had become a kind of anthem for weddings; it had been played at every wedding she'd attended in the past ten years. With good reason, too.

Andrew would never be as optimistic as she was—it simply wasn't in him. But, try as he did to ignore it, there had always been a streak of optimism in him. She didn't need more than that. She would be the cheerleader of their partnership and Andrew the practical one, the sensible one, insisting that he wasn't romantic when Kimberly knew that he was in fact the most romantic man she had ever met. He had his flaws, but as Julianne had pointed out, Kimberly had to love his flaws as well as his strengths. He was a human being.

She did love him, just the way he was.

"If you don't ask me to dance," she remarked, flashing him a flirtatious smile, "another one of Seth's cousins is going to beat you to the punch."

Andrew mirrored her smile, exhibiting that marvelously understated dimple of his. He slid his right arm around her waist and folded his left hand over hers. "You know," he commented, gliding about the cozy bedroom, "for a well-bred Southern lady, you're pretty forward, inviting a fellow to dance."

"It must be the corrupting influence of all those damn-Yankee college friends of mine," she drawled. "Mother warned me I'd find myself in a fix if I went to Barnard, that heathen 'naw-thren' school."

"What's Mother going to say when you tell her a heathen northern man plans to marry you and get you pregnant?"

Kimberly laughed. "She'll probably lecture you about the etiquette of wearing socks on Sunday morning."

"She and I are going to have some wonderful fights over the next thirty or forty years," Andrew predicted, pulling Kimberly closer and kissing her temple.

She nestled her head into the warm shadow of his neck and sighed happily. *Over the next thirty or forty years.* That was the optimist in Andrew speaking, the courageous, principled, optimistic man she knew he was, at long last ready to commit himself to the future, to welcome it with hope and love.

HMV·B·1

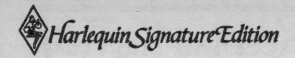

Harlequin Signature Edition

Carole Mortimer

Merlyn's Magic

She came to him from out of the storm and was drawn into his yearning arms—the tempestuous night held a magic all its own.

You've enjoyed Carole Mortimer's Harlequin Presents stories, and her previous bestseller, *Gypsy*.

Now, don't miss her latest, most exciting bestseller, *Merlyn's Magic*!

IN JULY

MERMG

Keeping the Faith

by
Judith Arnold

At the fifteen-year reunion of *The Dream* you met the six Columbia-Barnard graduates who founded the college newspaper. And you smiled as a long-term friendship turned to love for Seth and Laura in #201 *Promises*.

You've just seen Andrew and Kimberly overcome the prejudices of their past and once more embrace life—and each other—in #205 *Commitments*.

Don't miss the final episode, when Troy and Julianne take the most difficult and heart-wrenching step of their lives—and learn to live their dreams. Watch for #209 *Dreams* next month!

You may laugh, you may cry, but you will find a piece of yourself in *Keeping the Faith*.

Take 4 books
& a surprise gift
FREE

SPECIAL LIMITED-TIME OFFER

Mail to   **Harlequin Reader Service®**

In the U.S.   In Canada
901 Fuhrmann Blvd.   P.O. Box 609
P.O. Box 1394   Fort Erie, Ontario
Buffalo, N.Y. 14240-1394   L2A 5X3

YES!   Please send me 4 free Harlequin Romance® novels
and my free surprise gift. Then send me 8 brand-new novels every
month as they come off the presses. Bill me at the low price of
$1.99 each*—an 11% saving off the retail price. There are no
shipping, handling or other hidden costs. There is no minimum
number of books I must purchase. I can always return a shipment
and cancel at any time. Even if I never buy another book from
Harlequin, the 4 free novels and the surprise gift are mine to keep
forever.   118 BPR BP7F
*Plus 89¢ postage and handling per shipment in Canada.

Name   (PLEASE PRINT)

Address   Apt. No.

City   State/Prov.   Zip/Postal Code

This offer is limited to one order per household and not valid to present
subscribers. Price is subject to change.   DOR-SUB-1D